EVERY TRACE

EVERY TRACE

GREGG MAIN

HarperCollins*Publishers*

 For information address HarperCollins Publishers, Inc., 10 East 53rd Street, New York, NY 10022.

HarperCollins books may be purchased for educational, business, or sales promotional use. For information please write: Special Markets Department, HarperCollins Publishers, Inc., 10 East 53rd Street, New York, NY 10022.

FIRST EDITION

Designed by Nancy Field

Library of Congress Cataloging-in-Publication Data
Main, Gregg.
Every trace / Gregg Main. — 1st ed.
p. cm.
ISBN 0-06-019178-3
I. Title.
PS3563.A382668E9 1999
813'.54—dc21 98-25153

---

99 00 01 02 03 ❖/RRD 10 9 8 7 6 5 4 3 2 1

For Betsy

ACKNOWLEDGMENTS

Many people helped and supported me during the writing of this book:

Nancy Yost and Steven Fisher provided early encouragement for this work. Their editorial assistance and expert agenting have been indispensable and are very much appreciated.

At HarperCollins I would like to thank Marjorie Braman for taking a chance on an unknown writer; Dan Conaway for his many hours of hard work, remarkable insights, and inspiration during the editing process; and Constance Chang for her administrative help.

Murray Cohen, Nick Lombardo, and Ethan Luhks provided help over many years on many writing projects. I will always be indebted to them.

Finally, thanks to Andrew and Emily for their patience and understanding, and to Betsy, my first and best reader.

EVERY TRACE

CHAPTER 1

PETE DONELLY stared at the telephone in front of him before picking it up and dialing his sister-in-law's number. It was mid-October; outside the window the Dallas sky was a hard, shiny blue. Pete watched as a strong wind shook the sweet gum tree in their side yard, tearing orange leaves from it and blowing them out of sight. Yesterday, when Ellen had left, there had been no wind at all.

Ellen's sister answered the phone.

"Hi, Susan, it's Pete."

"Pete. Hi. How are you?"

"So-so. May I speak to her, please?"

Susan laughed lightly. She had an infectious laugh that usually made other people smile. But Pete wasn't smiling.

"Speak to who?" she asked.

"Come on, Susan. I know she's there. She called me from your house last night."

"Hold it. Slow down a second. What are you talking about?"

"Ellen. I need to talk to her."

Susan hesitated. "Ellen hasn't been here, Pete. I haven't seen her at all."

"But she said she was going to your house for a few days. She called last night and told me she was there."

"Is this some kind of joke?"

"Of course not."

"She hasn't been here."

Pete's stomach knotted into a ball as his mind raced back to the previous morning when he had carried Ellen's luggage out to her car. She hadn't wanted him to drive her to the airport.

Ellen had worn jeans and a deep purple sweater. It was a color she favored. Her wide blue eyes were set in a narrow face with delicate features. Her hair, which had been blonde when she was younger, was now a sandy brown. Pete put her bags in the trunk, and Ellen walked to the door of her car.

Pete said, "I hate you leaving like this. We need to talk."

"We've talked for days," Ellen said. "I need a break."

"All right. I understand." He leaned forward to kiss her, but Ellen turned her head, forcing him to brush at her cheek.

She got in her car without another word. Pete watched her back out of the driveway, head down the street and turn the corner. At seven that night she called to let him know she had arrived safely at Susan's house.

But she had lied.

Susan broke the silence. "What's going on here, Pete? Ellen called me last night, too. I thought she was home."

"I don't know what's going on. This is crazy."

Susan was silent for ten seconds. "Did you guys have a fight?"

"Yeah."

"Bad?"

"Pretty bad. Ellen didn't tell you?"

"No. What happened?"

Pete was silent. He was aware of the sound of his own breathing through the phone. It sounded as though he were gasping for breath. He didn't want to tell Susan the whole story. Pete liked Susan; he knew what she was going to think of him.

"You going to tell me or do I have to guess?"

"I was seeing someone," he said. "It's over now, but Ellen's pretty upset. I figured you knew." It surprised the hell out of Pete that Ellen hadn't told Susan. They were very close. "She said she wanted to get away for a while, and that she was going to your house." Pete paused. "I guess she's left me."

"Did she tell you that?"

"No. She said we could talk when she got back."

"Then I don't think she's left you. At least not permanently."

"If she calls you," said Pete, "find out where she's staying. And please tell her to call me."

Pete remained home most of the day, waiting for the telephone to ring. They lived in a two-bedroom home made beautiful by Ellen's love of gardening. She kept flowers blooming nearly year-round in the large gardens surrounding the house.

Part of the afternoon Pete sat outside on the back deck staring at Ellen's flower beds. He noticed that the lilies and daisies, along with a few others he didn't know by name, looked dry. Pete wondered if he should water them. There hadn't been any rain for almost a week, but Ellen had said nothing to him about watering. That indicated she hadn't planned on being gone for long.

LATE IN THE DAY Pete got on Central Expressway and drove downtown. He'd called Taylor Reed's office before leaving and spoken with Barbara, Taylor's secretary. She told Pete that Taylor would certainly make time to see him if he came by.

Taylor's company, Arroyo Capital Management, had its

offices on the twentieth floor of the Commerce Building. Pete entered the lobby of Arroyo and waited five minutes before Barbara appeared to usher him back.

Taylor's large corner office was decorated in English antique furniture, which he had been collecting most of his life. Taylor was one of Ellen's oldest family friends, having been close to both of Ellen's parents. He had known Ellen her entire life, and after her father died, Taylor had become a surrogate father figure to her.

Taylor stood and came around his desk when Pete entered. He was well over six feet tall, with thick silver hair. As always, he was impeccably dressed in an expensive suit. Nine years earlier, when Pete had first met him, Taylor had been a robust, energetic man, but the last few years had taken a toll. He'd had health problems, including triple bypass surgery, and had become very thin, even frail.

"Hello, Pete," he said. "Barbara told me you were going to stop by." Taylor put out his hand and Pete shook it. "Let's sit over here." Taylor indicated the sofa and chairs arranged around a dark, weathered coffee table. "Can I get you some coffee or a soda?"

"No thanks."

Taylor checked his watch as he sat opposite Pete. "It's good to see you, Pete, but I can see something's bothering you. What's the problem?"

Pete sighed before beginning. "I wondered if you'd talked to Ellen in the last few days?"

"No. I don't think I've spoken to her in more than a week. Why?"

Pete explained the situation without going into the reason he and Ellen had fought.

"I hoped she might have talked to you," Pete said. "Told you what she was doing, where she was going."

Taylor shook his head slowly from side to side. "No. She hadn't mentioned anything about going out of town to me."

"I think maybe she's left me, Taylor."

"Oh, I don't know about that," he said. "She'll call again. When she does, tell her you want her to come home. Don't take no for an answer. No matter how angry she is, I'm sure you two can work things out."

"I hope so," said Pete. "I just don't understand why she lied about going to Susan's."

"Maybe she thought it would be easier to tell you that instead of saying she wanted to be by herself."

"But where would she go to be by herself?"

"Maybe she hasn't gone anywhere. Maybe she's at a hotel right here in Dallas."

Pete hadn't thought of that possibility. He saw Taylor glance at his watch again. "I'm keeping you from something, aren't I?"

"No, no. I have a meeting in a couple of minutes, that's all."

Pete stood. "I'll take off. I just wanted to see if Ellen had said anything to you."

Taylor said, "I have someone who could check the local hotels if you like."

"That's all right. I can call around myself."

Taylor saw Pete out to the lobby.

"Try not to worry," Taylor said. "I'm sure she'll be home soon."

"It's just so strange," Pete said. "It's like she has a secret life or something."

Taylor frowned. "What do you mean?"

"She could go away anytime she wanted. I wouldn't stop her.

She didn't need to make up the story about staying with Susan. I just wonder why she did that."

"I don't blame you for being upset," Taylor said. "But I'm sure things will turn out fine. Call me tomorrow and let me know if you've heard from her."

AFTER THREE and a half hours Pete had checked on nearly fifty hotels and motels in Dallas–Fort Worth. None had Ellen Donelly registered. He had also called their credit card companies. There were no charges in the last few days for anything, especially not for a hotel or airplane ticket.

The phone rang at nine. It was Ellen.

"Jesus," he said. "Where the hell are you?"

"I'm at Susan's."

"You're not at Susan's. I talked to her today. What's going on?"

Ellen said nothing. Pete heard background noise over the phone—voices, a distant rumble. Ellen wasn't in a hotel room.

"I'll be home in a couple of days. I'll explain it then," she said. He heard a click and then the line went dead.

"Ellen!" he screamed, but it was too late. She'd hung up.

HE WAS DESPERATE and he was frightened. This was how Pete rationalized digging through the drawers in Ellen's desk.

She had a studio in an attic room they had finished off after purchasing the house. There was a computer and a printer on her desk, a large drafting table next to the wall, a four-drawer file cabinet, a large bookcase crammed with paperbacks and gardening magazines. Along the wall next to the drafting table were various portfolios full of Ellen's sketches and drawings. Another wall had canvases stacked against it.

Pete carefully looked through one desk drawer after another, rifling through the old letters, credit card receipts, sets of photographs, an old address book. Pete noticed his hands were shaking as he thumbed through these items.

Finished, he moved to the file cabinet. It contained copies of old tax returns, paid bills and other personal business. Another drawer was full of correspondence and papers that had to do with her mother's estate. Ellen's mother had passed away eight months before, and the estate had not been settled. Taylor Reed was her mother's executor, and he was handling the probate for Ellen and Susan. Pete glanced through these pages briefly and then put them away.

Next he sat down in front of the computer and turned it on. Pete pushed away the pang of guilt he felt as he began to search through the word processing directory. There were three subdirectories: "Personal," "Business," and "Other." Pete clicked on "Business" first and saw, as he expected, that this contained letters to various galleries regarding Ellen's drawings, along with correspondence with clients who had hired her to do portraits for them, usually of their children. In the "Personal" directory Pete found miscellaneous letters—to Ellen's sister, her mother, college friends. Pete skimmed through them but found nothing out of the ordinary, no clue that Ellen was planning to go anywhere or visit anyone.

Pete clicked on the third directory, and the computer asked for a password. Pete tried Ellen's middle name, then her maiden name, then her mother's maiden name. None of these worked. Pete's heart quickened, and he felt a rush of excitement. He was the only person besides Ellen who would ever turn on this computer, so he must be the one Ellen didn't want looking in this directory. Pete tried Susan's name for the password, then her middle name. He tried Susan's daughter's name. No luck. He wasn't sure if a password could be numbers or not, but he tried Ellen's birthday. Nothing.

"LET'S SEE," said Brian as he sat down in front of the computer. "Did you try her social security number?"

"Yes," said Pete. "452-86-3101. I tried every conceivable combination of it."

"There are nine digits. There are probably half a million combinations."

"All right, I exaggerated. I tried some of them."

Brian exited the word processing program and went into the file manager, clicking away at the keyboard and mouse. Brian taught history at North Dallas Community College, as did Pete, and they'd known each other for eight years. Brian was self-taught on the computer, and when Pete had called him about a way to get around the password, Brian offered to come right over. He was a tall, narrow man, with dark hair and a beard flecked with gray.

"So Ellen left, huh?"

"Yeah," said Pete. "Wednesday morning."

"Sorry, man. You have a big blowout?"

"A couple days before that."

"I've been having a bit of trouble in that area myself."

"What happened?"

"Nothing exactly. But Patty's acting very cold and pissed off about something. I don't know what the problem is, and to tell you the truth, I'm a little afraid to ask."

Brian and his wife had been having a rough time for the last couple of years. She'd taken the children and left him once, but then returned. Pete had little optimism about their long-term prospects.

Brian scrolled through pages of files, then stopped.

"Well, there are the files in that directory," he said, pointing to the screen. Pete bent over Brian's shoulder to get a better look. Indented below the word "Other" were two files simply named "One" and "Two."

"That's all that's in there?" asked Pete.

"That's it. I'm going to download these onto a disk and take them home. I've got a program called Password. It'll try six hundred thousand different words and names automatically to try to open the file."

"How long does that take?"

Brian slipped a diskette into the drive. "On my computer it takes about five hours. Your machine is slower. It'd take two or three times that long."

It was nearly midnight when Brian left. Pete was exhausted, but he wanted to check all the computer disks Ellen kept in the plastic box next to the computer. It took an hour, and all he found were backups to the files she had on the hard drive. The only ones missing were the two from the "Other" directory.

Later, lying in their bed, Pete thought about the first time he had seen Ellen. It was at a party one winter night eleven years before. They were both in graduate school at the University of Iowa at the time. Ellen was in the art department; Pete was getting his M.A. in History. Pete was instantly attracted to her, and he spent the next two weeks haunting student art shows and the halls of the fine arts department, hoping to see her again. When he finally did, they talked briefly and Ellen invited him to a bar where some of her friends were going. Pete gave her a ride in his car. As they talked he mentioned all the art he'd been looking at, hoping to run into her again.

Ellen laughed. "I love that," she said. "It's like you were on a quest."

"I tried Directory Assistance for your phone number first," he admitted. "You're not listed."

As he parked on the icy street outside the bar, Ellen put her hand on his shoulder. Pete flipped off the engine and looked at her.

"Do you want to kiss me?" she asked.

Pete was surprised by the question, and he didn't answer. Instead, he leaned toward her. They kissed for several seconds, and Pete felt his heart swell inside his chest. When she pulled away from him, all Pete wanted in the world was to kiss her again, right then, and continue kissing her for a long, long time.

"You can tell a lot about a person by the way he kisses," Ellen said.

"You can, huh?"

"Yeah."

He expected her to explain, but she didn't. Instead, she opened the car door. Pete jumped out and followed her to the bar.

Inside, sitting in a booth with three of her friends, Pete couldn't keep his eyes off Ellen. He stared at her for hours, forcing himself every once in a while to look away briefly, hoping that the others wouldn't notice his infatuation. He thought about kissing Ellen, and was hoping that she'd feel like coming over to his place when they left the bar. Pete didn't realize it at the time, but he was already falling in love.

CHAPTER 2

EVEN WITH THE WINDOW rolled down, it was hot in the car. Ellen had parked on the street a block up from Margold Video Distribution in central Los Angeles, not far from Western Avenue. The late-afternoon sun was burning through the side window. At five-thirty, when the men who worked in the warehouse got off, she would see the cars pull out of the parking lot. Franklin Walker had been employed at Margold for two years, ever since he had completed his parole in Texas and moved to California.

Ellen had been here before. Back in August, she had followed Walker's charcoal-gray Thunderbird from this spot. She was just watching him then, tracking him, getting a sense of his usual movements and habits. He had driven north on Western and then turned onto the Santa Monica Freeway, going west to La Brea Avenue, then headed north again, stopping at a bar near Santa Monica Boulevard not far from his apartment. Ellen had parked and followed him into the bar. Walker was sixty-three years old with a deeply receding hairline and a hard, weathered face. Ellen nursed a glass of wine as Walker had a few drinks with a thin, chain-smoking blonde in her fifties. They left and Ellen followed them outside, watching from the doorway as they drove away in his Thunderbird. She didn't hurry. Ellen knew they were going to his apartment and she knew where that was. Minutes later, when she drove past the front of his building, she saw the two of them walking up the sidewalk together. Ellen wondered if the woman knew her boyfriend had spent nearly thirty years in the state penitentiary at Huntsville.

Now Ellen was back. After arriving on Wednesday, she'd rented a car, checked into her hotel, then gone to a walk-in hair salon and had her hair cut. She purchased Revlon hair color at a drugstore, went back to the hotel and lightened her hair. Late in the day she drove to the Mail Boxes Etc. where she'd rented a box last August and picked up the package she'd mailed to herself from Dallas.

This morning she had driven to Walker's unattractive, pale blue apartment building. When Ellen didn't see the Thunderbird in its usual parking space, she parked her car around the block and went to check the building entrance. She was shocked to see that Walker's name on the mail slot had been replaced by Valdez. When she knocked on the apartment door, a young Latina woman told Ellen that she and her husband had been living there for over a month.

It was like being struck in the stomach. Ellen had a hard time breathing as she walked back to her car. She knew where he worked, but if he had changed jobs she would be in serious trouble. According to David Ellman, the private investigator who had finally located him, Walker had lived in the same apartment for the last two years, ever since he'd arrived Los Angeles.

Ellen hadn't bothered to learn where Walker's girlfriend lived when she was in L.A. last summer. That seemed like a costly error now. Her only hope was that he still worked at the warehouse. If she didn't see his car leave there this afternoon, she'd go to the bar she'd followed him to in August and wait, hoping he would show up there. Ellen worried all day that he might have left Los Angeles entirely, and if that were the case she didn't know what she would do. Years of work would be wasted, and she didn't know if she could go through it all again, especially alone.

She and her mother had always planned to be together when they confronted Franklin Walker. She remembered sitting in the hospital room with her mother when they both knew the end was near.

"Don't do it," her mother said. "I don't want you to do it alone."

"I want to. I know I can."

Her mother reached out with a spindly hand and patted Ellen's leg. It was awful the way she had deteriorated in the last month. Her face was nothing but pasty skin stretched tightly across her skull. "Sometimes I think I've been insane all these years. I'm afraid I made you insane, too. I want you to be happy and live a good life, have your own family. It's a terrible way to live, full of hate every day."

"I can't be happy until this is over, Mama. You know that. I was there."

"I know you were, darling. I know you were."

Ellen wiped her eyes with one hand. She missed her mother. She was the only person who understood. With her gone, Ellen had to keep everything to herself.

It was five-thirty. Ellen turned on the engine of the rented Toyota, letting it idle as she kept her eyes on the parking lot entrance. Things were going wrong. Unexpected things. But so far they were all minor. Today she would follow Walker to his new apartment or house. Then she would make sure he still lived alone. Once she determined that, the rest would go like clockwork. It would be a simple matter. But she mustn't lose her nerve. And she wouldn't. The pain of all those years, the fear, the raw, hot jolt she felt in her chest whenever she tried to remember her father, all of that had led her to this spot. She wasn't going to lose her fucking nerve. Not here, not now.

A car emerged from the warehouse parking lot. Ellen released the emergency brake and put her car in gear. She checked her side mirror and saw there was a line of traffic coming up her side of the street. When there was a break, two more cars pulled out of the lot. The second was Walker's Thunderbird. A shock of excitement shot through Ellen's body, and she nearly cried out with relief. She turned the wheels of the car and looked back over her shoulder. She had to let one car pass before she could pull into the street and follow.

Ellen remained one car behind Walker all the way to the freeway on-ramp. The car separating them continued on Western, and Ellen found herself right behind the Thunderbird waiting for the left turn signal. Once on the freeway she let him get several cars ahead of her. He moved into a middle lane, she stayed in the right. Ellen expected he might still get off at La Brea, and he did. He had moved but still lived in the same area. She followed cautiously, letting a couple of cars get between them once they were back on the surface streets. Not far from the freeway he turned left onto a residential street. She waited before turning onto the street, which she saw was Lexington. The Thunderbird was a block and a half ahead of her, and it turned right. Ellen sped up, turning down the same street.

The car had vanished.

Ellen accelerated to the next block, slowed as she reached the intersection and looked up and down the cross street. There was no sign of Walker's car. She raced through the next intersection and the next. Nothing.

Ellen circled back, fighting the panic rising in her chest. She cruised up a block, looking for his car. She went up and down all three streets he might have turned on, checking a couple of blocks in each direction without success. Heading back to Lexington, she noticed for the first time the narrow alley that ran between Lexington and the first street north of it. She stopped, peering up the alley. It was getting dark now. Ellen flipped on her headlights. She turned and drove slowly up the crumbling, uneven pavement. Each side of the alley was lined with small garages and open carports. If he'd put his car in one of the garages she'd be out of luck.

She spotted the Thunderbird in a carport in the middle of the block. Ellen stopped for a moment and looked back. It was the fourth building from the corner. She continued down the alley and parked on the street. A shiver of anticipation ran up her back as she turned off the engine and got out, grabbing her purse. She wasn't going to do it tonight, but it made sense to have the Smith & Wesson with her just in case something happened.

Ellen stepped briskly down the alley. She looked around the car, but there was nothing to indicate that the spot was reserved for a certain apartment. Ellen went to the side of the carport and saw two identical apartment buildings facing one another, a courtyard between them. The buildings were well maintained. In the gardens, yellow and white daisies bloomed along with two large birds of paradise. In the shady areas were pink and red impatiens. Franklin Walker had moved to a better building. There were lights on in about half of the units. Ellen didn't want to be seen loitering, so she kept moving, but then she saw a woman coming down the stairway from the second story of the building on her left.

It was the woman she'd seen with Walker in August. She carried a tall glass in one hand, a pack of cigarettes in the other. Ellen was startled, and she kept walking, not making eye contact with the woman as she passed the bottom of the stairs, the woman still a few steps up. Ellen went straight to the sidewalk and turned in the direction of her car. Dammit. He was living with the woman. That was why he had moved. Ellen hadn't planned for this, didn't know if she could manage with two people. Killing Walker would be no problem, but what would she do about the girlfriend? She was innocent.

As Ellen reached the car, she'd already made up her mind. She'd come back in the morning, see what time the woman left for work. If she was lucky, the woman would leave before Walker. Then Ellen could catch him in his apartment before he went to his job. The girlfriend wouldn't return for eight or nine hours. More than enough time.

When she called Pete that night from the pay phone, she was so preoccupied about Walker living with the blonde woman that she wasn't prepared when Pete angrily asked where she was. Ellen heard no concern in his voice, just that he was mad. Mad that she wasn't where she said she was and that she had deceived him. Well, he knew a thing or two about deception.

But Ellen knew she had to focus on the plan now, not on Pete and whatever the hell he was thinking. She'd deal with Pete when she went home. After this was all over.

CHAPTER 3

IN THE MORNING Pete called Brian to see if he'd had any luck discovering the password to Ellen's protected computer files. Patty answered the phone. She told Pete that Brian had left for school already. Pete knew then that Brian had not been successful. If the password program had worked, Brian would have phoned before leaving for school.

Pete sat at the kitchen table and went through their address book, telephoning friends to see if anyone had spoken to Ellen in the last week. It was an embarrassing ordeal. No one said anything directly, but he knew they all realized Ellen had left him.

After lunch Pete repeated his search of Ellen's studio, hoping to find something he'd overlooked. He found the plain, unmarked manila envelope in the third drawer of the file cabinet, stuck behind files of old tax returns. Inside was a life insurance policy on Ellen, listing Pete and Susan as the beneficiaries. The policy was issued on August 12 of that year, and it insured Ellen's life for $350,000. Pete was astonished. Ellen had never said a word about purchasing the policy.

In the kitchen he pulled the checkbook register out of a drawer and flipped the pages back to August. There was no entry for a check to Omaha Life.

Pete phoned Susan. She was at a loss to explain the insurance policy; Ellen had never mentioned it to her. Pete wondered if Ellen thought she might be ill. He called the offices of Ellen's internist and gynecologist to check on her last visits. She hadn't seen either doctor in months.

There was a phone number for Omaha Life on the declaration page of the insurance policy, but it was 1:20, and Pete had a class in twenty-five minutes. Pete got his notes and materials together, hopped in the car and raced to school, parking in a lot on the opposite side of the campus from the humanities building where he taught. Twice in the last two weeks he'd seen Tracy in the humanities parking lot. Each time she'd glared at him, and Pete could feel the hate radiating from her. Pete had never wanted to hurt Tracy, and it surprised him that she was so upset. She'd always known he was married, and Pete had never said he would leave Ellen for her.

He cut through the sciences building and hiked across the campus. Pete checked his mailbox in the department office, then went down the hall, stopping at Brian's office. He wasn't there, so Pete continued on to his class, which was "Introduction to American History." They had been reading a text on early colonization, which was lucky. Pete could lead this class in his sleep.

Pete let the class out fifteen minutes early. He gathered the papers the students had turned in, put them in his briefcase and left. Just outside the door he saw Tracy coming in his direction. For a second Pete thought he could duck back inside the classroom and avoid her, but she had seen him, so there was no point. He waited, watching her walk toward him.

"Hello," he said. "How are you?"

"Fine. We're doing *Macbeth,*" she said, referring to the tragedies course she taught. Tracy was tall, nearly as tall as Pete, and thin, with short dark hair. Her beauty turned heads, and she'd always exuded a sexual aura that Pete had found intoxicating from the first time he laid eyes on her. Now her brilliant dark eyes and pouting mouth, so irresistible a few weeks ago, filled him with self-loathing. "I've been leaving messages for you," she said.

"I know." There had been two in his office mailbox today.

"I never thought you'd treat me like this, Pete. It's really shitty."

He glanced behind him to make sure there was no one close enough to overhear her. When he looked back at her, Pete could see she was furious.

"So fucking worried what people might think," she spat out. "Never mind. I wanted to talk to you about our relationship. But I guess it doesn't mean enough to you."

"That's not true. We did talk about our relationship, a lot. It wasn't doing either of us any good."

She stepped up close to him, her eyes burning into his. "I thought you loved me."

"Tracy, we've been through this. I'm not going to go through it again."

Tracy snorted. "Screw you, Pete. All of a sudden you have such a great relationship with Ellen, is that it?"

Pete didn't respond. Tracy stepped past him, and Pete felt a pang of despair. "Tracy . . ."

She stopped and turned around. "What?" she asked.

"I'm sorry," he said.

"You're sorry. That's really great, Pete. I'm touched." She walked to the end of the hall and turned left.

Pete headed in the opposite direction. He stopped in the doorway of Brian's office. Brian was talking with a student. He looked up at Pete after a moment.

"Excuse me a second," he said to the young woman sitting opposite him. He stood and came out to the hallway. "You look terrible," he said after they'd moved a few steps away from the door.

"I just ran into Tracy," said Pete. "What happened with Ellen's computer files?"

"I ran the password program but it didn't work."

"Shit."

Brian said, "I gave the disk to a buddy over in Computer Science. If anybody can break it, he can."

Pete noticed the clock in the hallway. "Okay. I gotta run, but I'll call you tonight. Thanks."

PETE REACHED the insurance company from his office. The service representative at Omaha Life typed in the number of Ellen's policy on her terminal and told him that it had been paid for with a post office money order. She even had the serial number of the money order, which Pete wrote down. After a few more calls he got a number for post office information. He dialed it and got a man who told him when and where the money order was purchased. The date was August 6, which made sense since the policy was issued several days after that. It was where it was purchased that threw him. He phoned Susan immediately.

"She bought the money order in Los Angeles?" Susan asked.

"That's what they said. Did you know she had been there?"

"No. When did they say she bought it?"

"August sixth," he told her.

"How could she go to Los Angeles without you knowing?"

"I was away from August fourth through the ninth. I thought she was home, but obviously she wasn't."

"Where were you?"

"Camping with a couple of guys from school. We went up into the Ozarks." This was a lie, the same lie he had told Ellen at the time. He had actually spent those days with Tracy. He wondered if Ellen had somehow known. If she had, why go to Los Angeles and buy an insurance policy? It didn't make sense, but the fact that she'd done it on that weekend scared Pete. A vise of guilt gripped him so tightly that it took his breath away. He told Susan he would call her later and hung up the phone.

CHAPTER 4

Walker knew he had seen the woman before. He just didn't remember where. He'd gone out to the front of the building to get in his car, which he'd left out on the street the previous night after driving home from the Inkwell with Denise. The woman was at the entrance to the building, looking at the names on the mailboxes. She was in jeans and a dark shirt, with blonde hair. She had a large purse slung over one shoulder. As he approached, she turned her head and glanced his way. He saw the startled look on her face for an instant before she turned back to the mailboxes. Did he know her? She seemed familiar, and from the way she acted he'd say she recognized him. Was she looking for his name on the mailboxes? After he passed her and was out on the sidewalk, Walker looked back and saw the woman moving quickly through the courtyard toward the rear of the buildings. Maybe she was only startled because he had caught her looking at the mailboxes. He relaxed. If she was stealing mail, Walker didn't give a shit. She was welcome to the crap the mailman brought him.

He'd completely forgotten about her by the time he reached his job at the warehouse. It wasn't much of a job, but a sixty-three-year-old convicted murderer couldn't be choosy. The day passed without incident, the clock didn't drag any more than usual, and soon Walker was punching his time card and heading for home. That was when he saw her in the blue car behind him. She wore sunglasses, but he recognized her instantly. Walker only kept his eyes on the mirror for a second because now he was worried, and he didn't want her to notice him staring at her. She was fucking following him. There was no other explanation. No wonder she looked scared when he walked past the mailboxes. Shit. Why the hell was she interested in him? Whatever the reason, Walker knew it wasn't good.

In prison Walker had read *Say Yes to Success* by Eddie Rollins. Walker wasn't much of a reader, but this book cited example after example of hopeless losers like himself who were able to transform themselves into successful people by following a program of easy-to-learn techniques. Walker found it fascinating. Long ago he'd given up all hope of ever having any kind of a decent life, but maybe he shouldn't have. Eddie wrote that if a person gives up, then he deserves to be a loser. The wrong attitude was the major roadblock to success. After he finished the book, Walker used a coupon at the back to send off for audiotapes, which he listened to in his prison cell over and over again. Soon several of the other guys were listening to the tapes, and eventually they pooled their money to buy a set of videotapes, which they watched with fascination in the cell of a guy in on a second-degree murder conviction who had his own VCR.

Walker had now read all of Eddie Rollins's books and viewed all of his tapes. He felt that his life, though not a roaring success by any means, was a hell of a lot better than it used to be. He wanted to keep it that way. One of Eddie's main points was that successful people had the ability to turn negative situations into positive ones. Walker didn't know that this woman was going to create a negative situation, but he was inclined to think that was how it would turn out. Whatever happened, he sure as hell was going to do his best to turn the situation around and make it positive. Soon as he got home he planned to pull out one of Eddie's books and see if he could find some suitable advice.

The traffic started moving again. Walker glanced back again and saw that the woman was driving a small Toyota. Instead of driving straight home, Walker turned into the parking lot of a Lucky supermarket. The woman's car continued down the street. In the store Walker got the same things he always got: cigarettes, a couple of frozen dinners and some beer. When he walked back to his car, he saw no sign of the blue Toyota.

Turning down Lexington, however, he saw the car parked on the street near the entrance to the alley. There was nobody inside, so he tried to tell himself that it wasn't the woman's car. Those little Toyotas were common enough. Walker saw them all the time.

Inside his apartment, Walker immediately locked the door. She wasn't a big woman or particularly frightening, but she was following him. She didn't look like a cop, but shit, these days more than half the cops didn't look like fucking cops. Walker moved to a chair and sat down, his heart beating wildly in his chest. Why would a cop be following him? Since he got out of prison he'd been clean. Well, there was the one thing he'd done for Alan Barton, a thing he hadn't wanted to do, but there was no way he could say no to Barton. But that was in Phoenix almost a year ago now. Just a burglary, find some files in an office, take them out and give them to a man at the hotel. Walker hadn't even looked at the files. A clean job, and Barton had told him there was nothing to worry about. Now this woman was following him. Where had he seen her before? Phoenix? Maybe he'd never seen her before. She just reminded him of someone. That kind of thing happened to people all the time, he reasoned.

Walker pulled *Win, Right Now* off the shelf of the small bookcase. He opened it to one of his favorite chapters, "The Challenge of Overcoming Negativity," and started reading. Parts of it were hard for him to understand. Eddie Rollins was an intellectual. Walker had read some sections over and over for years, hoping that some of the more complicated ideas would become understandable to him over time.

There was a knock on his door and Walker stiffened. For several seconds he didn't move. Then, slowly, he got out of the chair and went to the door. If he got busted and thrown into jail, there was just no way on earth he could turn it into a positive situation. He looked through the small peephole. It was only Denise, the woman he went out with. It had been a mistake to move into the same apartment building where she lived. She wanted to see him every night, and sometimes Walker just wasn't in the mood. And Denise was a lush. That didn't bother him before, but now it got on his nerves. She knocked a second time, and Walker opened the door.

She wasn't bad looking for fifty-six—nice legs, a decent ass and waist. Her tits were big, but they sagged. All in all, she looked pretty good in clothes. Her face showed its age, but she had large eyes, and Walker used to like her short bleached hair. Hell, Walker knew he was no prize. For a long time it surprised the shit out of him that Denise wanted anything to do with him.

"Hi, hon," she said. "I was thinking of going over to the Inkwell." This was the bar where they often went together. Walker would drink beer. Sometimes he'd have a bourbon or two. Denise favored gin on ice.

"Not tonight," he said. He tried to give her a smile, but he knew it didn't look right.

"I've got some beer at my house," she said. "Come over. We can watch TV."

"I don't think so, Denise."

"Don't feel good, hon?"

He hadn't thought of saying that, but it wasn't a bad idea. "Yeah. Maybe that's it. I don't know."

"Can I get you anything? Want me to make you some soup or something? I've got five or six different cans at home."

Walker had never seen Denise eat food of any kind. She seemed to survive on cigarettes and gin. The fact that she had soup in her apartment amazed him.

"That's okay," he told her. "I'll get somethin' later for myself. Right now I don't feel like nothin'."

She put a hand to his cheek and Walker stiffened. "You feel clammy," she said. "Better take some aspirin. You're coming down with something."

She left and Walker closed the door behind her. He fell back into a chair and put his face in his hands. His chest was pounding so hard that he seriously thought he might be having a heart attack. It was when Denise touched her hand to his cheek that the memory flashed into his mind. At first he thought he must be wrong, he had to be wrong. But he wasn't. He knew who the woman following him was. He knew why she seemed so familiar. Jesus God. Once, a long time ago, he saw someone touch that woman's cheek much as Denise had touched his. A shiver crawled up his spine and his stomach turned over. Walker ran to the bathroom and threw up in the sink.

An hour later he called Alan Barton. He wasn't supposed to phone him, but this was an emergency. Walker didn't know if he had a home number or not. He'd only called it once before and then, as now, he got an answering machine. He left a message and hoped Barton would call him back tonight or tomorrow. Walker turned out the lights in his apartment, drank a few beers and looked out his front window every half-hour or so. There wasn't anything to see, just his neighbors going and coming. Around three in the morning, Walker finally managed to get to sleep.

CHAPTER 5

ELLEN HAD ONE old friend who lived in Los Angeles. John Ericson had been in the drama department at Iowa and was now a successful actor in Los Angeles. In Iowa Ellen had lived in the same apartment building as John, and they had become good friends. Pete called John to see if he'd seen or heard from Ellen lately, but he hadn't.

"I'll let you know if she calls," he said. "Are you sure she came out here?"

"No. But she was definitely in L.A. in August. You didn't see or hear from her then?"

"I was out of town most of August. If she called, she didn't leave a message."

If Ellen had gone to L.A. again on Wednesday, why didn't she want Pete to know? Why be so secretive? All he could do was ask why she was going, maybe try to talk her out of it. He certainly wasn't going to physically stop her from getting on a plane.

Pete called a friend who was a travel agent and had him check the passenger lists of flights to Los Angeles from Dallas–Fort Worth on the day Ellen left. Her name didn't appear on any of them. The travel agent then checked all the flights to San Antonio from Love Field. Again, Ellen's name didn't show up.

Ellen had worked at the bookstore in the Northpark Mall for a little over two years. She didn't care for the job much and, as far as Pete knew, she wasn't particularly close to anyone there. Still, he needed to see if Ellen had talked about leaving town to anyone at the store. Since she must have arranged to have some days off, she might have told someone what her plans were. The manager of the store was Dub Larwin. He was only twenty-eight, a tall, gawky man who loved books and hoped, according to Ellen, to have his own chain of bookstores one day. When Pete arrived on Saturday morning, Dub was in his cramped office, which seemed barely large enough to contain his long arms and legs.

"Sit down," Dub said. He had long brown hair that he combed behind his ears and wore glasses. He moved a stack of files from a chair, setting it on top of another group of files on a cabinet, and Pete sat down. Dub swiveled around in his desk chair to face him.

"How's Ellen enjoying her time off?" Dub asked.

Pete said, "That's why I stopped by today. Something kind of weird has happened. I can't find Ellen."

Dub stared at him in surprise. "What do you mean?"

Pete explained briefly, telling Dub they'd quarreled, but that Ellen had promised to be home by now. "I was hoping she might have said something to you or someone else here about her plans."

"No," said Dub, thinking about it. "All she said to me was that she was tired of working here. I asked if she had another job, and she said no. I was sorry to lose her. She was a good employee and everyone liked her. God, I hope she's okay. This is scary."

"Wait a minute," said Pete. "You mean she quit?"

Dub hesitated. "You didn't know?"

Pete shook his head. "When?" he asked.

"Let's see," said Dub. "Her last day was about three weeks ago. I can check the exact date for you."

"No. That's okay. It doesn't matter." This meant Ellen had given notice long before they had the blowup over Tracy. And that for more than two weeks she had pretended to go to a job she no longer had. Quitting the bookstore must have been unrelated to Pete's affair. But why hadn't Ellen told him about it?

"Do you have any idea where she might be?" asked Dub.

"Maybe Los Angeles."

"Did you talk to Vera about this?" asked Dub.

"No. Who's Vera?"

Dub was surprised again. He seemed embarrassed for Pete.

"Ellen's friend," he said. "She works here. I thought you knew her."

"No."

"Well, they seem like pretty good friends, is all. They'd take lunch together a lot."

"Is she here now?"

Dub shook his head. "She's off today."

Dub gave Pete Vera's phone number. Pete tried it right then from Dub's office, but he got her answering machine. Pete left a message asking her to call him at home.

From the mall Pete drove north on Central toward Brian's house. He and Patty had moved into a large home in a new development about a year before. Some of the homes had only recently sold and the new owners had yet to do any landscaping. Pete pulled up to Brian's house and parked. It was past eight now. Surely he wouldn't be interrupting their dinner.

Brian's two kids were running around downstairs, screaming at the tops of their lungs, when Patty opened the front door. Patty had gotten a lot bigger in the few weeks since Pete had seen her.

She must now be about seven months pregnant, he realized. Pete felt a quick stab of sadness pierce him when he saw Lily, Brian's five-year-old, dart past. He and Ellen should have had a child.

"Hi," he said to Patty, who looked like she hadn't slept in a week.

"Hi," she said. "The asshole's in the kitchen." She stepped back to let Pete in and then closed the door. "Have you heard from Ellen yet?" she asked.

"No."

"When she does call, tell her she's my hero."

Pete stared at Patty, too surprised to say anything. She turned, yelling to the children that it was time to get ready for bed. They screamed horribly and ran from her.

Brian was sitting at the kitchen table working on a beer when Pete walked in. He gave Pete a weak smile.

"Hey, homey," he said. "Hear from Ellen?"

"No. Your friend have any luck on the computer files?"

"Not yet. He reformatted the files, but they came out gobbledygook."

"Shit."

"He's got something else he's gonna try. Don't worry, he likes this kind of stuff. It's a challenge to him now. He'll keep working on it."

"Okay," Pete said. "Patty acted weird when I came in."

"What did she say?"

"She said Ellen's her hero. What the hell's that mean?"

"We better go outside." Brian grabbed a couple of beers and they went out the back door, sitting at the redwood table on the patio.

Brian twisted off the cap of his beer. "Patty's pissed off," he said. "She's threatening to leave again. That's why she said that about Ellen. Because Ellen had the guts to do what she wants to do."

Pete nodded. It sickened him to think that his marriage could now be compared to Brian and Patty's. "What happened?" he asked.

"She found out about May," said Brian.

"Who's May?"

"I've been seeing her for a couple of months. I thought I told you about her."

"No. She's in one of your classes?"

"Not now. Last semester."

And she's probably all of nineteen years old, thought Pete.

Brian continued, "I told Patty it was the first time it'd happened, and it wouldn't happen again."

"She believed you?"

"No." Brian chuckled bitterly. "She didn't believe me. But I don't want to lose my family, Pete. I've been wrong. I know that." Brian took a long pull from his beer. "I've known it for a long time."

THAT NIGHT Pete found himself checking the pockets in all of Ellen's clothes. He found a couple of dollars and pieces of scratch paper with brief grocery lists and notes on them, nothing of relevance. The phone rang while he was still searching. He answered it in the bedroom.

"Hello," he said.

"Hello," a woman said. "Is this Pete?" The voice had a Southern accent, Georgia probably.

"Yes."

"This is Vera Retson. I'm a friend of Ellen's at Hunter's

Bookstore. I'm returning your call." Pete explained why he had called earlier in the day.

"I haven't talked to Ellen for about two weeks," she told Pete. "She didn't mention that she was going out of town to me. Do you think she's all right?"

"I hope so, but I'm concerned about her. Do you remember what you talked about two weeks ago?"

"Jeez . . . nothing important. I was asking her what she'd been up to since she left the store. That kind of thing. I hadn't seen her in a little while, so we were catching up. I thought she might want to take another class."

Pete waited a moment. "Class?"

"Yeah," she said. "We took the handgun safety class together last winter. Then once a week or so we'd go out to the Northside Gun Club and practice. Sometimes we'd go out to lunch before or after."

"I . . ." He stopped himself. Pete didn't want to sound like a total idiot, but he had no idea Ellen had ever shot a gun in her life. "So you'd practice shooting once a week?" he said finally.

"That's right. Lots of times we'd go Thursday afternoons. It's not too crowded there during the day. You go at night, you need reservations. The last couple of months we only went a couple of times together. Ellen said she was pretty busy." Vera hesitated. "Gosh, I hope you hear from her soon."

"Me too." Pete promised he would let Vera know when he heard something. It shook him up to think Ellen was learning to shoot a gun and hadn't told him about it. Did she own a gun? He supposed she did. Where in the hell did she keep the thing?

Pete was still sitting on the edge of the bed next to the phone when it rang again. He picked it up. Taylor Reed said hello.

"You haven't heard from Ellen yet?" he asked.

"No," said Pete. "Neither has Susan."

"I thought as much, since you hadn't called," Taylor said. "I took the liberty of calling a friend of mine at the police department this morning. He had someone look for her car out at the airport."

"Did they find it?"

"Yes. It's at DFW in Lot Six."

That meant Ellen hadn't taken a commuter flight to anyplace close by. All those flights left from Love Field.

"You're sure it's her car?" asked Pete.

"Yes."

"Do you know any reason that Ellen would go to Los Angeles?"

"Los Angeles?" Taylor thought a moment. "No. Is that where you think she is?"

"Maybe," said Pete. "She went there once last summer without telling me." Pete explained to Taylor about finding the insurance policy.

"Why would she do that?"

"I don't know, but she's been doing some strange things. I'm starting to get a bad feeling about this."

"What kind of strange things?" Taylor asked. He was starting to sound worried now.

"Today I found out she quit her job three weeks ago without mentioning it. And she's been taking shooting lessons."

"Shooting lessons?"

"Yeah. Now she goes somewhere, maybe L.A., and she hides that from me. It's weird."

"Maybe you should contact the police in Los Angeles."

"I will. But I'm going out there myself. I don't know where to start looking, but I'll figure something out once I get there."

Taylor was silent for several seconds, then said, "I'll call my friend at the police department. We should file a missing persons report. And I know someone in Los Angeles who may be able to help you. A private detective who did some work for me once. He's very good. Hold on a minute, and I'll look up his number."

CHAPTER 6

ON SATURDAY Walker didn't see the woman's car on his way to or from the supermarket, and he started to hope that maybe he was wrong about the whole thing. In the afternoon he even cruised around the neighborhood looking for the blue Toyota. Barton hadn't called back yet. Walker figured he might call tonight. If he did, Walker would tell him the whole thing had been a false alarm.

It was dark when he returned to his apartment from running some errands. He was just reaching his front door when Denise said hello. Walker hadn't seen her, and it startled him.

"Sorry, hon. I didn't mean to scare you," she said. "You feeling any better?"

"Yeah," he answered. "Didn't see you." She was in the shadows under the stairway that led to the second-floor units.

"I just tried knocking on your door," she explained. "I was going upstairs and I heard someone coming. I thought it might be you. Mind if I come in?"

"Guess not." He wasn't in the mood for her, but he was too beat to argue. Walker unlocked his door and turned on the light. Denise followed him inside and sat on the green-checked sofa he'd bought last year at Krause's when they were having a blowout sale. She had her glass of gin in an insulated cup. Walker closed the door.

"You probably had a touch of the flu," she said.

"Yeah. I'm tired."

"That kind of thing wears you out."

He got a beer from the refrigerator and sat down opposite her.

"I've got some chicken cooking at my place," she said. "Let's go up."

Actually, what she had was KFC warming in her oven, which didn't bother Walker. He liked it fine. Denise put a piece of chicken and some coleslaw on her plate, but she didn't eat any, concentrating instead on her drink, which she refilled two times. Finally, Walker asked if she was going to eat her piece of chicken, and she said probably not, she wasn't so hungry tonight. She passed it to Walker and he ate it.

A few hours later Walker sat up in Denise's bed. She was asleep, snoring loudly. Walker looked at the bedside clock—it was past three in the morning. He shouldn't have stayed with her, since he was expecting Barton to call. Well, if he had, he had. Walker couldn't spend all his time waiting for him to call back.

Walker slipped out of her bed and put on his clothes. Denise didn't stir. Not surprising, the way she had washed down the gin. Walker made sure he locked her apartment door as he left.

He went down the stairs to his apartment, turned to his right, reached into his pocket for his keys and realized they weren't there. He patted his other pocket. Not there either. Fuck. Had he left them at Denise's place? He didn't think so, but it was unlike him to leave them in his own apartment. It was because he was tired, he thought, staying up all night worrying about that woman. He grabbed the doorknob and turned, hoping he'd forgotten to lock it. Not tonight. He shook the knob in frustration. Wouldn't be so bad if it wasn't three in the goddamn morning. He wasn't going to wake the manager now, and he wasn't sure he could wake Denise.

He heard a noise in the darkness behind him, then a voice.

"Open the door and go inside." It was a woman's voice. Walker's heart stopped: the woman stood a few feet away and held a gun in her right hand pointed at Walker's chest. It was a revolver, a good-sized piece. Probably a fucking .38. She'd been waiting for him.

Walker breathed in and out, trying to calm the fear that was crawling up his chest. He'd never been surprised by someone holding a gun before.

"Open the door and go inside," she repeated.

"I can't."

"I'll kill you. I don't care."

"I locked myself out."

This stopped her for a few seconds. Walker could tell she was thinking. She didn't believe it. But she knew it might be true.

"What were you going to do?"

"I don't know. I was thinkin' about tryin' to get in a window."

"What window?"

"Around the side there. The bedroom window."

"You're lying. Open the door or I'll shoot you."

"Why? What'd I ever do to you?"

She hesitated, then said, "You killed my father."

It sent a shudder through him to hear her say it. So he was right the other day: it was her. He remembered her as a kid. Four or five years old. In his mind he saw her father putting his hand to her cheek and whispering to her. *Damn that fucking day.*

"I don't know what you're talking about," he said.

"Dallas, 1965. You killed a man. My father."

"I never killed no one. I never lived in Dallas," he said. "You got me mixed up with some other person."

"I know who you are, Walker. My mother and I spent quite a lot of money finding out all about you. Now get that door open."

Jesus, who would've thought the little girl he saw that day would turn into this.

The woman cocked the pistol. Shit. She might really shoot him.

"Listen, lady. I don't wanna die. Believe me. But I can't open the fuckin' door. I left the keys upstairs." He looked her straight in the eye, hoping she would realize he was telling the truth. Walker thought that if she told him to crawl through the bedroom window, he might be able to work something.

She thought about it, then nodded toward the corner of the building. "All right. Go to the window." He walked to the end of the building and turned. She stayed a couple steps behind him, not too close. Walker was acutely aware that the gun was still cocked. He hoped to hell she wouldn't pull the trigger by accident. Once he crawled through the window, he would make a move when she tried to follow him. No way she could climb in that window and keep the gun on him the whole time. Maybe it was lucky as hell that he forgot the key. Eddie Rollins said that all men get their lucky breaks, it's just that not everybody knows how to recognize them.

Walker stopped in front of the window. It was cracked open, just like he had thought.

"Go ahead," she said.

He had to take the screen off. Walker pulled up at the bottom edge, but it wouldn't come easily. He forced it, bending the screen a bit, but it came out. He put it down on the cement.

"Walker!" The voice, a loud whisper, came from around the building. It was Denise. *What the fuck?* "Walker!" she said again.

"Who's that?" the woman asked.

"A friend."

"What's she want?"

"I don't know."

"Go to the corner and see. Say the wrong thing and I'll shoot you. I don't give a shit if you die."

She moved back a couple of steps as he walked by, all the time keeping the gun right on him. She seemed comfortable with the gun—it looked like she had some experience. If he took off running for the street, she'd probably drop him with one shot. He went to the edge of the building and stopped. Denise was hanging over the edge of the second-floor balcony, a terrycloth robe tied loosely around her, her right tit flopping halfway out.

"What?" he asked.

She'd been looking down at his front door. She turned her head at the sound of his voice. "You forgot your keys," she said, letting them dangle from her outstretched hand. Fucking Denise. She'd had enough gin to put four people under, but she wakes up and finds his goddamn keys in the dark.

The woman said, "Get them." She was behind him, blocked by the wall from Denise's view.

He moved away from the building and thought again about running. He'd have a second or two of surprise, but that wouldn't be enough. It'd take him at least five seconds to cross the court-yard. Walker stopped right below Denise, and she dropped the keys down to him.

"How were you going to get in?" she asked.

"There was a window open."

"Now you can go in the front." The upstairs door closed, and she was gone.

Thanks a lot. Now I'm probably a dead man. He went to his apartment door. The woman waited a few seconds, then came sliding along the side of the building until she was next to him. Walker used the key in the lock, and she followed him in. He heard her push the door shut and throw the deadbolt.

"Go to that chair and sit down," she said, pointing.

Walker did as he was told. The woman pulled a stool out from the bar and sat opposite him. She was a good five feet away. There was one lamp on in the dim room. The woman stared at him for a long time. Walker kept his eyes on hers as long as he could, then he looked away.

"You've changed a lot," she said.

"You got the wrong person. I never killed no one."

"You were there," she said. "You were an accomplice to the murder of my father. That makes you as guilty as your partner."

Walker looked down at the floor for a few seconds. There didn't seem to be much point in denying it. She knew who he was.

"The other man did it on the spur of the moment," he said. "I didn't know it would happen. I didn't want it to happen."

"Who was the other man?"

Walker didn't say anything.

She waited awhile. "Not talking now? Well, you better talk pretty damn quick. I've spent my whole life hating you. You ruined our lives. Killing you will make me very happy."

"I was in prison a long time. I paid for what happened."

"Not enough."

Walker was silent. How could he argue with her? He could see the hate in her eyes. Hell, he'd probably feel the same way about somebody killing someone in his family. Except his daddy. He'd have been happy to have that bastard dead when he was a kid.

She held the gun steady. Her hand wasn't shaking. She'd had shooting lessons probably, could aim, pull the trigger, hit the target. But now she was into something that she'd never practiced. Walker thought he could wait her out. Wait for her to slip. Turn the negative into the positive. He'd almost had a break before, he'd really get one if he was patient. The woman was nervous and scared. She had to be, doing something like this. She'd slip. When she did, he'd have to be ready.

"I want to know who was with you the day my father died. I want to know who shot him."

"He's dead."

"I don't believe you."

"It's true. He got shot and killed years ago. He was holding up a store. Liquor store, I heard."

"How'd you find out about it?"

"You hear things in prison."

She stared at him for a long time. "You're lying," she said. "I can tell you're lying."

"I'm not lying, lady."

"My name's Ellen. Don't you remember? You asked me my name once."

Walker remembered. He wished to hell he didn't, but he did. "Guess I forgot," he said.

"Forget my father's name, too?"

"No."

"Tell me his name."

"Come on. What good's this gonna do?"

"Tell me my father's name."

He stared at her, gritting his teeth. "Victor Samuels," he said finally.

"You know how old he was when you killed him?"

"I keep tellin' you I didn't kill him."

"He was only thirty-one. And you might not have shot him, but you sure as hell were there."

Walker moved his eyes away. The hate in her face was so fierce that it was hard to look at it. She might really kill him, no matter how afraid she was.

"I want you to tell me who shot my father. You've got six hours to tell me his name and where he lives. If you don't, I'm going to shoot you in the back of the head just like your partner shot my father."

"How do I know you won't shoot me anyway?"

"You don't. But if you don't tell me the truth, I definitely will."

"Okay," said Walker. "His name was Crowe. Larry Crowe. He got killed seven, maybe eight years ago. Check up on it. You'll see."

"What were you doing in my father's office that day?"

"We wanted the typewriters, adding machines. Anything else we could sell easy. I had a habit then. I needed the money fast."

"A habit?"

"Heroin."

"You were addicted to heroin?"

"That's right."

"Stupid liar," she hissed. "I know all about you. We paid investigators to find out everything about you. You were a drunk, not a junkie. You're lying about your partner, too. He's alive. You've got a little less than six hours to tell me who he is. It's your life or his. Take your pick."

They sat in silence. He looked at the gun. She was resting it on the top of her knee. The fucking thing was still pointing straight at him. She looked like she could sit there for six days, waiting.

"Lady," he said. "What happened thirty years ago was a terrible thing. Believe me, I wish to hell it'd never happened. We didn't go in there plannin' to kill nobody. It happened. I'm sorry it was your daddy." He hesitated, running his hand across his brow. "Killin' me isn't going to make anything better. You get caught, and it'll make things a whole lot worse. I know. You may think you want your revenge, but every day you spend inside you'll wish to hell you'd never even heard the word."

"I won't get caught."

"You can't know that for sure."

"We spent a long time planning this. I won't get caught. If I kill you, who's going to care besides your friend upstairs? The cops aren't going to give a shit."

"Maybe they won't. But they'll know it's a murder, and they'll investigate. They'll look into who might have a motive."

"Stop worrying about me," she said. "You should worry about yourself."

"Right now, you can walk out of here and drive away. Nothing'll happen to you. No one'll know you were here. You don't wanna kill nobody."

She glanced at her watch. "Time's a-wasting."

"Shit, lady."

"Take off your shoes," she said.

"How come?"

"Just do it."

Walker bent over, untied one shoe, then the other. He slipped them off his feet.

"Now take the laces out of the shoes."

Walker looked at her for a moment and then did it.

"Tie the laces together. Then use the laces to tie your ankles together."

Walker wrapped the laces around his ankles and started to tie them.

"Wrap them around again," she told him. "They're long enough."

Walker wrapped the laces around his ankles again and started tying a knot.

"Make it tight," she said. "And knot it twice."

He finished and sat up in the chair. "That okay?" Christ, he was in a fix now.

"Yeah," she answered. Keeping the gun on him, she reached with one hand into her purse and pulled out a pair of handcuffs. Jesus. She got those fucking things on him and his chances of getting out of this mess were going to be zero. There might always be a way to turn a negative situation positive, but Walker was starting to think this present situation would tax even Eddie.

"Stand up now," she told him. He stood up slowly.

"You don't need those," he said. "I'm not goin' nowhere with my feet tied like this."

"Turn around," she said. "Then put both hands on top of your head."

Shit, just like a fucking cop. He turned around, which wasn't all that easy since his ankles were bound, and put his hands on top of his head. She stepped up behind him, jamming the barrel of the gun into his back. Then she slipped the cuff around his left wrist and yanked the arm down behind his back.

There was a knock at the door. Walker froze and felt the woman flinch. For a second neither moved, then Walker twisted to his right, bringing his right elbow down and driving it into the side of her head. There was a crack and she fell to the floor. He turned around and saw she was bleeding from her nose, a stream of it running into the carpet. He turned and fell because of the shoelaces around his ankles. She still had the gun in her hand. He reached over her to grab it, and she came alive under his weight, thrashing and turning, hitting at his face. He twisted her wrist and the gun fell onto the carpet. Walker got his fingers on it, lifted it up and smashed it against her head. Then he hit her two times hard in the chest, hearing something snap. Shit. Walker stopped. She was out cold.

There was another knock on the door. "Walker?" he heard Denise say. "You okay?"

He got to his feet and tried to move, forgetting that his ankles were tied, and he nearly fell again. Walker hobbled as best he could to the door, unlocked it and opened it a crack.

"You all right?" asked Denise. She was still in her robe, though at least now she had it wrapped around her. Dark makeup was smeared around her eyes, and her hair was twisted by sleep. She was a sight, but he couldn't be pissed off. She was a nosy bitch, but she'd probably just saved his life.

"I'm fine," he said. He heard stirring behind him.

"What was that noise?" Denise asked.

"I was lying down on the sofa," he said. "When you knocked, it surprised me. I rolled off."

"Sorry. I thought I heard voices after I gave you the key." There was a low moan behind him. If Denise heard it, he didn't know what the fuck he'd do.

"Guess I was talkin' to myself. I was pissed off about forgettin' my keys. Good night." He heard the woman moan again, barely audible. Walker pushed the door closed.

"Don't feel like a nightcap, do you?" she asked, raising her voice.

Walker opened the door an inch.

"No. I need to get some sleep." How could she think about a drink? It was four in the morning. He was going to have to get her in AA. "I'll talk to you tomorrow," he said.

"But—"

"'Night, Denise."

He closed the door again and locked it. Turning around, he saw that the woman was on her hands and knees now, not moving, still dazed, out of it. Walker had the gun in his right hand. He turned it around, holding the barrel tight, the metal cold in the palm of his hand. He waited a few seconds, then heard the faint steps of Denise climbing the stairs to the second floor. Shuffling over to the woman, Walker raised the gun over his head and brought it down hard on the back of her skull. It made more noise than he expected, and she collapsed to the floor. What the fuck did she think she was doing? He thought of her thirty years ago, the little girl in Dallas, and it made him sick. She had seemed so sweet then. This time she'd brought it all on herself, threatening to shoot him. He'd told her to leave, walk away, go home, but she wouldn't. Now look what she'd done.

He hobbled to the kitchen and pulled a knife from the drawer. Sitting on the linoleum, he sawed at the shoelaces, freeing himself. Back in the living room, he saw that the woman was still. He went to her purse and looked for keys. He found a set, went through them and got the key to the handcuffs. After he unlocked them, he knelt down next to the woman and cuffed her hands behind her back. She was bleeding like a pig from the back of her head. He went to the bathroom and got a towel, which he held to the wound. The blood soaked into the towel, drenching it.

Jesus. Just his luck, she'd bleed to death in the apartment. Walker got another towel and held it to her head. Finally the bleeding stopped. If she woke up he didn't want her to start moaning or screaming, so he had to do something about keeping her quiet. There was some packing tape somewhere. Last Christmas he had sent a package to his sister in Midland. He'd bought the tape to seal up the box.

Walker threw the blood-soaked towels in the trash and washed his hands. Then he looked in the kitchen for the tape. It was two inches wide, a thick reinforced plastic. Once he had it, he started looking for the scissors to cut it. They were around somewhere, but it took him about five minutes to find them. He went back to the woman and checked to see if she was still breathing, then taped her ankles together. *See how she likes it.* He rolled her over, cut a piece of tape and put it over her mouth. There was a large pool of blood soaked into the carpet. He'd use another towel to soak some of it up, but it was going to look like shit. No way you could clean up a mess like that. The hell with it. He couldn't worry about that now.

He grabbed the woman under the arms and dragged her into the bedroom, leaving her on the floor between the bed and the closet. Back in the living room he picked up the phone and started to dial Barton's number, but then stopped and hung up. He'd wait to see if the woman lived or not before he called again.

CHAPTER 7

SATURDAY AT NOON Pete waited in the lobby of a Norm's coffee shop on Pico Boulevard about five miles north of the Los Angeles airport. Pete had arrived in L.A. four hours earlier. He rented a car and got a room at the Day's Inn. He called the private investigator Taylor had recommended, and the investigator suggested meeting at this restaurant. On his way, Pete had stopped at the police station in West Los Angeles and filled out a missing persons report on Ellen.

Norm's was probably a chain, but Pete didn't know of any in Dallas. The place was full of elderly people. Pete was the youngest customer by two decades, maybe three. It gave him an odd feeling. After he sat down on the orange Naugahyde bench and took his eyes off the booths filled with gray- and white-haired patrons, he noticed the posters on the walls advertising various specials. The food was cheap—five-course dinners for $6.95 including coffee and dessert. Breakfast specials for 99 cents. That explained all the senior citizens. Well, Pete was on a budget himself, and it wouldn't hurt to know about a place like this.

Pete looked up as a man in his late sixties entered, taking off a pair of sunglasses. Thick gray hair was matted around his ears, but the top of his head was entirely bald. His face was broad, with a meaty nose that looked like it had been broken more than once. He was a tall man, a bit heavy, and wore a tight gray sport jacket over a white shirt and a limp tie. He looked at Pete and walked over.

"Donelly?" he asked.

Pete stood up. "Yeah. Mr. Saunders?"

"Call me Marvin."

As they shook hands, Pete noticed the detective's jacket was frayed at the cuffs. This guy wasn't what Pete had expected. Taylor had said the man was a veteran, but Pete hadn't known he meant retirement age.

They sat in a booth next to a large window that looked out on the busy six-lane street. It was a little past noon, and the traffic was relentless. Pete passed Marvin a manila envelope.

"These are the flyers you wanted."

"Good." He opened the envelope and pulled out a sheet of paper with a photograph of Ellen on it. Along the bottom was her name, age, height and weight. Pete had just had them printed at a copy shop near his hotel. "Perfect. These all for me?"

"Yeah. I kept a hundred for myself."

"So your wife's been gone four days now?" Marvin asked.

"Three days. She left Wednesday morning." It seemed unbelievable to Pete that his world had blown apart in so short a time. "She called me Thursday night and hung up on me when she realized I knew she wasn't at her sister's house."

A young waitress appeared and took their order. A perky woman with short dark hair and freckles running across her nose, she knew Marvin well, calling him by name. Evidently he was a regular at Norm's.

Pete went over the whole thing with Marvin. He told him about searching the house and finding the insurance policy. He explained how he found out that Ellen had purchased a money order from a post office in Los Angeles to pay for the policy. He finished by telling him what he had learned from her manager at the bookstore and her friend Vera.

Marvin said, "You don't know for certain that she flew to L.A.?"

"No. All I know is that she came out here in August without telling me about it. And she left her car at the Dallas–Fort Worth airport on Wednesday. This morning when I parked out there I saw it. I had a travel agent check flights to L.A. on the day she left. Her name wasn't on any passenger list. So I don't know where she is. She could be in Vermont for all I know."

Their lunch arrived, and Pete looked at the plateful of food set in front of him. He had no appetite. He hadn't since Ellen left. Mechanically, he put a piece of fish in his mouth and began chewing.

Marvin said, "Well, L.A. is the only lead you've got, so it's the best place to start. But let's keep our minds open to other possibilities." He dipped a shrimp in the seafood sauce and deposited it in his mouth. Marvin chewed and swallowed. "This is out of character for her, far as you're concerned? Traveling out of town without telling you where she's going?"

"Yeah. Totally."

"But she's done it twice. At least twice."

"That's right. Thursday night when she called I could hear something in the background."

"What?"

"Voices. And some sort of rumble."

"Traffic?"

"I don't think so. But she was obviously at a pay phone."

"You think she could have a boyfriend? I know that's an unpleasant thought, but since you were involved with someone else maybe she is, too."

Pete said, "It's possible." Odd that the idea hurt so much, given the circumstances, but it did. "I've never had any feeling that something like that was going on. I asked her sister about it. She and Ellen are pretty close, and she said she didn't know of anything."

Marvin pushed his plate away and grimaced. "I shouldn't have eaten so much," he said. "Too greasy." His voice was tight. Obviously in some pain, he held one hand knotted into a fist against the front of his chest. Then he reached inside his jacket pocket and took out a small bottle. He opened it, shook out a pill and put it in his mouth.

"You okay?" asked Pete.

"Fine in a minute," he said. "My whole life I've loved to eat. Pisses me off that I have such a bad time with it now. That's a little better." Marvin relaxed a bit.

"Is it an ulcer?"

"Yeah. That and more. My stomach lining's shot. But shit, I've still got to eat." He wiped his mouth with the napkin. "This insurance policy you found at your house."

"Yeah?"

"You and your wife have any other insurance besides that?"

"We both have hundred-thousand-dollar policies. Then I've got a small policy through the school where I teach. That's all."

"And she bought this policy for three-fifty on herself and didn't tell you?"

"Yeah."

"Has she ever visited L.A. besides last August?"

"We were out here about six years ago on a vacation. We stayed a few days, then went up to San Francisco."

Marvin picked up his glass of water and sipped it. "How did she pay for her plane ticket in August?" he asked.

"She didn't charge it on any of our credit cards. I checked our old bills. On Thursday I called the card companies to see if there had been a recent charge for an airline or a hotel. There wasn't."

"So she used cash, probably. You haven't noticed an unusual withdrawal of cash from your bank account?"

"No."

He said, "She's up to something, isn't she?"

"Yeah. Maybe she's just trying to make me suffer. I hope that's all it is. But there's something strange about the whole thing. I'm afraid that something else is going on besides her being angry at me."

"There might be," said Marvin.

Though it was near the end of October, the weather was hot and bone-dry. A gust of wind scuttled brown leaves across the sidewalk as Pete and Marvin walked to the parking lot. They reached Marvin's car—a ten-year-old Buick in mint condition.

"So where do we start?" Pete asked.

"I need a check for fifteen hundred dollars. That's for the first week. After that it's two hundred a day plus any expenses."

"You think it will take more than a week?" asked Pete.

"I hope not. But you never know."

"Okay," said Pete. He pulled his checkbook from his back pocket.

"Besides the recent fight over your affair, were there any other problems?" asked Marvin.

"No. Not really." The biggest disagreement they'd ever had until this was whether to try to have a child or not. That was years ago now. They hadn't even talked about it recently.

Marvin nodded. "Okay. I'll see what I can dig up. Since we know she was here in August, I'll find something."

"What can I do?" asked Pete.

"Call her friend out here again. Try to think if there's anyone else she might have visited or called. It's odd she'd be here twice and not call anyone she knew."

Pete wrote out a check and handed it to Marvin.

FOUR AIRLINES flew from Dallas to Los Angeles. Pete drove back to the airport and went to the ticket counter of each one. He left a few flyers with the shift supervisors and explained the situation. All the people he spoke with promised to post Ellen's photograph in areas where flight attendants and other employees would see them. Pete wrote his name and hotel phone number on the bottom of each.

Back at the hotel Pete called his home number and checked the messages on his machine. There was one from Susan, who said she'd heard nothing. Pete called her back, then phoned John, Ellen's friend from Iowa who lived in L.A. John promised to telephone everyone he could think of who knew Ellen in college to see if anyone had talked to her recently.

Though he was exhausted, Pete couldn't sleep. After lying on the bed for almost an hour, he went to a window. He was on the sixth floor and could see the freeway a few blocks away. Traffic was heavy in both directions, cars flowing ceaselessly, all full of people, hundreds of thousands of people. He wondered if any of them had seen Ellen in the last few days. Pete slid the window open and listened to the steady rumble. The air flowing over his face was warm and dry. The city was so huge and imposing that he felt like there was no way he could ever find Ellen. A tear fell from his right eye and coursed slowly down his cheek. Within minutes the dry breeze had evaporated every trace of it.

CHAPTER 8

IT WAS A DREAM more real than any other. Ellen was a small girl sitting on the floor of her room. She was playing with the new dollhouse she'd gotten as a birthday present. The mommy and daddy sat in the living room listening to music on the radio and talking. The children were playing upstairs. There was a dog. He came up the stairs to find the children. *Ruff, ruff,* the dog barked at the kids. Ellen and Susie didn't have a dog. Ellen wished they did. It wasn't fair. Almost all her friends had a dog. Some had cats, too.

"Hey, pumpkin," her daddy called from downstairs. "Want to come for a ride in the car?"

"Yeah!"

She left the dog in the children's bedroom and ran downstairs. Her mother brushed her hair quickly, and she went out the kitchen door with her father.

He opened the front door of his black car and she climbed up onto the seat. He went around the other side, getting in behind the wheel. He started the car and slowly backed down the driveway.

"I've got to go by my office," he said. "Then maybe we can stop and get some ice cream."

"I want chocolate."

"You do? You think the ice cream store will have chocolate?"

"Yes."

"Are you sure?"

"They always have chocolate."

He laughed and she laughed with him. Ellen liked going places with her daddy. His car smelled good, and he was always being funny. Also, Susie never went because she was too little. Ellen liked being alone with him. At home Susie was always trying to make him hold her. They couldn't even play Candyland without Susie messing it up.

They got on the highway and drove to his office, which was downtown. It was a brick building. Daddy unlocked the door, and they went inside. They climbed the stairs to the second floor. There was a long hallway there. His company was at the end of the hall. He had his keys out and put one key in the lock on his door and opened it. There were words on the door and a picture of an oil rig. They entered and he let the door close. He started forward, then stopped. He was listening to something.

"Stay here, pumpkin," he said to Ellen. "I'll be right back."

Ellen stood next to a gray metal desk, leaning her back against the cool rounded edge. It was dim—her father hadn't turned the lights on. There was a second desk in front of her. On it was a calendar, a ceramic cup with pens and pencils in it, and a neat stack of papers. Next to the desk a typewriter sat on a small table.

Ellen heard voices. She went to the doorway where her father had gone. Through it there was a hall that led to lots of offices. One was her daddy's. The voices got louder. Then she heard a thump. The floor vibrated with several more thumps. Something fell with a crash. Ellen was scared. She moved back, went around the desk and carefully pulled the chair out. It was on wheels. She crawled under the desk and pulled the chair in after her. There were no more noises for a long time. Then she heard footsteps. A person came into the room and stopped. Ellen could see his scratched black shoes through the four-inch space between the desk and the floor. Ellen clasped her hands over the back of her head and put her face down on the floor just like they did at school when they practiced for an air raid.

The man said, "She ain't here."

A second man spoke. "I saw her come in with him. Look outside. Be quick about it."

The door opened and closed. She heard more footsteps as someone else came into the room. "Crap," she heard the second man say. The footsteps went away. Ellen wanted her daddy. She pushed the chair away and crawled out from under the desk. Standing, she thought about going through the doorway where her father had gone. But the loud noises had come from there. The car was outside. She could go to the car and wait. Ellen wasn't afraid of the car. She liked her daddy's car.

She was halfway down the stairs when a man appeared at the bottom of the steps. He had wavy hair, a pale face and a large jutting chin. When he smiled, Ellen saw that he had a silver tooth in front.

"Hi, there. I been looking for you, girl. Let's go upstairs. We gotta figure out what we're gonna do." He climbed the stairs toward her. When he was just two steps below, Ellen turned around and started back up.

He took her into her daddy's office and closed the door. She heard a key turn. The man had locked it. Her father sat in the chair at his desk. She went to him and climbed into his lap. He put his arms around her and kissed the top of her head.

"You okay, sweetheart?" he asked.

"Yeah." She felt him shaking underneath her. "Are you cold?" she asked.

"No. I'm not cold." But he kept shaking. "Everything's going to be okay," he told her.

"I'm scared," she said.

"We'll be okay in a little while."

"Is that a bad man?"

"He won't hurt us."

They waited silently. Ellen kept her hands folded in her lap. She heard an occasional car or truck pass by.

The dream jumped ahead and Ellen was standing at the door, trying to open it, but it was still locked. She was crying.

"It's okay, sweetheart," her daddy said. "Don't worry about it."

"I'm sorry," she said.

They heard a car drive up quickly and stop with a screech. A car door slammed. Her daddy got up and went to the window.

"The police," he said. "They've come to help us."

The door to the office flew open, and the bad man stepped in. His face was red and angry. "Come on, you sonofabitch! He wants to see you!"

Her father didn't move. Ellen looked back to the man. He held a gun in his hand. It was pointed at her daddy.

"Move your ass right now!" he screamed. Ellen felt her eyes burning and she started to cry. Her daddy bent down and looked at her.

"Don't cry, sweetheart," he said. "We're going to be okay. You be a brave girl and wait right here for me, okay?" He put his hand against her cheek. Ellen looked into his brown eyes and saw that he was frightened. She cried harder. He kissed her on the forehead and said something that she couldn't understand. He went around the desk and left. The bad man with the gun closed the door again, and she was alone.

Ellen went to the window. She wasn't tall enough to see out of it. Dragging a chair over, she climbed up and looked. There were three police cars outside the building. One was parked right next to her daddy's car. Policemen were walking toward the building. They had guns in their hands.

She heard a loud bang. The policemen got down on the ground. Some crouched behind the cars. Ellen heard more bangs. Then it was quiet. She crawled under her father's desk and put her forehead against the scratchy carpet. She wanted to go home. She wanted her mommy.

Then Ellen smelled smoke.

THERE WAS SOMETHING wet on her face. She felt a pounding in her head and was sick to her stomach. Slowly, she realized her hands and feet were stuck together. Ellen tried to move her hands apart. She couldn't.

Opening her eyes, she saw a wall. She had a hard time deciding if she was close to the wall or not. There was nothing to use as a reference point. There was a pale shag carpet leading to the wall. One side of her face was against the carpet. It was scratchy. She remembered trying to handcuff the murderer. Did that really happen? Had she really taken the gun and pointed it at him and tried to force him to tell her the name of the other man? Maybe she had dreamed it. She dreamed about the murder so often. But what was this? This could be a dream, too. A sick dream where her head was exploding and she lay on a carpet looking at a wall that was close or far, she couldn't tell which. Maybe she was dead. She closed her eyes. If you were dead, would everything still hurt so intensely?

She remembered the murderer turning. She had looked away and he had turned and hit her in the face. He had kicked her, she thought. Kicked her in the head. God, her head hurt. Ellen opened her eyes again and looked at the wall. It was very far away, she decided. Trying to turn her head, Ellen was overwhelmed by a blinding pain so intense that she gasped for breath and nearly passed out. Lying very still was best. If she was very still, the pain subsided enough for her to think. She had confronted him. He had beat her. She wasn't dead, but he would kill her. He was a murderer and she'd threatened his life. Ellen wondered if there was any way someone could find her. Pete wouldn't even be looking for her yet, had no idea where she was. But that didn't matter. Soon she'd be dead. In a certain light it was a terrible thing she'd tried to do, yet she and her mother were justified. The man who shot her father had gotten away. Walker went to jail, but not the other man. The man who shot Daddy. She remembered her mother sobbing on her shoulder when she was a girl, climbing up onto the bed and holding Ellen as she cried and cried, Ellen's pajamas becoming soaked with her mother's tears. "That bastard killed him and got away with it," she would weep. "He got away with it." Ellen knew even then that she would someday find the man who got away. Now she had failed. She and her mother had planned it for so long that she never really considered failure. But they had never planned for Ellen to do it alone.

She heard a man say, "You awake?"

Ellen tried to move her head, but the blinding pain came again. When she opened her eyes, she could see him leaning over to look at her. She remembered he had a silver tooth in her dream. She'd never recalled that before.

"I thought I mighta killed you," he said.

She tried to open her mouth but couldn't. Maybe her jaw was broken. Nothing seemed to work. Her hands, her feet, her mouth. He thought he might've killed her. She couldn't understand why he hadn't. He would kill her soon, and Pete might never know what happened, what she had been trying to do. She wondered how many days she had been gone, but her head was muddled, she couldn't think. She hadn't called Pete for a couple of days at least. He might have called the police by now. Maybe the police could trace her. She wished she had told Susan where she was going. She almost had, wanting her to know about it, but Susan wouldn't have understood. Susan didn't see their father walk out the door, didn't see the look in his eyes when he touched her face that last time. Susan hadn't dreamed about that day and waked up screaming, choking, trying to get out from under the desk and away from all that black smoke.

Without warning she was moving and her head was flooded by the white-hot pain. Opening her eyes, she saw nothing but red and white spots flying in every direction. She stopped moving. The spots faded, and Ellen saw the murderer's face in front of hers. She was sitting up. She tried to scream as he pulled the tape away from her mouth, but she didn't hear any noise. The murderer held a glass to her lips.

"Drink some of this," he said.

She swallowed, and it was the most wonderful sensation she'd ever had. She swallowed more and more, greedily wanting every drop in the glass. She hadn't realized how parched she was. How long had it been since she'd had something to drink? How long had she been unconscious? Ellen finished the water in the glass.

"More," she tried to say.

"That's enough for now," he said.

She thought she would start to cry. How could he not let her have any more water? She tried to say, "Please." What she heard was only a moan.

"You'll get sick. In a little while I'll give you more."

A little while? What did he mean? An hour? Two? A day? She couldn't wait. Water. Please, God, if he'd just give her some more—

She was moving again, and the pain came screaming back and the room disappeared in red. As the murderer gently placed her back on the floor, Ellen wondered if she would be dead or alive tomorrow. Then she felt herself falling into a dark hole where there was no pain and no thirst and no dreams. There was nothing.

CHAPTER 9

PETE CALLED SUSAN in the morning, then left the hotel. He drove to the post office where Ellen had purchased the money order to pay for the life insurance policy. It was in a commercial block of storefronts and small office buildings. At one end of the block was a new corner strip mall.

The post office was closed because it was Sunday, but Pete walked a couple of blocks in each direction, handing out Ellen's picture to every store and business that was open. He didn't stop until he ran out of the flyers. Then he went back to his car. It was only 12:15. From a pay phone he called John Ericson to see if he'd had any luck calling University of Iowa alumni, but John didn't answer. Pete left a message. Then he pulled out Marvin's business card and looked up the address on his map. It wasn't far away.

Twenty minutes later he was parked in front of an apartment building on a shady, tree-lined street a couple miles west of the post office. Pete went inside. The lobby of the building was full of white-haired men and women. On one side seven people sat watching a television game show. In other parts of the room people were reading or talking. One old guy sat by himself playing with a Gameboy.

By the time Pete got on the elevator with a small silver-haired woman who walked with a cane, he realized this was a retirement home. And he'd given Marvin fifteen hundred dollars. Jesus Christ. The woman got off at the second floor. Pete held the door open for her while she inched her way out. He rode to the next floor and found number 330. He knocked. A short, plump woman opened the door. Her face was smooth, practically wrinkle-free.

"Hello?" she said, looking at Pete's chest.

"Hi," Pete said. As soon as he spoke the woman raised her eyes to his face, and Pete realized she was blind. "I was looking for Marvin Saunders," he continued.

"Come in, please," she said, stepping back. "I'm Louise, Marvin's wife." She held out her hand. Pete took her small hand in his.

"I'm Pete Donelly," he said.

Pete entered, and Louise closed the door. "Marvin," she called. The detective came in from another room.

"How you doing?" he asked Pete.

"Okay. I was in the neighborhood, so I thought I'd stop by. I wasn't sure if you worked out of an office or not."

"This is my office now. Have a seat."

It was a small apartment with an efficiency kitchen. The living room had two chairs, a small sofa, a television and a coffee table. Next to the kitchen area was a small square table with a phone and some papers on it. The apartment gave off a slightly medicinal odor.

"I was just doing some work on your case," Marvin said, nodding at the table.

"Good." Pete sat down. "Have you always worked out of your apartment?" he asked.

"I used to have an office," Marvin said. "But seventy percent of what I do is make phone calls. At my age it makes sense to cut down on overhead."

Pete wanted to ask what Marvin's age was. He was wondering if he could get back part of the fifteen hundred dollars he'd paid him. The old guy had worked less than twenty-four hours; Pete ought to be able to get at least half of it back. He'd get another investigator out of the phone book. By tomorrow he'd be better off. Ellen would be better off. A day would be lost, but he needed someone who could work his ass off for a couple of days and find his wife. Marvin was a nice enough guy, but he lived in a place that was one step away from a rest home, for Christ's sake.

"I'm sorry to hear about your wife, Pete," Louise said.

"Well," said Pete, "I hope we'll find something out pretty soon."

"I'm sure you will," she said. "Marvin's always been very good at finding people."

Marvin said, "I called all the motels and hotels in the area surrounding the post office on Ninth. She's not registered at any of them under her own name. I'll try the likely hotels around the airport next. You check to see if she'd ever been registered at the place you're staying?"

"No," said Pete. "I didn't think about it."

"You can do it tonight. I heard you went out to the airport."

"How'd you know that?" he asked.

"I haven't been sitting on my butt here. Well, I have been sitting on my butt." He snorted. "But I've been making calls. I called the airlines this morning."

"I thought maybe somebody would remember seeing her."

"Good idea. Somebody did."

Pete looked at him, not saying anything. It took a moment for what Marvin said to register.

"Someone recognized her?"

"Yeah. A stewardess. When I called Far West, the supervisor told me someone named . . ." Marvin stood and went to the table. He picked up a note pad. "Her name is Lisa Battiston. She remembers seeing Ellen on one of her flights."

"When?"

"Last week. She can't remember the exact day. Lisa's flying today, but she'll be back in L.A. around three."

LISA BATTISTON'S SHIFT was ending after doing a round trip from L.A. to Dallas to New Orleans and back. Pete and Marvin waited in the terminal for her flight to arrive. The crew deplaned about ten minutes after the last passenger. Lisa was a thin woman with henna-tinted hair and tired eyes. She looked to be in her early thirties. Marvin introduced both himself and Pete, and they went to the bar inside the terminal to talk. Pete bought Lisa a glass of white wine. Marvin had a gin and tonic. Pete saw Marvin slip two pills into his mouth before he took his first sip of the drink. Lisa looked at the photos that Pete had brought of Ellen and remained confident that she had seen Ellen on one of her flights. She wasn't sure what day it had been, only that it was within the last week.

She said, "I don't know why I remember her, but I do. Maybe I chatted with her for a minute or something."

"You can't remember anything else about her? Anything she said? Something that struck you about her?" asked Marvin.

"No. Sorry. I'll keep thinking about it. Maybe something will come to me. But I see a lot of passengers in a week, let me tell you. I couldn't even tell you that she was on the L.A. flight. If you say she was, fine. But I did a couple of Denver and Salt Lake runs last week. All I know is that I saw her."

They finished their drinks, and Lisa took them to an office where they were able to get two copies of the passenger list for the Dallas to L.A. flight Lisa worked the day Ellen left. Pete checked the list. He thought Ellen's alias might strike a chord with him, but none of the names meant anything. Thirty-two women boarded the flight in Dallas that day. Eight of them were stopping in L.A. to make a connection to another destination. Of the twenty-four who stayed in Los Angeles, it was obvious that seven were traveling with family members with the same last name. That left seventeen names of women traveling alone to Los Angeles. Marvin underlined them. Most likely one of those names was used by Ellen. If they were lucky, Marvin said, she had used the same name when she registered at a hotel.

"So what do we do now?" Pete asked as they drove away from the airport.

"A good question."

Pete looked over at Marvin, who was staring straight ahead. The sun was burning through the side window onto his face. His skin was gray and spotted; it sagged around his cheeks and neck.

Pete said, "You must have some idea."

"We could start checking hotels, I guess, but there are a hell of a lot of 'em out there and we've got seventeen names. We could spend weeks calling places and asking them to check and not find the right place. And she might've used a different name at the hotel."

"Shit," said Pete. "How about the hotels and motels around the post office?"

"It took me about an hour today when I called asking about her. That was just one name. Now we've got seventeen."

"So what do we do instead?"

"I don't know off the top of my head."

"Then we should start calling the hotels and asking them to check for any of these names."

"It'd take weeks," said Marvin. "There are thousands of hotels in Los Angeles."

"We can narrow it down. We'll try everything close to the airport first. Then around the post office where she got the money order."

"It's a waste of time."

"What else are you going to do?"

"Right now, I don't know."

"Shit, Marvin." Pete clenched his teeth in anger as he double-parked in front of Marvin's building. "How can you not know what you're going to do? I'm paying you to find my wife. I'm scared to death about this."

"Then let me work my way. I spend the next two weeks calling hotels all over, we won't be any better off. You do that if you want. I've gotta think. I'll think of something."

"What if you don't?"

"Don't worry. I will."

Marvin opened the car door and climbed out.

"How can you know you'll think of something?" Pete asked.

Marvin leaned down to look at Pete. "Kid, I've been doing this for over forty years. I always think of something."

He slammed the car door, and Pete watched the hulking figure walk slowly to the entrance of his building, noticing for the first time that he had a slight limp. *Jesus, what a package*. Marvin unlocked the front door and stepped into the lobby of his building. Driving away, Pete's stomach felt like it had turned to rock. Should he have fired Marvin? He had been on the verge of doing it. But if he had, then where would he be? It wasn't like he had someone else who could take over on a moment's notice.

When he returned to the hotel there was a message from John Ericson saying he'd had no luck finding anyone who had heard from Ellen in recent months. Pete tried calling John back, but again got his answering machine.

It was Sunday night now, three days since Ellen last called. As he lay in his hotel room Pete thought about a time he'd come across Ellen and her mother, Lois, unexpectedly. Pete and Ellen had been married about four years. At that point Ellen was teaching two drawing classes in the evenings through SMU Extension. She had just had a show of her work in a St. Louis gallery, and she had spent quite a bit of time up there before the opening. Pete was teaching at North Dallas Community College. This day he wasn't feeling well, and after his last class was over, he headed home instead of working in his office. He came in the side door, stepping into the kitchen, which was empty. He walked through the room and, without meaning to, realized he'd sneaked up on Ellen and her mother. They were sitting on the sofa quite close to one another. An open file folder was on the coffee table in front of them. Ellen was reading a typewritten report or article. Pete noticed it was several pages long and the pages were stapled in the corner. He watched them for several moments before Lois looked up. She was shocked when she saw him. She actually gasped.

He said, "Hi. I didn't mean to scare you."

Ellen was surprised, too. Her face reddened, and she quickly put the papers she was holding down on the table. "Hi," she said. "You're home early."

"I don't feel good. I thought I'd lie down. What're you two up to?"

"Nothing," Ellen said. Lois put the pages Ellen had been reading inside the file folder, picked it up and stood.

She said, "I'll be going, then. Sorry you're not feeling well, Pete."

"You don't have to leave."

"No. I've got things to do. And if you're not well . . ." She glanced at Ellen. "I'll talk to you later, okay?"

"Yeah," Ellen said. "Thanks for coming by."

Lois walked to the front door and left. Ellen smiled at Pete, her face still slightly flushed. "You think you're getting the flu?"

"I hope not. Your mom didn't have to run off."

"She was leaving soon anyway."

"What were you doing?"

"Nothing. It was just . . ." She stopped without finishing and put her hand to his forehead. "You've got a fever. I'll get you some aspirin."

"Thanks. I'm going to lie down." Pete felt so lousy he didn't really notice that Ellen had ignored his question. He went to their bedroom, kicked off his shoes and stretched out on the bed. Ellen came in a few minutes later and sat next to him. He opened his eyes and looked at her. She handed him the aspirin and a glass of water.

"Mom was talking to me about her will when you walked in. She's thinking of changing it into a living trust or something. She wanted to know what I thought."

At the time he didn't think anything about it. But now, lying in the hotel, he wondered if Ellen had lied to him. When Lois died her estate had not been placed in a trust. The probate process had been complicated and was still, almost nine months since her death, not settled. He remembered how strange Ellen and her mother had acted that day. It was several years ago now, but he wondered if Ellen had been keeping a secret from him even then. If so, her mother had been part of it. But Lois was dead now. She wasn't part of what Ellen was doing.

Grasping at straws, he thought. *You're just grasping at straws.*

CHAPTER 10

WALKER TRIED to wake the woman up again to give her more water, but she wouldn't come to. A couple of times he tried trickling a little water into her mouth. She seemed to swallow some, but then she would start to choke on it, and that scared him. The back of her head looked bad, but it wasn't bleeding any, so he didn't do anything to it. He put a pillow under her head and threw a blanket over her. She'd pissed on herself, so he kept the bedroom door closed because of the smell. If she woke up he'd give her dry clothes to put on.

His situation, though improved from when she had the gun on him, was hardly what you'd call positive. It'd take a lot of work before he could say he'd succeeded in turning this mess around, but he now believed it was possible. If he did succeed, he thought he would write a letter to Eddie Rollins. It was just possible Rollins would read the letter on one of his TV specials or mention it in his next book.

Walker had gone through the woman's purse. She had two sets of ID in there. One set with her real name, another set with a different name. Walker couldn't tell the fake driver's license from the real one. It must have cost her plenty to get it. There was more than a thousand dollars in cash in the purse, a set of keys, and, separately, a hotel key and a car key from a rental agency.

There were two things he knew he needed to do right away. First, he had to get rid of the woman's car, which must be parked nearby. Second, he had to go to her hotel and get her belongings. It was possible, even likely, that she had his name and address written down somewhere in her hotel room. Once she was reported missing, he couldn't have the cops finding anything with his name on it.

Walker left the apartment in the morning to look for her car. It didn't take long. The blue Toyota he'd seen her driving was parked two blocks away with a Budget car rental sticker on the back bumper. Now he needed a plan.

He went back to his own car, then drove north to a shopping center in Hollywood, several miles from his apartment, parking on the side street next to the lot. After he dumped the woman's rental there later, he'd walk to his car and drive home. Walker took a bus west on Sunset, then transferred to a southbound bus on La Brea. He got off a few blocks from home.

The woman was still asleep, her breathing steady. Maybe she was going to be all right after all. He didn't know how he would handle it if she did wake up, but maybe Barton would have called by then. Walker went into the kitchen and looked around. He knew he should eat something. It was past noon, and he hadn't had anything all day. But he wasn't hungry. Too much shit going on to be hungry. Back in the living room he turned on the television. Soon he fell asleep sitting on the sofa.

The doorbell rang and woke him. His apartment was dark, the television still on. He stood up, thinking about the woman, and took a step toward the bedroom but then remembered someone was at the door. Must be Denise. What time was it? He glanced at his watch and saw it was almost eight. He switched on a light and opened the door.

"Hi, hon. I wasn't sure you were home," Denise said. "I didn't see any lights."

"I fell asleep," he said.

"Bad day?"

"I didn't feel so good."

"I'm sorry," she said. "Still under the weather, huh? You feel up to a drink or something?"

He couldn't let her into the apartment, so he said, "I wouldn't mind getting out. Just for a little while."

Walker stepped back inside to grab his jacket off a chair and then went out, making sure the door was locked after he closed it.

Usually they would take Walker's car, but he didn't have it now. He told Denise it was in the shop, and asked her to drive. It was early and the Inkwell only had a few customers. Walker got their drinks at the bar and carried them to a booth where Denise waited.

"Where do you want to go for dinner?" Denise asked after she'd had her first pull on the gin.

"I'm not much hungry," he said.

"Not tonight, hon. When Darlene is here."

Walker stared at her blankly. He didn't know what the fuck she was talking about.

"My sister," she said, annoyed. "Remember? You promised you'd go out to dinner with us."

"Right. Right. It slipped my mind is all. When is it?"

"Day after tomorrow. Don't go forgettin' about it again. Darlene's lookin' forward to meetin' you."

"Okay." Walker knew she'd never let him forget about it now. He tried to think what day it was today, but he didn't know. The thing with the woman had made him totally lose track of things.

"What's wrong with your car?" she asked.

"My car?"

"You said it's in the shop."

"Needs new brakes. Not a big deal."

Denise lit a cigarette and looked at him. "You seem a little out of it tonight. You feelin' worse? We can go home. I got some beer at my place."

"No. I'm glad to get out for a while. I'm still fightin' that damn flu."

They had a few drinks and then Walker said he was tired. He wanted to get back to his apartment. Denise put her arm around him as they walked to her car, which meant she wanted him to come up to her place.

Back at their building they stopped near the stairs.

"Want to come up?" Denise asked. "I'll buy you another beer."

"Not tonight."

"Maybe you should sleep up at my place. You need somethin', I can get it for you."

"No, thanks. I'd rather be in my own apartment."

"Okay, then. I can stay down here. You need someone to look after you."

God, she was becoming a major pain in the ass.

"Not tonight," Walker said and slid into his apartment, leaving Denise standing alone in front of his door. He thought she would knock, but he was wrong. After a little while he heard her climbing the stairs to her apartment. Denise knew something was going on with him, but Walker couldn't worry about it now. He hoped she'd just think he was sick and leave it at that. And he hoped to hell she wouldn't come looking for him in the middle of the night to make sure he was all right.

At ten Walker left his apartment again and walked to the woman's rental car. He slipped on a pair of cotton work gloves before he unlocked the door and got inside. It was a cool night, the first they'd had in a couple weeks, and as he drove toward Santa Monica it got foggy. He parked in the lot at the Holiday Inn, well away from the entrance. As he walked through the clinging damp to the hotel entrance, he removed the gloves and stuck them in his back pocket. Walker had changed into his best clothes—a long-sleeved plaid shirt and cotton slacks. He hoped he looked like someone who'd be staying at the hotel, but he really had no idea what people who stayed in a Holiday Inn looked like.

The lobby of the hotel was deserted except for two people working at the registration counter. They didn't give him a second glance as he walked to the elevators. He pushed the call button, and the doors slid open immediately for him. Walker stepped in and rode to the fourth floor. He went to his left down a hallway, reached the end, turned left again and found Room 416. Taking the key from his pocket, he opened the door and went inside.

Before turning on the light, Walker slipped the gloves back on. He hit the light switch and surveyed the room. To his left was a closet; the sliding doors were closed. Beyond the doors next to the wall was an aluminum stand with a suitcase on it. The suitcase was closed but not latched. A paperback was on the night table between the two beds. Walker took a step and then slid open a closet door. There was one jacket and one dress hanging inside. Moving past the suitcase, he stopped in front of the dresser. There was nothing on top of it except a Holiday Inn magazine and an arrangement of tourist brochures. It didn't look like the woman had touched them. Why should she? She wasn't here to sightsee. Methodically, he opened every drawer in the dresser and found them all empty. In the bathroom he found her makeup bag. A toothbrush and a few other articles were out on the counter. He put everything in the makeup bag. He pulled her shampoo out of the shower, added this to the bag and left the bathroom.

He checked under the bed and in the drawers of the night tables. There was nothing there. He put the paperback in the suitcase, folded the dress and jacket from the closet over it, and closed and latched the suitcase. He glanced around one last time before wiping the room key clean on the bedspread. Walker put it on top of the dresser. He picked up the suitcase and makeup bag and walked out. In the hallway he removed the cotton gloves.

"Taxi, sir?" the uniformed doorman asked as Walker came out of the hotel lobby with the two bags.

"No," he said, not stopping. "Thanks anyway." He crossed the semicircular driveway and went into the parking lot. He was glad for the fog. It would make it difficult for the doorman, or anyone else, to get a good look at him. He unlocked the trunk of the Toyota and put the bags inside. Before getting in the car, Walker looked around to make sure no one was watching him.

He heaved a sigh of relief as he pulled out of the lot and turned east onto Pico. The worst was over now; no one had questioned him or even looked at him with suspicion as far as he knew. He hadn't left anything behind. *The hotel will think she checked out. They'll charge her room to her credit card.*

Walker took the freeway to La Brea, drove four miles to Sunset and went right. The parking lot where he wanted to leave her car was nearly deserted when he reached it. A few cars were parked near the department store, but that was it. Probably belonged to night maintenance or security men. Walker stopped the Toyota in the middle of the lot without turning off the engine. He could see his own car parked on the street a few hundred feet away. This wasn't going to work, he realized. It was much too easy for someone to notice him leaving the car, taking the bags out of the trunk and going to his own car. Someone watching from a store window. A person driving by could notice him getting in his Thunderbird. Hell, there might be a homeless asshole watching him from the shadows right now. They were everywhere these days. He'd have to wait and switch cars during the day when the parking lot was full. He'd get out, maybe walk into a store, then leave and get in his own car. No one would notice him. He'd be one of a couple hundred people parked in the lot. Walker put the woman's car in gear and drove back home.

He parked a block from his building and carried the bags down the alley that ran behind his complex. All the lights were out in the apartments as he slipped into the courtyard and made his way to his door. Inside his apartment, Walker set the bags down, went to his bedroom door and opened it. The woman was still unconscious.

There was a manila folder in her suitcase. Walker took it out and opened it. Inside was a copy of a page from a map book that showed the neighborhood where he used to live. His old address was written along the top of the page. The street was brightly marked with a yellow marker. Walker set the page down. A copy of a different map showed where he worked. Also in the folder were the woman's airline tickets. He put everything back in the folder and stuck it in the suitcase.

In the morning, around nine, Walker drove the woman's car back to the shopping center and dumped it, returning in his Thunderbird. Walker went in the room to check on the woman when he returned and saw that her eyes were open. She turned her head and looked at him. He could see she was scared. Good. Less likely she'd try something if she was scared.

He said, "I'll be back in a minute." Walker turned and went to the living room. He opened her suitcase and removed a pair of underpants, jeans and a shirt. He took them into the bedroom.

"I'll untie you," he said. "You can change your clothes. Go into the bathroom and clean up. But if you try to get away, I'll stop you. You understand what I'm sayin'?"

She nodded her head slowly up and down.

Walker cut the tape around her ankles first and pulled it free from her socks. He moved to her hands and unlocked the handcuffs. He glanced down at her face. Her eyes were closed again. "You awake?" he asked. She opened her eyes and looked at him. "Your dry clothes are here on the bed," he said. "You go to the bathroom and get yourself changed. You well enough to do that?" She nodded. "Okay. I'm gonna stand over there by the door. I don't trust lettin' you outta my sight. So just go ahead now." He backed up toward the doorway and stopped.

She didn't move for a few moments, then she pushed herself up from her side until she was sitting awkwardly. The first thing she did was put a hand to the back of her head, carefully touching the blood-caked hair and scalp. Using both hands, she tried to get up off the floor but only got halfway before she fell back into a sitting position. Walker didn't know if she was dizzy or what. He went over and put out his hand to her.

"Here," he said.

She looked at his hand but didn't take it. Instead she tried to get up on her own again. This time she made it.

He told her, "Bathroom's right down the hall."

She picked up the clothes from the bed and followed him,

moving slowly. In the hall Walker pointed to the bathroom door. "In there. You can close the door most of the way, I guess. Don't latch it."

She used one hand to steady herself as she took the few steps to the bathroom. The light came on and she pushed the door until it was almost closed. Walker heard the water turn on in the sink.

The woman spent about ten minutes in the bathroom. When she came out she looked much better; she'd washed most of the blood off her face. The tape was missing from her mouth.

"How you feel?" he asked her.

"About like I look," she answered. Her voice was a hoarse whisper. "Back in there?"

"That's right."

She went back into the bedroom. Walker flipped on the light as he entered the room behind her.

"Can I sit on the bed?" she asked. She spoke so quietly Walker could barely hear her.

"Yeah."

She sat facing him, keeping her eyes on the floor. Walker studied her for a few moments. She wasn't a large woman. He figured she weighed one-fifteen at the most. It took some guts for her to come after him like she did. She had held the gun easily, he remembered, keeping it pointed right at his chest. She'd have killed him if he didn't tell her what she wanted to know.

He asked, "You hungry? Or thirsty?"

"No. I drank some water in the bathroom."

"You need anythin' before I tie you up again?"

"There's one thing I'd like."

"What's that?"

"I want you to tell me who the man was that shot my father."

"Lady, you're outta your mind." He taped her mouth shut, put the handcuffs on her and tied her ankles with rope. Walker turned out the light and left her lying on the bed. Back in the living room, he sat down. What the hell could he do with her? There was only one thing to do and he knew it. Walker felt a stab of guilt, but it wasn't his fault. She had come after him. Threatened to kill him. Shit. She still wasn't giving up, either. Still wanted to know who pulled the trigger. The little girl had grown into one tough lady, that was for sure. Well, maybe he would tell her what happened that day. It was what she had come to find out. Maybe that'd make it easier for her. Dammit to hell. He'd had rotten fucking luck his whole life and nothing was changing. This was a situation that even Eddie Rollins wouldn't be able to turn into something positive.

The phone rang. Walker answered it. It was Barton. Finally. Walker told him to sit down. He wasn't going to believe what the fuck had happened.

CHAPTER 11

MONDAY MORNING Susan called Pete just as he was about to leave the hotel and drive to the post office where Ellen had purchased the money order in August.

"I'm in Dallas," Susan told him.

"What're you doing there?"

"I was thinking yesterday about how close Mama and Ellen were. If Mama was still alive I think she'd know where Ellen went. So I decided to fly up here and look through her house. I thought there might be something that would help us."

"Did you find anything?" Pete asked.

"I found a safe deposit box key that I hadn't known about. The box is at the Bank One in Preston Center. I called the bank. It's in Mama and Ellen's name."

"That's strange."

"Did you know about it?"

"No."

"The bank will let me open it, but they want Taylor there to represent Mama since he's the executor of her estate. And they want you there to represent Ellen."

"Can't you do that?"

"No. You're the closest relative."

"You think I should fly back?"

"Can you?"

"I'm not sure I should. Ellen's out here somewhere. I know it."

"What if you got a flight back tonight? We could go to the bank tomorrow morning, then you could fly right back. It might be important."

Pete thought about it. "All right," he said reluctantly.

"Thanks," she said. "She should have called one of us by now, Pete."

"I know."

"She might be mad at you, but she isn't mad at me," Susan said, sounding on the verge of tears. "Something must have happened to her. Otherwise she would have called to let me know she's all right."

Pete knew this was true. Ellen would never make her sister suffer like this if she had a choice.

"Maybe nothing bad has happened," he said. "It's possible she's fine, and there's a good explanation for all this. We just haven't figured it out."

"God, I hope you're right. You really think she's out there?"

"Yeah, I do. See you tomorrow morning."

PETE GOT TO MARVIN'S apartment at ten-thirty. He sat at the small table across from Marvin as Louise made coffee. Pete told Marvin that he was flying back to Dallas that night.

"How long are you staying?"

"Just a few hours. I'll be back tomorrow night."

"There might be something in that bank box that's helpful," Marvin mused. "Taylor's the executor of your mother-in-law's estate?"

"Yeah. He was one of her oldest friends."

Marvin nodded in understanding. "I got a line on something this morning."

"What?"

Louise brought coffee over and put it on the table in front of Pete.

"Thanks, Louise," he said.

"You're welcome."

She glided back into the kitchen, poured another cup of coffee and brought it out to Marvin.

"Thank you, sweetheart," Marvin said.

"No problem." Louise turned and bumped the empty chair to Marvin's left. "Whoops," she said and went into the living room.

Marvin picked up his coffee and took a sip. "Last night I realized I should check with the car rental companies. Ellen must've rented a car. She wouldn't come out here and ride around in a taxi, right? Or at least that's unlikely. There are only six companies with counters in the terminal where Far West is, so last night I called all of them and checked names against the names from the passenger list."

Pete stared at Marvin and waited. This was a great idea. Pete didn't know why he hadn't thought of it himself.

Marvin continued, "Six women out of the seventeen rented cars."

"Only six? That'll make it a lot easier to check with the various hotels."

"Yeah. But listen to this. One of the women rented a car for four days, but she hasn't turned it back in yet. It's two days late now."

"What was the name?"

"Paula Bradford."

Pete shook his head. The name meant nothing to him.

"Paula Bradford's car is still out there. Budget called the hotel where she said she'd be staying, but she's checked out."

"What hotel was it?"

"The Holiday Inn in Santa Monica."

"To rent a car this woman had to have ID."

"She did. Credit card. Driver's license. If this is Ellen, she had fakes."

THE HOTEL was in the south part of Santa Monica less than a quarter-mile from the beach on a small rise, giving west-facing rooms a nice ocean view.

The assistant manager, an overweight man named Lowell, took Marvin and Pete into his office. Lowell sat behind his desk, turned to his computer and tapped a few keys. "Let's see," he said. "Paula Bradford made the reservations on September twenty-fifth for three nights. She arrived on the afternoon of the fourteenth and left sometime last night."

"What time last night?" asked Marvin.

"It doesn't tell me that," said Lowell. "Let me check the front desk." He picked up the phone and punched in three numbers. After waiting a few seconds he said, "Can you look up what time Paula Bradford checked out yesterday? She was in Four-sixteen." He glanced at Pete and Marvin. "They're checking." He waited, listening. "Thanks a lot," he said, hanging up and facing Pete and Marvin again. "Apparently she didn't stop by the desk when she left," said Lowell. "The maid found her room vacated this morning with the room key left in it. She could have left anytime yesterday afternoon or evening, even early this morning."

"Any calls in or out of the room yesterday?" Marvin asked.

Lowell went back to the computer screen and scrolled down through the file. "No," he said.

"She stayed more than three nights," said Marvin.

"That's right," said Lowell. "The two extra nights were charged to her credit card."

"Which was under the name of Paula Bradford?"

"Of course."

Pete leaned forward. "Did she make any long distance calls to Dallas the first couple days she was here?"

Lowell scrolled back up the file. "No," he said. "No calls at all."

Ellen had called both Pete and Susan. Pete remembered the noise he'd heard in the background when she last called him. She'd been in a pay phone that time.

Marvin asked what the woman had given as her home address.

Lowell hesitated before answering. He said, "That's personal information and there are strict rules about releasing that. Paula Bradford might not be your wife, after all. I think I've given you pretty much everything I can."

Pete pulled one of Ellen's photographs from the folder he'd brought and put it in on the desk in front of the man. "This is my wife. Does she look familiar, Mr. Lowell?" He slid another photo in front of him. "Here's a photograph of the two of us together. She's my wife. I love her, and I'm afraid she might be in trouble."

Lowell looked at the photographs. He shook his head. "I don't recognize her," he said. "But I can imagine how worried you must be. I'm sorry I can't do more to help, but . . ."

Marvin shifted in his seat as if uncomfortable. "I know you've got a job to do, Mr. Lowell, but you've got to think about Pete here. The home address of Paula Bradford might help us determine if she was his wife or not."

Lowell sighed, tapping his pencil against the desk. He said,

"I'll tell you what. Give me a few minutes. I'll call the vice president up in San Francisco and see what he says. You wanted to leave a picture of your wife?"

"That's right. We've got flyers printed up," Marvin answered.

"Give me fifteen minutes. I'll see what my boss says."

Pete and Marvin took the elevator to the fourth floor and walked down the hall, stopping in front of Room 416 for a moment.

Pete asked, "Are we looking for anything?"

"A maid," Marvin said.

A couple minutes later they came upon a housekeeping cart parked in front of an open doorway. Marvin leaned into the room and spoke to the woman, asking for a moment of her time. She stepped out into the hallway, apprehensive. Marvin asked her a question in Spanish, and the woman shook her head no. Marvin showed her a photograph of Ellen, and again the woman shook her head. Marvin thanked her and walked back to Pete.

"It was worth a try," he said.

They rode the elevator down to the lobby. Pete thought there was a decent chance that Ellen was the woman who had stayed here, but unless they could get some confirmation of that, unless someone remembered seeing her, it was hard to know whether they should keep looking elsewhere or not. There were six other women from the flight who had rented cars that day. Ellen might be one who had turned her car in on time.

When they returned to the front desk and asked to see Lowell again, he was on the phone. They took chairs in the lobby to wait.

Pete asked Marvin if he'd ever been to Dallas.

"Never have," he said. "I hear good things about it."

"It's not bad. I'm not a native. I grew up in Des Moines. Ellen and I moved there after we got married."

"How long has that been?" Marvin asked.

"Eight years."

"That's a good amount of time."

"How long have you and Louise been married?"

"Forty-eight years last March."

"Wow," said Pete. "Forty-eight years." And his marriage had smashed to pieces after only eight.

"It hasn't all been easy," Marvin added, seeming to sense Pete's feelings. "We had our rocky periods. It was especially tough when Louise lost her sight."

"How'd that happen?"

"Glaucoma. It got worse and worse in her mid-thirties. By the time she was forty, she was blind. Boy, was she pissed off at the world for a couple years."

"Can't say I blame her."

"Neither can I," said Marvin. "But it was tough living with her then. And her blindness made so many things difficult for a while. Sometimes it was hard to remember that we still loved each other."

"But you stayed together."

"Yeah," said Marvin. "We did."

Lowell came out to the lobby then and walked over to the two men.

"I talked to my boss," he told them. "He said there was no way we could give out the address of a guest. I'm sorry. Maybe you should go to the police. If they asked us for the address it might be a different story. Don't worry, I'll make sure your wife's picture gets circulated among the employees. If she was here, I'm sure someone will remember her."

Pete drove Marvin back to his apartment. On the way Pete said, "Sorry about last night. I was impatient."

"Don't give it a second thought. I wish we'd found her the day you got here. Things don't usually work that way, though."

"I don't want you to think I'm ungrateful. Checking the car rental agencies was a great idea. I think she probably stayed at the Holiday Inn." Pete pulled up in front of Marvin's building and stopped.

"I told you I would think of something. Call me tomorrow after you look in that bank box."

"I will."

BEFORE DRIVING back to his own hotel, Pete stopped by the Holiday Inn again. He went back to the fourth floor and walked down the hall toward Room 416. To his surprise, the door was open. Looking in, Pete saw a young housekeeper just coming out of the room.

"Excuse," she said shyly, looking down. "More towels." She was a very young woman, no more than eighteen.

"I'm not staying here," said Pete. "But I wondered if you might remember the woman who was in this room a few days ago?" He pulled a photograph out of his shirt. The young woman came closer to look at it. Her name tag said "INEZ."

"Ahh," she said. "I remember this lady, okay. She was here for some days. Her hair was more . . ."

"Shorter?"

"Yes. More shorter."

"So you remember her?" There was a tingling sensation in the back of Pete's neck.

"*Sí.* Okay. I saw the picture downstairs. I cannot read the English. My friend tells me she is gone lost?"

"That's right. I'm trying to find her."

"I am . . . sorry. She was nice lady."

"You talked to her?"

"I talk to her two times in the morning. I come to clean her room and I find her still here. She was nice woman to me."

"Why do you say she was nice?" Pete asked.

"Okay. She give me nice tip two times." Inez smiled happily as she remembered this.

"How much did she give you?" asked Pete.

"Twenty dollars. I hope you find your wife."

"Thank you."

"Sometime while she here, I worry for her."

"Why?"

Inez frowned.

"Why were you worried?" Pete glanced at her name tag again. "Inez, anything you can tell me might be important. Please tell me what made you worry."

"I do not open her purse," Inez said. "Already it open." She stopped and looked at Pete to see if he believed her.

"Don't worry. I know you wouldn't open anyone's purse."

Inez smiled tightly and nodded her head. "Okay. It was a big purse. *Negro.* Black. You can fit many things in it." She indicated the size with her hands. Pete knew the large black bag she was describing. "I clean her room, and it was on the bed. You know, maybe she was downstairs having something to breakfast. I moved the purse and it was very heavy. I do not open. But I look." She stopped and looked at Pete fearfully.

"You're not going to get in trouble, Inez. What did you see in the purse?"

"Okay. There was a gun in the purse. That was why I was worried for her. I know she must have trouble to carry a gun like that."

Pete had to wait five minutes before the assistant manager, Lowell, came out and ushered Pete back to his office. Pete sat down and told him that Inez had positively recognized Ellen's photograph as that of the woman who had stayed in Room 416.

Lowell nodded his head. "All right," he said. "I think I can go ahead and give you that address you wanted earlier. It seems certain it was your wife here. The hotel has to be careful, you understand."

Pete said, "Yes. I understand your reason for being cautious."

"Hold on just a second," Lowell said. He swiveled around to face his computer screen and typed in some commands. "Here it is," he said after ten seconds. "Paula Bradford listed her home address as 935 Hamilton Street, Dallas, TX 75025. Is that your address?"

Pete shivered. He said, "No. It's not our address. But I think I know where it is."

Lowell frowned at him. "Where?" he asked. "I'm sorry. It's none of my business, but you had the strangest look on your face."

"I'm not sure," Pete said. "It's . . . I'll have to check on something." Pete jotted down the address on a piece of paper. "Thanks for your help, Mr. Lowell." Pete stood and shook hands with him.

"Good luck to you," he said to Pete.

Pete walked out to the parking lot in a state of shock. *What in the hell's going on?* Pete wasn't sure, but he thought the address Ellen had used—935 Hamilton Street—was the address where her father, Victor Samuels, had his office. It was the address where he had been murdered.

CHAPTER 12

Walker stopped the cart in front of the frozen food case and stared at the stacks of dinners inside it. Too many damn choices. He wished he had some idea about what the woman liked to eat, but there was no way of knowing. Standing there in the grocery store, doing a normal thing with all these other people around, it was hard to believe the mess he was in. There was no way it wouldn't turn out bad. Real bad. Walker knew he shouldn't give in to these negative feelings, but how could he help it? He'd beaten the woman, nearly killed her, and now he had her tied up in his bedroom. How the fuck was he supposed to have positive feelings about that?

Walker slid open the glass door and started pulling dinners out. All different kinds. He remembered staying with his sister and her husband, Arnie, when he was released from Huntsville. Chrissie was the only visitor he had ever had in the thirty years he was in prison. She came to see him eleven times and wrote letters to him three or four times a year. When he stayed with her, Chrissie had just bought an Italian cookbook and she made manicotti one night. Walker had never heard of the stuff before, spaghetti and meatballs being his only experience with Italian food, but it was good. Real good. Seeing the frozen manicotti in the food case, Walker wondered why he had never picked up a box before. He put two boxes in his cart, took a few more things and moved on. In the next case he pulled out four Mama Giotto's combination pizzas. That should do for now. Breakfast was the next thing. Walker didn't have a clue about breakfast. He took a couple of packages of waffles out and looked at them. How many kinds of waffles could there be? He pulled out a third box, looked at it. He picked the whole-grain kind because he figured the woman was probably the type of person who cared about healthy foods.

Barton wanted Walker to keep the woman alive for a day or two. That's the way he put it—"Keep her alive another day or two," as though killing her eventually was just the most obvious thing in the world. Barton was checking things out in Dallas, making sure no one knew what she was up to. Walker thought that the woman must have been on her own. If anyone was in it with her, they'd have showed up looking for her by now.

In the cereal aisle he put a box each of Wheaties and Raisin Bran in the cart. He stopped in front of the granolas. Walker had never tasted granola, but it must be popular based on the amount of it that the store carried, and he knew it was healthy. He grabbed a box and tossed it in the cart.

"When'd you start eatin' cereal?"

Walker turned in surprise. Denise was behind him with a shopping cart that contained a gallon of Popov gin and a bag of Milky Ways.

"What're you doin' here?" he asked.

"What's it look like?"

"I thought you went to the Ralph's."

"You're the one always tellin' me the prices are better here." She glanced in his cart. "Expectin' company?"

"No. Why?"

"Got enough food there for a month."

"That way I don't have to come back so soon."

Denise pushed her cart up next to his.

"You eat cereal?"

"Sometimes."

"I never seen you."

"I figure it's better than eatin' a doughnut off the truck every day."

"Guess you're right about that. You go to work today?"

"No. I'm still not a hundred percent. Guess I better get goin'," he said.

"What else you need to get?"

"Some beer and some apples."

"Don't let me hold you up. I'm goin' that way."

She followed him to the produce section, where Walker picked out a few apples and pears, then got a small bunch of grapes. Denise put a single apple in a plastic bag, setting it next to the gin and candy. She tagged along to the cooler, where Walker got beer, then walked with him to the checkout line.

"Where you parked?" she asked as they emerged from the store into the hazy afternoon sun.

Walker pointed. "Over there."

"Me too."

They pushed their carts across the asphalt. Walker stopped when he noticed the man standing near his car. He was about six feet tall, maybe a bit more, with a thick neck and shoulders. He had long hair pushed back behind his ears and wore blue-mirrored sunglasses. Walker had never seen the man before, but he knew exactly what he was.

"See you later," he said to Denise.

"Want to do something tonight?"

"Maybe I'll feel up to it. I'll let you know."

Denise turned toward her car, and Walker continued to his. The guy was leaning against the back of the car next to Walker's. His arms were covered with elaborate tattoos.

"How's it going?" the guy asked as Walker reached his car. He dropped the cigarette he'd been smoking to the ground.

"All right," said Walker, unlocking the trunk of his Thunderbird.

"Franklin Walker, right?" asked the man.

"That's right." Walker turned to face him.

"We have a mutual friend in New Orleans," said the guy. "My name's Dale."

"What's goin' on, Dale?"

"Our friend wanted me to check things out with you. See if you needed any help."

"I'm doin' okay," said Walker. "Don't need any help right now."

"That's good," said Dale. "I'm glad to hear that. No problems, huh?"

"No problems."

Dale pulled a folded piece of paper from his shirt pocket and held it out to Walker. "Here's a number where you can reach me. You need any help, call anytime. Day or night."

Walker took the paper. "Thanks," he said.

"No problem. I'll let our friend know everything's cool."

"Right," said Walker. "Everything's cool."

"See you around, Franklin."

Dale turned and walked away. Walker watched him for a moment, then began putting the groceries into his car. When he glanced up again, Dale had left the parking lot and turned up the street. Walker wasn't surprised that Barton had sent someone to check on him. He'd halfway expected it, but it still troubled him. Having to worry about an animal like Dale wasn't going to make things any easier.

After he got the groceries into the apartment, Walker checked on the woman and saw that she was sleeping. He put all the food away, barely squeezing the frozen dinners into the freezer, then opened a beer and sat down. He had time for one sip of the beer before there was a knock at the door. He'd known Denise would be down, but he didn't think it'd be so soon. The woman's suitcase and bag were on the floor to the left of the TV. Walker jumped up and carried them into the hall. The stain on the carpet was another problem. He had planned to get some more stain remover at the store, but he'd forgotten it. He'd tried cleaning it up with one kind the day before, but it didn't help much at all. As he grabbed a towel from the bathroom, there was a second knock on the door.

"Just a minute," he called. He spread the towel over the stain, then closed the door to the hall. Walker went to the front door, unlocked and opened it.

Denise started to take a step in. Walker instinctively got in front of her, blocking her way.

"Walker, what're you doing?"

He checked over his shoulder. Everything looked okay except for the towel on the floor. *What the fuck?* He stepped back, and Denise entered. She had a tall glass of gin in one hand, her cigarettes and lighter in the other.

"What's with you?" she asked. Denise sat on the sofa, crossing her legs as she pulled out a cigarette and lit it.

"Nothin'."

"You don't want me to come in, just tell me."

"No, it isn't that. It was . . . I don't know."

She eyed him for a half-minute, smoking. Walker took a swallow of his beer.

"Who was that you were talking to?" she asked.

"What?"

"In the parking lot at the store. I saw you talking to some guy."

"That was just some guy," he said. "It was nobody."

"I never seen anything like it," she said.

"Like what?"

"The way being sick has made you act so different."

"I'm feelin' better now."

"I'm glad of that."

Denise put her cigarette in an ashtray and stood. She took two steps toward the hall. Jesus! Walker jumped to his feet.

"Where you goin'?" he asked.

"The bathroom."

"Wait a second," he said. "You can't."

She stopped. "Why not?"

Walker put himself between her and the hall door. Why the fuck had he ever let her in?

"You just can't," he said. "Sorry."

"I can't use your bathroom?"

"No. It's a mess."

"So what else is new?" Denise tried to go around him, but he moved to block her way. Walker realized he had stumbled onto the perfect excuse. Denise was always complaining that his apartment was filthy, especially the bathroom. She kept her own place as neat as a pin. Dusted and vacuumed at least three times a week. The bathroom was always spotless. So was the kitchen. Of course, Denise never ate anything, so it was easy for her to keep the kitchen clean.

"I been sick in there," he told her. "I haven't had time to clean it up yet."

Denise stared at him in disgust. "Jesus, Walker. That's just . . ." She tried to think of a word, but nothing awful enough came to her. Walker saw her shudder. Denise picked up her cigarettes and glass. Thank God she was leaving. She stopped at the door and glanced back.

"You know what's happened to us?"

"What?"

"Our relationship has gone stale."

Walker wondered where she'd come up with that one. Probably saw them talk about it on Rosie O'Donnell or Jenny Jones. He didn't know how she could watch that talk show shit day after day. She was always telling him about the jerks she'd seen on those shows. Guys who dressed up like women. People who'd dumped their kids and then decided they wanted them back because now they were going to be good parents. Like his daddy taking him and Chrissie out of the home that cold morning when Walker was eight. He'd been afraid of the tall, sour-smelling man, but he couldn't remember why. He found out soon enough, that was for damn sure. His daddy was alive today, he'd probably be a regular on Jerry Springer.

"What do you say to that?" Denise asked.

"I don't know what to say."

"Well, you think about it." Denise walked out.

Walker went to the door and turned the button to lock it. Be just like her to turn around and march right back in to tell him what a pig he was. He opened the door into the hall, picked up the woman's suitcase and took it into the bedroom. Stupid of him not to put her stuff in here before.

The woman was awake now. Her eyes followed him as he carried the suitcase to the far side of the bed and put it down. He went back for the smaller bag and her purse. After putting them down, he glanced at her. She stared back at him with the same deep blue eyes she had had when she was a girl. For a few seconds the woman disappeared and in her place was the four-year-old girl, frightened, staring up at him, barely conscious. Walker's heart ached. He blinked.

"You need to go to the bathroom or anything?" he asked.

She turned her head slowly back and forth.

"All right. I'll be back in a little while, then."

He sat in the living room, turning off all the lights. If Denise came back he wanted her to think he'd gone out or was asleep. There was no point in seeing her again tonight. Walker needed to be alone so he could think things through. Barton would be calling tomorrow or the day after to tell Walker to kill the woman. If he didn't do it, Barton would send Dale. Walker had to figure out what he was going to do then.

CHAPTER 13

PETE'S PLANE arrived at one in the morning, Dallas time. Leaving the airport parking lot, he drove slowly past Ellen's car to make sure it was still there.

It took him a half-hour to get home. Pete parked in the driveway. The air inside the house was stuffy and stale. In the living room, Pete flipped on a lamp. He put his keys on a table and noticed a light coat of dust on it.

He went to the kitchen to get something to drink. Opening the refrigerator, he looked to see what was inside, deciding on orange juice. He removed the container and poured himself a glass. Pete drank half of it and then reopened the refrigerator to see if there was anything to eat. He had his hand on a plastic container when he heard the noise. At first he couldn't think of what it was, but then he knew. It was the sound of one of the stairs creaking.

Someone was in the house.

Every muscle in Pete's body tensed. His heart was pounding in his throat as he slid open a drawer and pulled out an eight-inch knife. He moved from the kitchen to the service porch. Pete knew he should go out the back door now, run to the neighbor's house and call the cops. But whoever was here would be gone by the time the police arrived. Pete moved past the door. There was another creak, and he froze again, listening.

Pete slipped into the bathroom, which had two doors. The second door, now closed, led to the hallway. He took the handle in his left hand and turned it. It made a pop as it opened, and Pete heard running in the hall. He swung the door open and ran to the living room just in time to see the screen door slam shut. Three long strides took him to the door. He pushed it open and burst out to the porch. A man was running across the street, angling away from Pete's house. He carried something in his arms. Pete went to the top step of the porch and stopped. He heard something behind him, but before he could even begin to turn, he was struck hard on the back of the head. The next thing he knew he was lying on the porch, the rough concrete against the left side of his face. It took him a few moments to realize what had happened, to remember the noise behind him. The back of his head hurt. Pete lifted his right hand and carefully felt an enormous lump swelling back there.

He sat up slowly, then stood and went inside the house. Putting some ice in a dish towel, he held it against his head while he called the police. He tried to remember what he could about the man he'd seen running across the street. He wore dark clothes, Pete recalled, but he hadn't noticed anything beyond that. His hair was dark—brown or black, Pete suddenly remembered. Pete climbed the stairs to Ellen's studio and looked in. The desktop computer was gone, though the monitor and the keyboard were still on the desk. Pete went downstairs and checked the rest of the house. Nothing else seemed to be missing.

The police carefully looked through the house and found where a back bedroom window had been broken. One of the patrolmen filled out a report, and Pete signed it. The officers left.

It seemed strange that the burglars had taken nothing but the computer. The police had told him the men had probably been in the house no more than a few minutes. Pete was lucky. If he had come home an hour later he would've been missing half the house. And if he'd been hit a little harder he'd probably be spending the night in the hospital.

Pete nailed the broken window shut. In the morning he'd call someone to fix the pane of glass. He was tired, so he got in bed, but once there he found that he couldn't sleep. He thought of calling Susan to tell her what had happened, but why wake her? He'd see her in a few hours. Eventually, Pete got out of bed and went up the stairs to Ellen's studio to look around again.

He opened all three drawers in the file cabinet and skimmed through them. Nothing appeared to have been touched. He sat at the desk, opening all the drawers there. Again, everything seemed fine. His eyes moved up from the drawers and stopped on the clear plastic box where Ellen stored her diskettes. The box was empty. Carefully, he touched the edge of it and turned it sideways so that he could see all of it. Pete stared at the place where the computer had been. He could understand taking the computer. It was worth something. But why take the disks? No one would, except someone who wanted the information that was on them. And that meant it wasn't the value of the computer the men wanted, it was what was saved on the hard drive.

Pete stood, went downstairs and tried to think it through. Someone wanted her computer files. Why? Because they didn't want him, or anyone else, to read what was in the files. It seemed incredible, but Pete thought this must mean someone in Dallas knew where Ellen was and what she was doing. And they must think there was something on her computer or disks that might be harmful. Pete thought about the protected directory that Brian had made a copy of. He'd call him first thing tomorrow.

Before going back to bed, Pete called the police department and informed them of the missing diskettes.

AT SEVEN-THIRTY in the morning Pete called Brian.

"Did you find Ellen?" Brian asked.

"Not yet. Your friend have any luck with those files you downloaded from the computer?"

"No. He says Ellen must have used some security program to protect them. He could get around a simple password easy enough. Do you guys own any security software?"

"I don't think so."

"Okay. He's gonna keep trying."

"It's important," said Pete.

"I know. I'll call you in a couple of hours."

Susan met him at the door of her mother's home, throwing her arms around Pete and hugging him tightly for several seconds.

"How was the flight?" she asked.

"All right, but you won't believe what happened last night."

She let go of him. Susan was taller than Ellen, with lighter hair, which was tied back in a braid. She had pale, almost translucent skin, a narrow nose and blue eyes the same color as Ellen's. Today there were dark shadows under her eyes. Susan looked exhausted.

They went inside, and Pete told her briefly about the burglary. Susan's daughter, Caitlin, was playing in a small portable playpen. Seeing Pete, she grabbed the side of the playpen and pulled herself to her feet.

"How's my niece?" Pete asked, walking over to her. He

reached down and picked her up. "What a big girl you're getting to be. Aren't you?" He carried Caitlin to a chair and sat down with her on his lap.

"They took the computer and the disks?" Susan asked in disbelief.

"I think it means someone knows what she's doing," said Pete. "And they don't want me to find out."

"What?"

"It's too strange," said Pete. "Ellen disappears and then someone breaks into our house and all they take is her computer and her disks. It's got to be related."

"But who would know what she's doing?"

"I have no idea. Oh, I almost forgot." He reached in his pocket and pulled out a piece of paper. "I didn't tell you yet, but we found the hotel she stayed at."

"You did? When?"

"Yesterday afternoon. I'm sorry. I'm so tired my brain's gone. She stayed at the Holiday Inn in Santa Monica from Wednesday until sometime late on Sunday under the name of Paula Bradford. Does that name mean anything to you?"

"No."

Pete looked down at the slip of paper in his hand and read the address there. "For her home address she wrote down 935 Hamilton Street. Is that the address I think it is?"

Susan nodded. "That was where my father's office was. Why on earth would she use that?"

Pete shook his head. He didn't have the answer to that either.

Susan took him upstairs to Ellen's old bedroom. Ellen and Susan had cleaned out much of the house since their mother had died, but some pieces of furniture remained. Susan opened the closet and pointed to a blue shoe box on the shelf.

Susan said, "The key was in there. I took down the box to see if anything was in it. I could hear it rattling around."

"Nothing else was in it?"

"No."

"I wonder if it's been there all this time, or if Ellen put it there recently?"

"The bank said there were two keys issued. I think this must be Mama's key."

Forty-five minutes later they were in the car, driving to the bank.

"There's something else I found in the house that was kind of interesting," Susan said. "It doesn't have anything to do with Ellen."

"What?"

"I found some old letters in the attic to Mama. They were love letters."

"From your father?"

"No. From Taylor."

"Taylor Reed? You're kidding. How old were they?"

"They're from twenty-five years ago. He wanted to marry her, and I guess she didn't want to get married again."

"Did you know there was a romance between them?"

"No. But we were pretty small then. I remember they used to go out to dinner together a lot."

"Think Ellen knew there was a romance?"

"No."

"It seems a little weird to me," said Pete.

"Why? Mama was single. My dad had been gone several years. I wish she had married Taylor. Instead she spent all those years full of hate, unhappy."

Caitlin fell asleep in the car on the way to the bank and

remained sleeping as Susan gently transferred her to the stroller. Taylor Reed was already waiting for them inside the bank. Always well dressed, today he had on a dark gray suit with a wine-colored tie. Taylor kissed Susan and shook hands with Pete. His hand felt cold and dry.

"Any word?" he asked Pete.

"Yesterday we found out she stayed at the Holiday Inn in Santa Monica."

"But she checked out?" asked Taylor.

"She left Sunday night or Monday morning."

"And you don't know where she went?"

"No. Marvin's working on it."

"Let me know if I can help. This kind of business can get expensive if it goes on long."

"Thanks." Pete then told Taylor about the burglary at his house.

"My God," said Taylor. "Are you okay?"

"I'm fine," said Pete. "But I think the burglary's related to Ellen."

"Why?"

"They took her computer and her computer disks. That doesn't make sense unless someone doesn't want me to see what she has saved on her computer."

"But what could be on her computer?"

"Something that has to do with her trips to Los Angeles."

"This is incredible," said Taylor. "Are the police in L.A. involved?"

"Not yet. I filled out a missing persons report. That's about it."

An assistant vice president of the bank took them into the vault. Susan inserted the key she had found in her mother's house into one of the locks, and the vice president inserted the bank's key in the other lock. Both keys were turned and the box pulled out. Pete carried it into a small room, which they all crowded into. He set the box on a counter, and Susan opened it. She gave a short gasp. The box was full of cash, all neatly bundled.

"Susan, why don't you take it out and count it," Taylor told her. He had brought a pen and pad of paper with his company logo on it to inventory what was inside the box. Susan began removing the money and counting it. There was over fourteen thousand dollars, in hundreds, fifties and twenties. Under the cash was a manila envelope. Susan removed it and undid the clasp. Inside was a document. Pete saw that it was an Agreement of Purchase and Sale between Ellen's mother and a company called Delta Partners.

"Do you know what this is?" Susan asked Taylor.

"I think so." He took the pages from Susan and glanced at it. "This is the sales agreement between your mother and the company that purchased your father's business," he said.

"I wonder why she had it in here?" Susan asked.

"It's the type of thing she would want to keep in a safe place," Taylor replied. He handed it back to Susan, who replaced it in the envelope.

Taylor had everyone present sign the inventory. They put the money and the sales agreement back in the box, returned the box to the vault and said goodbye. Taylor had the bank make a photocopy of the inventory for Pete.

Pete and Susan drove away from the bank in silence. Caitlin was still sleeping. Finally, Susan asked, "What do you think?"

"I don't know. I guess it explains where Ellen got the money to pay for these trips to Los Angeles. And the insurance policy. Other than that, I don't know what in the hell it means."

Susan put Caitlin down in a portacrib when they returned to

Lois's house and made coffee. Pete sat at the kitchen table with her.

"I wish she was just having an affair or something," Susan said. "She got mad at you and went off to be with her boyfriend."

He must've had a pained look on his face, because Susan immediately apologized.

"I'm sorry," she said. "I don't think that's the case. It's just that I'd rather that than have her hurt or something."

"I'd rather that too," he admitted. "But that isn't what's going on."

Susan looked at him across the table, waiting.

"I'm starting to wonder if this has something to do with your father's murder," he said.

"How could it?"

He shook his head. Neither Ellen nor her mother had ever put the tragedy behind them. Pete recalled the first time he'd been with Ellen when she had a nightmare. Her scream had nearly scared him to death. He sprang up, heart pounding, thinking at first that someone was in the room attacking her. It took a few seconds for him to realize Ellen was asleep. He tried to wake her, but she fought him, pushed and scratched at him, all the time screaming so loudly that he was afraid a neighbor would call the police. Finally she woke up, and Pete held her in his arms as she sobbed. Ellen refused to tell him what the dream had been about that night, though a few days later, when he asked again, she told him the story of what had happened to her father.

It was more than a year later that Pete learned Ellen hadn't been completely truthful with him that day she first told him about the murder of her father. Now, he wondered if he'd ever learned the truth.

"If you think about it, it seems possible," he said. "Ellen traveling to Los Angeles in secret. She takes out a life insurance policy as if she were in danger. You said that if your mother was alive she'd probably know where Ellen was. Well, this was the thing that destroyed your mother's life, and it's haunted Ellen."

Susan said, "It's been over thirty years. What could she be doing?"

"When they investigated the murder, was there any connection to Los Angeles that you remember?"

"I don't think so. I never heard anything like that."

"And Ellen used that address at the hotel," he reminded her. "Why in God's name would she do that?"

"I don't know." Susan thought about it. "Maybe you're right. But if it is related to the murder, what is she doing?"

"Your mother never mentioned any new development or theory about the murder in the last few years?"

"No. The only thing I remember her talking about was that Franklin Walker got out of prison."

"That's the man who shot your father?"

"One of them."

"He got out of prison?"

"Ellen never told you?"

"Not a word."

Susan wearily massaged her temples for a moment. "It drove Mama crazy that he was being released. She wrote to the parole board, the warden at Huntsville; I think she even wrote to the governor. He served something like twenty-nine years, but Mama didn't think that was nearly long enough."

"I think I'd agree with her. How long ago did he get out?"

"About three years ago."

"Do you know what happened to him?"

"How would I know that?"

"Your mother never mentioned anything?"

"No."

Pete felt a wave of nausea roll through him. Everything seemed to fit. He wished it didn't, but it did. "I wonder if Franklin Walker could be in Los Angeles now," he said.

"Pete." Susan looked at him in alarm.

"Maybe she wanted revenge. It drove your mother crazy that he got out, right? Maybe it drove Ellen crazy, too. She still wakes up screaming about it more than thirty years later. Maybe she wanted to get even with the man who did this to her."

"Ellen's not violent," said Susan.

"She had a gun with her in Los Angeles."

"What?! What kind of gun?"

Pete told her about his conversation with the hotel maid.

"I don't believe that."

"The maid wouldn't make that up, Susan. And I know Ellen was taking shooting lessons."

Susan was silent.

Pete continued, "She took them with a friend of hers from the bookstore. She didn't tell either one of us about that, did she? Why not?"

"This can't be right," Susan said, a hint of panic in her voice.

"Christ. Maybe it's not," said Pete. "I hope it's not."

CHAPTER 14

THERE WAS SMOKE. At first she only smelled it, but now she could see it. She opened her eyes and the room was black with it. Like nighttime. It was very hot and the smoke burned her eyes and it hurt to breathe. Where was her daddy? He should come back and get her. She was choking now, and she screamed for him over and over, but he didn't come. Then she was choking so much that she couldn't scream. Ellen put her head down on the floor, and the smoke was like a fuzzy blanket, covering her up, protecting her, making her safe from the bad men and the guns. Something reached through the fuzzy blanket and grabbed her leg.

Ellen woke from the dream trying to scream, but her mouth was taped shut, so the sound was muffled. She saw the murderer standing over her, and she couldn't remember where she was or what had happened. Her head ached terribly and her arms and shoulders were numb. The murderer bent down and talked to her in a low voice, but she didn't understand what he was saying at first. Then she stopped trying to scream and listened to his hoarse whisper in her ear.

"You were having a dream. You have to keep quiet. If you're quiet, I'll take the tape off your mouth."

Ellen knew where she was now. She knew what had happened. How long had she been asleep? She had no idea what amount of time had passed. Vaguely she recalled changing her clothes and washing her face in the bathroom. Was that hours ago or days? And how long was it since she left Dallas? Pete must be looking for her by now. She hoped to hell he'd called the police.

"That's better," the murderer said. "Nice and quiet. Do you want a drink of water?"

Ellen nodded her head. She was dying of thirst. He walked away and Ellen wondered again why he hadn't killed her. There must be a reason. Ellen supposed she shouldn't worry about it. She was lucky; maybe her luck would continue. The murderer returned with a large glass of water. Ellen turned her head and saw him set it on top of a white chest of drawers.

"I'll untie you and take the tape off your mouth, but if you try anything, you'll be sorry. Okay?"

Ellen nodded again. He untied her ankles and then pulled her legs out straight, causing shooting pains up the backs of her legs into her back. She hadn't realized that she was bound with her legs pulled up behind her. The murderer helped her sit up on the edge of the bed and removed the tape from her mouth. Finally, he unlocked her handcuffs. She eagerly took the glass of water in both hands and drank half of it quickly.

"Your head hurt much?" he asked.

"Yes."

"I brought some aspirin. Want some?"

"Yeah."

She swallowed two aspirin with the rest of the water. She handed the glass back to the murderer.

"Want more?"

"Yes, please."

He left, and she looked around the room. There was one window with the drapes drawn. A closet with sliding doors that were closed. There was a dresser about five feet high with six drawers in it. Next to it was a plastic clothes hamper. The carpet in the room was old and worn.

The murderer returned with another glass of water and Ellen drank all of this, too.

"Are you hungry? Want some lunch?" he asked.

She hadn't thought about it, but she realized she was. She probably hadn't eaten for days. "Yes," she said.

"I've got green chile enchiladas, lasagna, chicken pot pie, and pizza. Or I could make you a sandwich. What do you want?"

Ellen couldn't think. What had he said? Enchilada? Pizza? It was a question for a restaurant. "Anything," she said. "I don't care."

He let her walk to the bathroom then. Her legs were so stiff and sore that she could barely move. The murderer instructed her to close the door but not to latch it. She sat on the toilet and urinated, then went to the sink and looked at herself in the mirror. The left side of her face was black with bruises and badly swollen, the white of her eye blood red. The injuries along with her bleached hair made the face in the mirror unrecognizable. Ellen tried to see the back of her head, but it was just a mess of dried blood in her hair. She needed to wash that out.

The murderer stood in the hall waiting when she opened the bathroom door. "Your lunch's in the microwave," he said. "It'll take a few minutes. I'm givin' you lasagna."

She sat on the edge of the bed again. The murderer stood in the doorway watching her. She asked, "Can I take a shower sometime? I'd like to wash my hair."

"All right." A bell sounded in another room. "That's your food," the murderer said and walked away.

Ellen considered going to the window, opening it and screaming for help. She'd be dead before the police could ever arrive. Better to wait until she was stronger, though she didn't dare wait too long.

He brought her food back on a plastic tray. She put it on her lap and began eating. The food tasted good, and she ate all of it.

"Thanks," she said.

He took the tray from her. "You're welcome. You want to lie down or sit?" he asked her.

"I'd rather sit for a while," she said.

"Okay. I need to ask you some questions." Walker waited, but she didn't say anything to that. "I need to know why you came," he said.

Didn't he know? Hadn't she told him? Maybe she wasn't remembering things the way they really happened. "I thought that was pretty obvious. I came to find out who shot my father. You know who he is."

"I know who he was. He's dead now. I told you that before. That's the only reason you came here?"

It made her angry that he still was lying about this. The anger seemed to clear her head. "That's the only reason," she said. "And I know you're lying to me."

"I'm not lying, lady."

"You were in jail for thirty years. Someone sent you money every month for all that time. That made life inside Huntsville a whole lot easier, didn't it? After you got out someone helped you move out here. Someone helped you get your job. Who was that person?"

He was stunned. She could see the look of disbelief in his eyes. "My sister," he stuttered. "She sent me the money."

"No, she didn't." *He's so stupid.* He could hardly put two logical thoughts together, and he had helped murder her father, destroyed her family. It infuriated her. "Your sister is Chrissie Watkins," she continued. "She lives in Midland with her husband, Arnie. He's worked for Ashland Oil for twenty-five years. Chrissie wrote to you. She visited you about ten times while you were in prison, but she never sent you any money."

The look on his face was so funny that Ellen almost laughed out loud. But she didn't want to make him angry. The murderer averted his eyes from Ellen and stared at the dirty carpet for a few moments. When he looked up at her again she was smiling at him. "You don't have a lot to smile about, lady," he said.

She said, "I know that. But I can smile if I want to. There might not be that many times left to do it."

"Shit," he said. "I wish to hell you hadn't done this."

"Why? You don't want to kill me?"

"Why do you have to talk like that? What good's it gonna do talkin' like that?"

"I'm just trying to be honest." *He doesn't want to kill me,* Ellen thought, and she suddenly felt happy. Maybe there was hope. It didn't mean he wouldn't do it if he thought he had to. What Ellen had to figure out was the best way to convince him that there was no need to kill her.

"Sorry," she said. "I'm not really myself yet."

"Yeah," he said. "You got hurt pretty bad."

"I guess so."

"Who else knew you was coming here?" he asked.

"No one. My mother did. But she's dead." She stopped for a moment and then continued. "This all began as her idea. She paid for the detective to find out where you were and everything."

"How do I know she's really dead?"

"I don't know. You could call Dallas and check it out, I guess."

"When did she die?"

"Eight months ago. She had cancer."

"You did this all on your own? Came out here. Found me, threatened to kill me. You didn't tell anyone what you were doing?"

"I didn't want anyone to stop me. And I didn't want anyone to be able to connect me to the murder. I was going to kill your partner. If you didn't give me his name, I was going to kill you."

"You're married?" he asked.

"That's right."

"Your husband doesn't know?"

"I told him I was visiting my sister in San Antonio. I was calling him every night, pretending I was there."

"When was the last time you talked to him?" he asked.

"I'm not sure. I don't know what day today is."

"It's Tuesday."

She frowned, thinking. "I came here Saturday night?"

"Yeah."

"I talked to him that day," she lied.

"So your husband must be looking for you."

"I guess he might be."

"Would he think you'd come to Los Angeles?"

"No. There's no way he'd know that."

"You have friends out here?"

"A couple. But I haven't talked to them. I didn't want anyone to know I was here." Ellen wished she had called John Ericson. He was one of her best friends, and Pete, once he started looking for her, would definitely call John. He might have already done it by now.

"How were you going to kill him?" the murderer asked.

"It doesn't matter, does it?" she asked. "You say he's already dead."

"If he was alive, how would you do it?"

"The same way he killed my father."

"I saw the fake driver's license in your purse. You buy your airline tickets under that name?"

"Yeah."

"You were being careful."

"I was going to commit murder."

The murderer stared at her for several moments. "You shoulda let it alone," he said.

"I couldn't."

"Just made a big fuckin' mess for everybody."

He stood then. He retaped her mouth, handcuffed and tied her, and left her lying on the bed.

She thought a long time about what she should do. It seemed inevitable that he would decide to kill her. But he didn't seem to want to do it, and that should give her some time. In a day she would have some of her strength back. Then, if she got a chance, she could get away. Until then she'd be nice to him. Not give him a reason to kill her. He was trying to make sure that no one knew where she was. Maybe she could be vague enough to keep him guessing. He wouldn't kill her until he was satisfied that no one knew where she was. Perhaps, in the end, he would decide he didn't need to kill her. Not likely, but you never knew. Unlikely things happened.

Like Pete and that woman.

It was such a shitty thing he did to her. Ellen took a slow deep breath. She was letting herself get worked up, and after all, it wasn't that important now. Still, it hurt. And that woman—Tracy—was so beautiful. That made it worse. Too bad Ellen had named Pete one of the beneficiaries on her insurance policy. He sure as hell didn't deserve the money now.

Ellen wished she could sleep. The minutes crawled by and she realized how incredibly boring being held prisoner was going to be. Maybe if she complained about it, he'd bring in a radio for her to listen to. Or even tie her into a sitting position so that she could read. No. He'd never let her have her hands free. Forget it. The radio was a good idea. She couldn't see a reason he'd object to that.

She heard voices. They were coming from inside the apartment. Someone else was here. A neighbor? A friend? The girlfriend, probably. Ellen had forgotten about her. She had dropped the keys to him that night, she remembered. Ellen wondered how close they were. So close that he'd tell her about Ellen? No. Which meant that when they saw each other, they'd be going upstairs to her apartment, leaving Ellen alone. If she could get her hands free, she'd be able to get away.

She remembered the day she and her mother first talked about trying to find the murderer. They were sitting in the garden room of her mother's house. It was late afternoon in winter and very cold outside. The wind rattled the glass walls of the room, which was quite cold, being nearly impossible to heat during the winter. Ellen didn't mind the temperature. She and her mother both wore sweaters, and even though the back yard was bare now, the trees just trembling sticks poking up at the gray sky, Ellen enjoyed the view.

"Sometimes I think about trying to get revenge," her mother said. She didn't say what she was talking about. She didn't need to.

"I do, too," admitted Ellen. "I don't know if that's healthy or not, but I fantasize about it."

"Why wouldn't it be healthy?"

"Because I'm dwelling on it. I don't think I should dwell on it." Ellen paused to take a sip of tea from the mug she held in her lap. "But I can't help myself."

"Of course you can't." Her mother didn't say anything else about it until Ellen was getting ready to go home. Ellen had pulled her coat on and picked up her purse.

"I was serious earlier," she said. "About trying to get revenge."

"I was, too. I think about it all the time."

"But I want to do something about it. Really do something."

Now Ellen wasn't quite sure what her mother was getting at, and she looked at her. Her mother stared back, her face set and serious, her eyes bright and intense.

"Like what?" Ellen asked.

"I hired a private investigator, for one thing."

"Mama. To do what?"

"I wanted to see if he could find out who shot your father. The police bungled the investigation. You know that. We've always known that. If they'd been tough with Franklin Walker, he'd have told them who was with him that day."

"What did the investigator learn?"

"Nothing. He couldn't find out a thing about who the man might be. Franklin Walker was a loner who'd always committed burglaries and robberies by himself. In prison he's a loner, too. The investigator talked to people there. Walker isn't close to anyone."

"I can't believe you did this."

"I'm tired of sitting around thinking about how our lives were ruined. Only one thing will make me feel better. I decided to try and do something about it. I did find out some things about Walker that might be useful."

"Like what?"

"He'll probably be out of prison in a year."

Ellen couldn't believe it. "His sentence is up?"

"No. He's going to be paroled. It makes me sick. He was there when your father was shot. He's as guilty as the man who did it." She stopped. Her voice had been rising. When she continued, she was calmer. "Another thing I found out is that somebody sends him money every month."

"Who?"

"Mr. Limright, that's the investigator's name, couldn't find out. It's a post office money order that comes once a month with no return address on the envelope. It must be from the man he's protected all these years. The man who shot your father."

"Not necessarily."

"Who else would send him money?" she asked.

"A relative, maybe."

"He only has a sister, and she isn't sending him the money. Mr. Limright checked."

"How?"

"I don't know how. I didn't ask him. This is his profession. He knows how to do these things. I'm paying him to give me reliable information. He knows I don't want him to make anything up."

Ellen had put her purse down on the table again. "I'm not sure this was a good thing for you to do," she said.

"Why not?"

"I don't know. It scares me. What good does it do to get all upset about this again?"

"Again? I've never stopped being upset by it. Have you?"

"No. Not really."

Ellen left then. She didn't want to talk about it anymore, but that was how it began. A week later her mother brought it up a second time. The idea of actually doing something about her desire for revenge both frightened and thrilled Ellen. At first she didn't take it seriously. They talked about it, but as time went on and they continued to talk, Ellen realized they would do something. It wasn't just speculation. Lois paid another investigator to dig into Franklin Walker's past, and he couldn't find a hint about who his partner might have been either.

Slowly, over a period of many months, their plan was formed. Walker was released from prison and for a while, infuriatingly, they lost track of him. Then an investigator found him in Los Angeles, working for an adult video distributor. This worried the detective because he discovered that the owners of the business had ties to an organized crime family in the East. Could Walker's partner be connected to organized crime? If he was, would they ever be able to find him? And if they did, how could they kill him without the mob hunting them down? These were questions they spent months discussing, and when they finally solved them to their satisfaction, they discovered new problems and wrestled with ways to solve those.

CHAPTER 15

Detective Lamar Harris of the Dallas Police Department was a tall, heavy black man in his mid-forties wearing an expensive suit with a black and gold tie. They sat in the living room as Pete explained his theory of why Ellen's computer had been stolen. Harris wrote down several notes on a pad of paper while Pete spoke.

When he'd finished, Pete took the detective up the stairs to Ellen's studio and showed him the plastic box where the computer diskettes had been stored.

"And the computer was right here," said Harris, pointing to the place on the desk where now only the monitor remained.

"That's right," said Pete.

"We can dust that box for prints," Harris said. "Did you touch it when you were looking around?"

"Just the edge of the box right there." Pete pointed out the spot.

Harris looked around the room. "Nothing else taken?"

"Nothing."

They went back down the stairs to the living room.

"I don't know anything about the murder of your wife's father, of course," said Harris. "But I'll request the files on that case.

They'll be stored on microfiche after all these years. Now, you said your wife's car is parked out at DFW?"

"Yeah. I checked on it last night when I got my car out at the airport."

"And it's been there since Wednesday?"

"That's the day she left. She checked into the Holiday Inn in Santa Monica that afternoon."

"You said you filled out a missing persons report in L.A. Did you do that here?"

"Taylor Reed did. He had a friend in the police department look for Ellen's car at both airports on Friday. That's how we found out where it was. Taylor said he'd file a missing persons report."

"Do you know who his friend is?"

"No. But you could call Taylor and ask him."

Harris nodded. "The report should have been filed on Friday or Saturday, I guess. I'll find out who took it. And I'll see what I can find out about this Franklin Walker character."

"Thank you."

Harris picked up the pad of paper and stood. He told Pete a crime scene technician would be by to fingerprint the disk storage box. The technician arrived a little more than an hour later, lifted several prints from the box, then took prints from Pete for comparison purposes.

Pete tried reaching Taylor at his office to let him know that Detective Harris might be calling him, but Barbara, his secretary, said he was out for the afternoon. Pete called his home and got the answering machine. He left Taylor a message.

CATHERINE REYNOLDS lived in an antebellum mansion set on two acres overlooking White Rock Lake in east Dallas. Pete called before driving out, and Catherine told him he could come by anytime. She'd be home all afternoon.

Catherine had been a lifelong friend of Ellen's mother. The two grew up together in Highland Park, were sorority sisters at SMU and remained in Dallas all their adult lives. If Ellen's mother had confided to anyone about a desire to seek out Franklin Walker, Pete reasoned, it would have been Catherine Reynolds.

She answered the door moments after Pete rang the bell. Catherine was a thin woman, her jet-black hair streaked with gray. She wore dark framed glasses, the lenses slightly tinted. Catherine smiled warmly at Pete and offered her cheek to him, which he dutifully pecked at. She then led him into a large family room, where she poured Pete a glass of ice tea from a crystal pitcher. The windows of the room overlooked a long, sloping lawn that led down to the dark waters of the lake.

Pete told Catherine about Ellen's disappearance and his suspicion that she was trying to find Franklin Walker. Catherine was horrified by the story. Pete asked if Ellen's mother had ever talked to her about Franklin Walker.

"I think you already know the answer to that," she said. "Poor Lois talked entirely too much about Franklin Walker and the murder for over thirty years. It wasn't at all good for her. A person has to let go of grief eventually, otherwise you can never live a normal life. I told Lois that over and over again, but she wouldn't listen to me."

"Did she ever mention wanting to find Walker after he got out of prison?"

"No. She was very bitter about him being paroled, of course. She talked about that constantly for a time. But I never heard her say she wanted to find the man or confront him. I can hardly imagine Ellen would ever do such a thing, either."

"Maybe I'm wrong," Pete admitted. "But something's happened to Ellen. Today Susan and I unlocked a bank box that Lois and Ellen had. The contract for selling Victor's business was in there. She ever talk about that?"

"Not in years. Lois discussed it with me way back when she sold the business, of course. Taylor Reed handled the entire transaction for her. She was happy with the price she got for it. I remember that."

"She and Taylor dated for a while, didn't they?"

Catherine looked at him in surprise. "Who told you that?"

"Susan. She found some letters Taylor wrote to Lois."

"Lois dated Taylor for a few months before he enlisted in the service near the end of World War II. Taylor went in right as he turned eighteen. It was before Lois met Victor."

"The letters Susan found were written after Victor's death."

Catherine nodded. "I see. Yes, I suppose they would be. I'm very surprised that Lois saved them. That was a very difficult situation for her. She genuinely liked Taylor. He was always so helpful to Lois, and wonderful to the girls. But she never loved him. She enjoyed spending time with him, but he wanted to be married. It was quite awkward for a while."

"Taylor finally got over it?"

"More or less."

"What do you mean?"

"Well, he seemed to finally resign himself to the fact that Lois was not going to ever marry him, but then Lois went out on a few dates with Eric Haffner after he moved to Dallas. It was nothing serious, though Eric was an extremely handsome man then. Lois told me Taylor had a fit about it."

"Really?"

Catherine leaned forward in her chair, putting down the glass of ice tea she'd been holding. "Taylor showed up at Lois's house late one night, stinking drunk, and made a huge scene. He said some awful things."

"What?"

"Well—" Catherine looked away, staring out the window at the lake for a few moments. "Taylor's an old friend, so please don't repeat this, not even to Ellen."

"All right."

"I don't like saying this, but Lois told me Taylor threatened to commit suicide that night."

"What! I can't imagine Taylor doing anything like that."

"No, neither can I. It isn't like him at all. But he really loved Lois, and he was drunk. I'm sure he was extremely embarrassed about the entire episode the next day. And, of course, it was asinine of him to be jealous. Lois wasn't in love with Eric Haffner. She never loved anyone but Victor."

SUSAN AND CAITLIN were flying home to San Antonio that afternoon, and Pete was giving them a ride out to Love Field. He was just leaving the house when the phone rang.

"Hey, bud," said Brian.

"What's up?"

"The computer guy just called. Bingo. He's printing out the files right now."

"What's on them?"

"He didn't say. He just broke the security. I'm going over there now. Want to meet at El Fenix in an hour and a half?"

"Yeah."

Pete drove to Lois's house, picked up Susan and Caitlin, and headed for the airport.

Susan said, "I've been thinking about the possibility that Ellen was trying to find Franklin Walker in Los Angeles."

"Yeah," said Pete.

"If she or Mama wanted revenge for my father's death, I don't think they'd go after Walker."

"Why not?"

"Because he spent thirty years in prison. He was punished."

"But you said your mother didn't think that was long enough."

"True," Susan said. "But Franklin Walker didn't actually shoot my father. He was there, but he didn't do it. At least, the police didn't think he did."

"Why'd they think that?"

"They found the gun in the alley behind the building. Walker's fingerprints weren't on it. Someone else's were."

"So maybe Ellen went to Los Angeles to find the other man. Franklin Walker's partner."

"How could she? The police spent years trying to find him."

"I don't know," said Pete. "Maybe your mother or Ellen figured something out. Or remembered something."

"Maybe."

"Or Franklin Walker is in L.A. And Ellen went there to track him down because he knows who was with him that day."

"But he would never say," said Susan. "Not in all these years."

"No," said Pete. Then something struck him and it felt like a trickle of ice water running through his chest. "If this theory is right, if she left because she was trying to find Franklin Walker or the other man, then the person who broke into our house last night might be the man who shot your father."

"Oh, Jesus," Susan muttered.

"If Franklin Walker's in Los Angeles, I'll find him."

After saying goodbye to Susan and Caitlin at the airport, Pete drove out Lemmon Avenue to the restaurant where he was to meet Brian.

Cheap and popular, El Fenix was a cavernous restaurant with big formica tables and velvet paintings on the walls. It wasn't quite six when Pete stepped inside. The place was mobbed, as usual, and Brian had yet to arrive. Pete gave his name to the hostess and waited for ten minutes before they had a table ready for him. Once he was seated, Pete ordered a beer. Five minutes later Brian showed up. He had a manila folder stuffed with a couple of hundred sheets of paper.

"Hey, homey," he said, sitting across from Pete. "Sorry I'm late, but I had to wait for it to finish printing." Brian handed the heavy folder to Pete.

"What is it?" Pete asked, opening the folder.

"Looks like a play to me."

"A play?" Pete stared at the first page. It said "Act I" along the top. Below this the setting was typed in capital letters: INTERIOR SUBURBAN HOUSE—1964. Brian was right. It was the manuscript of a play. Pete paged through it quickly.

"Did you read any of it?" he asked Brian.

"No. I waited for it to finish printing and came straight here. There were two files in the directory. The first was an outline for the play. The second is the play. Did you know she was writing this?"

"No." Pete was reading a scene fifty pages into the play. A girl and her father were locked in a room. The father was bound to a chair; the girl was crying. Jesus Christ.

Pete closed the manuscript and set it on the table. Even though he'd expected the files to contain something about Ellen's father's death, he wasn't expecting this. Why hadn't Ellen told him she was writing about her father's murder? How did he fail to realize that something had come unhinged in her life? How had they grown so far apart in the last couple of years, both of them having secrets from one another? Pete had wanted a good marriage. He'd wanted them both to be happy. How the hell did this happen?

"What is it?" said Brian. "You look scared."

"I am scared," Pete said.

They ordered dinner, and Pete told Brian everything he'd learned about Ellen, and his suspicions about why she went to Los Angeles. After dinner they walked out to the parking lot together.

Brian said, "I hope she's okay, bud. I really do."

"I know. I appreciate your help with this."

"No problem."

"Can you do me another favor?"

"Name it."

"Get on the Internet and see what you can dig up about a company called Delta Partners."

"Sure. Who are they?"

"They bought Ellen's dad's business. I don't know if they still exist or not."

"I'll see what I can find."

Pete unlocked his car door.

"How are things going with Patty?" Pete asked.

"Touch and go," said Brian. "Still touch and go."

AS HE ENTERED the airport parking structure, Pete noticed the smell. The windows were rolled up in his car, the heater on, but the acrid smell of something charred seeped in. It was a bitter smell Pete recognized as burning rubber or plastic. He thought someone's engine must have caught fire. The smell was not overpowering, and he thought it probably had happened several hours before, though the smell still lingered in the poorly ventilated lot. Pete went to the third level and the smell became stronger. He drove along the perimeter of that level and turned down the aisle where Ellen's car was parked. He saw the orange cones first. As he got closer, he realized the lane was blocked off with yellow tape. In a trance Pete stopped his car, turned off the engine and got out.

Ellen's car was completely destroyed. The tires had burned away, so her Nissan sat on the steel wheel rims. The windows were blown out, the interior scorched down to a maze of wires and springs with the steel undercarriage beneath it. Pete stepped under the yellow tape and slowly circled the shell of Ellen's car, his feet crunching on wet cinders that lay around the car like a black carpet. Everything that could possibly burn had burned. There wasn't a square inch of white paint left on the body of the car, not a scrap of cloth or plastic in the interior. Pete looked up at the concrete ceiling. It was blackened for twenty yards in each direction. His eyes returned to the charred vehicle. What could have been in the car? he wondered. It hadn't occurred to him before that he should search it, but now he wished he had. Whoever was doing this was taking no chances. Ellen, if she was still alive, was in terrible danger.

"Hey, asshole!" someone yelled at him. Startled, Pete looked toward the voice. A security guard in a small electric cart had stopped the next aisle over. "Get the hell away from there."

"When did it happen?" asked Pete.

"Four in the morning. Now get the hell out of there or I'll arrest you right now."

Four in the morning. About three hours after the burglary at his house. Pete turned without a word and walked back to his car. Inside the terminal he called Detective Harris and left a message. He boarded his flight to Los Angeles fifty minutes later.

CHAPTER 16

Walker took the turkey dinner out of the microwave and put it on a plate. He stuck the second dinner in, set the timer, and pushed the start button. As the microwave whirred, he carried the first dinner into the bedroom where Ellen was tied up.

"I fixed turkey for dinner," he said. "I hope that's okay with you."

He unlocked the handcuffs, untied her feet and removed the tape from her mouth.

"Can I use the bathroom?" she asked.

"Sure."

He stood in the hall while she was in there, even though Walker was feeling pretty confident she wouldn't try anything nuts now. She was too smart for that. She'd take off if she could, but she wasn't going to try something unless she had a real chance.

The toilet flushed and she came out. In the bedroom she sat on the edge of the bed and started eating her dinner.

"How is it?" he asked.

"Pretty good."

"I'm having the same thing. I like the Select Menu turkey. For Italian I like Family Favorites best."

"You always eat frozen dinners?"

"Pretty much. Want something to drink? I didn't bring you nothing."

"A glass of water."

"All right."

He left her alone. Hell, he figured he could trust her for a half-minute or so. In the kitchen he got her a glass of water, and the bell rang on the microwave. Walker took his dinner into the bedroom with the water.

"Here you go." He handed her the glass and sat down on the chair he'd brought into the bedroom a couple of days before. It was a lot of work taking care of the woman. He had to feed her, make sure he remembered to let her go to the bathroom every few hours, and check to see she was covered at night so she wouldn't get cold. But for some reason, Walker didn't really mind all the time he'd spent caring for her. Even though she had come to kill him, he found himself liking her. It wasn't like he felt she was a friend. It was different than that. Maybe it was because he kept remembering her as a little girl and how scared she'd been. Walker had felt sorry for her then. Shit, he still felt sorry for her.

"These frozen dinners you microwave are something," he said to her. "For somebody like me who can't cook, it's great."

"You eat dinner with your girlfriend much?" she asked.

"Sometimes." For a second Walker wondered how she knew about Denise, but then he remembered that Denise had dropped the keys down to him the night the woman showed up with the gun. "Lotsa times we just go out for a drink. She doesn't eat much."

"Does she know about me?" the woman asked.

"Hell, no." Did she think he was crazy? "I ain't told nobody."

"I just wondered."

"I tell somebody, they might call the cops. I don't want to go to jail again, lady. Not never."

"I don't blame you. But what are you going to do with me?"

Walker turned his eyes away from her. She sure had a knack for turning nice conversation bad. He wondered if she did the same thing to other people or if it was just because she hated him in particular.

"I don't know what to do with you," he said. "I wish to hell you'd never showed up here."

"Me too."

Walker continued eating. The woman finished most of her dinner and set the plate aside. She drank the rest of her water.

"Want anything else?" Walker asked.

"No, thanks. I'm full. If you let me go," she said, "I won't tell anyone."

Walker chuckled. He took a bite of the corn from his plate. It was mixed in with a thick white sauce. Walker had no idea what it was, but it was very good.

"I'm serious," she said. "I won't go to the police. I had a gun. I was going to kill you if I had to. I don't want the police to know that. Let me go. I'll be very thankful to go back to Dallas alive. You won't see me again."

Walker said, "I know how much you hate me, lady. I don't even blame you. You go to the police and say I beat you up and held you prisoner, who they gonna believe? You or me?"

"I won't do that. I swear I won't."

"You don't turn me in to the cops, it's because you're comin' back to try and fuckin' kill me again."

"No," said Ellen. "You could've killed me, but you didn't. I'm grateful to be alive. I'm grateful to you."

She sounded like she meant it, and Walker found himself

moved by her words. What was it about her that got to him?

"I don't hate you anymore," she said.

"I'm glad a that," he said.

"You won't go back to jail," she said. "Because I won't tell anybody."

He nodded his head slowly. Walker wanted to believe her, but he couldn't bring himself to accept that it was really true. She was smart. Smarter than he was. She might just be trying to trick him into letting her go. Then she would want him in fucking jail or dead. But if he didn't let her go, then what? There was no getting around the fact that Barton wanted her dead.

"You know who Eddie Rollins is?" he asked her.

The woman thought a minute. "I've heard the name," she said.

"He's my favorite writer. He wrote a book called *Dare to Succeed*. That's his most famous one. Another book he wrote is called *Anybody Can Be a Winner*."

"That's right. He's the self-help, positive-thinking guy. He does those TV infomercials."

"Yeah. See, Eddie Rollins says you can turn even the most negative situations into positive ones. The situation we got here is pretty goddamn negative, but I figure there's got to be some way to make it positive. Eddie Rollins could."

"I'm sure there's a way to do that," she said.

Walker ate the last bite of his corn and put the plate down on the floor next to his chair. "Sometimes I wonder if this is some sort a test for me," he said.

"What do you mean?"

"Like I've got the worst possible situation in the world, but if I turn it around and make it positive, maybe my whole life will change. And maybe Eddie will write about me in one a his books. He does that, you know. Talks about people that have succeeded in life using his ideas. Maybe me and you'll be in one a his books." He smiled broadly at her. The idea thrilled him.

"Maybe," she said. "It's certainly possible."

Walker thought of something. "Only one problem," he said.

"What?"

"Eddie'd have to use different names for us. Otherwise we both might be in some trouble with the law."

"I guess you're right. We'd still know it was about us, though. It wouldn't matter to me."

"Yeah. Me neither. And Eddie'd know our real names and everything." He smiled at her, and she smiled back at him.

"Maybe I could help you," she said.

"How's that?" he asked.

"If we both wrote him letters about what had happened, it might have a better chance of getting in a book."

He said, "You'd do that?"

"Yes."

It was a nice thing for her to say. She was a nice woman, he guessed, even if she had been out to kill him and Barton. Maybe she wouldn't have been able to do it. Lord knows, it wasn't that easy.

"Guess I better get rid a these plates," he said, reaching down to pick his up off the floor. "Need anything else?"

"No."

Walker took the plates and glass into the kitchen, setting them on the counter near the sink. He went back to the bedroom. The woman still sat on the edge of the bed. Walker realized he never thought of her by her name. Ellen was the name of a small girl he had met once, and it was hard to call the woman that.

"You think about it a lot?" he asked her.

"Yeah," she said.

It didn't surprise Walker that she knew what he meant.

"I don't remember what happened that day," she said. "But I think about it all the time. And I have nightmares about it. I remember the nightmares."

"What kind a nightmares?"

"It starts off with my father asking me to go to his office. Then we get there and hear a noise. I don't know if this is the way it really happened or not. It's the way I dream it."

"What else do you dream?"

"I see you in my dream. You meet me on the stairs and take me to a room where my father is. I dream about being out of the office and looking for a phone. And I dream about the smoke. I'm under the desk and smoke is everywhere. You had a silver tooth."

"Huh?"

"You had a silver tooth back then, didn't you? In the front? You do in the dream."

"Yeah. That's right. You called the cops, right?"

"I—" Ellen's voice caught in her throat. She paused, pulling her emotions into check. "I'm not sure."

"'Member the fire?" he asked.

"Only about the smoke under the desk," she said. Her voice was shaky. "I can't breathe. I'm scared. I usually wake up right at that part."

Walker said, "I think about it a lot. I guess I must think about it pretty near every day."

Walker sat quietly for a moment, then said, "Guess I better do your handcuffs now." He picked them up from the top of the dresser. The woman—Ellen—stood and turned around, putting her hands behind her back. Walker cuffed her wrists. He tore off a piece of tape and applied it to her mouth.

After he had her bound and lying comfortably on the bed, Walker went to the refrigerator and got a beer. He quickly rinsed the plates and forks they'd used for dinner, putting them in the dishwasher.

In the living room he drank his beer and wondered about letting the woman go. She seemed sincere when she said she wouldn't go to the police. And Walker had to admit she had a point when she explained why she wouldn't want the police to know what she had tried to do.

A very negative situation had definitely been improved, Walker thought. It wasn't exactly positive, but it was pointing in that direction. He felt good about that. The whole thing could have been a disaster. He'd almost killed her. Thank the Lord he hadn't. If he had, for sure he'd have ended up in San Quentin for the rest of his life. Or the woman might've killed him. He wasn't sure which outcome would've been worse. He got up and went to the refrigerator to get another beer. As he opened it, the phone rang.

"Hello," he said.

"It's me," said Barton.

"Yeah. Hi."

"She still alive?"

"Yeah."

He didn't say anything for a few moments. "I did some checking in Dallas. It doesn't look like anyone knows what she's doing. Her husband has been out to Los Angeles, though. He knows she went there. She's still in your apartment?"

"Yeah."

"You'll have to get rid of her."

Walker didn't say anything.

"Dump the body somewhere nobody'll find it for a long time.

The desert or something. That's the best thing to do."

Walker still didn't respond.

"You there?" Barton asked.

"Yeah."

"What's wrong?"

"Nothin'."

"If you don't want to do it, I'll send Dale. That's no problem."

"No. I can handle it."

"Good. Do it right away. I'll come out in a few days. I want you to move someplace else. New city. Understand?"

"Yeah."

"Do it right away." Barton hung up.

CHAPTER 17

Flying back to Los Angeles, Pete read the outline and then the full manuscript of the play Ellen had written. To say Pete was horrified by what he had read didn't do justice to his feelings. The terror that the young girl in the play felt was so overwhelming Pete could barely continue reading the play as he approached the conclusion. It was unbearable, and Pete realized he had never truly appreciated the horror Ellen had suffered at the age of four. She always said she didn't remember what happened that day; she only knew what happened when she dreamed about it. Ellen was reluctant to talk about the dreams, and Pete never pressed her to confide in him.

He assumed the play was based on her nightmares, and now Pete certainly understood why she woke up screaming. He knew little about drama and nothing about writing a play, but Pete could not remember ever reading anything as harrowing as this. *Poor Ellen,* he thought as he finished reading the draft all the way through. *No wonder she wanted to do something to put an end to this.*

It was a little past nine at night when Pete arrived at the Holiday Inn in Santa Monica. A room was more expensive here than at the hotel where he'd stayed before, but Pete wanted to stay in the same hotel where Ellen had been. There was a message waiting for him to call Marvin. Pete phoned as soon as he got to his room.

"Something's come up," said Marvin.

"What?"

"They found the car she rented."

"Where?"

"In a shopping center on Sunset Boulevard in Hollywood. It was there part of the day and then overnight, so a security guard called it in. It's a big parking lot. There's lots of traffic in and out. No one noticed the car being left. I went around with Ellen's picture. No one remembered seeing her."

"Shit," said Pete.

"It doesn't make things any worse than we already thought," offered Marvin.

"Maybe not. But some things happened in Dallas."

"What?"

Pete gave Marvin a quick summary.

"Okay," said Marvin gravely. "So what we need to do is find Franklin Walker."

"Right away," said Pete.

"The rental company picked up the car already. I checked it out, and there was no sign of a struggle, anything like that. They're not going to clean the car because I want the police to go over it. I'll call Roy Trenton about that first thing tomorrow. He's the detective I already talked to about Ellen. A decent guy. It'd be a godsend to find somebody's prints in that car. And I'll get him looking for Franklin Walker."

"We have to find him."

"Another thing was that the security guard who noticed the car sitting there all night saw something funny a couple nights ago."

"Sunday night?"

"Yeah. The night Ellen left the hotel. The guard was inside the Sears there, and he saw a car pull into the parking lot and stop right in the middle of it. It was a Toyota, just like your wife rented, but he can't swear it was blue. It was night, so all he can say for sure was the car was a dark color. Anyway, he said the car sat there for at least a minute. The security guy thought something might be going on, so he watched, but then the car drove off, went out to Sunset and turned west. He didn't think too much of it, but last night when he got to work at eleven he sees a car looks just like it parked in the lot. Same make and model. It sat there all night, and he walked over to it in the morning and saw the rental sticker on the back bumper. That's when he called it in."

"He couldn't tell who was driving the car the first time he saw it?"

Marvin shook his head. "Too far away."

"What do you think was going on?"

"If it was Ellen's car that first night, I think the driver, whoever it was, was looking for a place to dump it. They were checking out the lot. It looked okay, so the person came back the next day when the lot was full and left it."

"Were the keys in the car?"

"Under the seat."

"There's no reason Ellen would have left the car like that."

"No," said Marvin. "There's not."

EARLY THE NEXT MORNING Pete reached Detective Harris in Dallas. Harris told Pete that the fire department had determined an incendiary device had been placed under Ellen's car sometime before four in the morning on Tuesday. No witnesses had been found who saw anything unusual in the parking structure prior to the fire breaking out. As far as Franklin Walker was concerned, he seemed to have disappeared. The first six months after his release he had lived quietly in a halfway house in Richardson. Following that, he had checked in monthly with his parole officer in Fort Worth. When he successfully completed his parole requirements, he left his last known address. Harris suspected Walker had left the state, but could find nothing on him in the computer.

"He hasn't been arrested anywhere, I can tell you that with some certainty," said Harris. "I'm trying to find out if he's been working, but so far no luck."

"Concentrate on Southern California," said Pete. "I think he's out here."

"I am."

After hanging up with Harris, Pete telephoned Taylor's office, telling his secretary that it was urgent he speak with him. He spent several minutes on hold before Taylor came on the line.

"Yes, Pete," he said. "What is it?"

"I think I know why Ellen came to Los Angeles," Pete said.

"Why?"

"To find Franklin Walker."

Taylor was silent. Pete could hear him breathing steadily over the phone.

"You know who he is?" asked Pete.

"Of course," said Taylor quietly. "That's a name I'm not likely to forget. Are you sure about that?"

"No. But it's the only thing that makes sense at this point. Did you ever have any idea that Ellen or her mother wanted to find him?"

"No."

"Did you know Walker had been released from prison?"

"Yes. Lois talked about it. It was very upsetting to her at the time. It must've been three years ago now. Was Ellen upset about that?"

"If she was, she never talked about it to me. To tell you the truth, I didn't even know the man's name before yesterday."

"So you think this Walker person is in Los Angeles?"

"Yeah. The police are trying to locate him, but he seems to have dropped off the face of the earth. Listen, Taylor, someone torched Ellen's car yesterday morning."

"Torched? You mean it was set on fire?"

"Yes."

"But it's at the airport, isn't it?"

"That's where it happened. I just got off the phone with the police. It was deliberately set on fire."

"My God." Taylor seemed stunned.

"Did you tell anyone that her car was out at the airport?" Pete asked.

"What? No. Just you. Why?"

"I'm just wondering how the person who did this knew where her car was. I told Susan, Marvin and Detective Harris, but that's it."

"Detective Harris?" said Taylor.

"He's with the police department. He came out to the house yesterday because of the burglary."

"Ah," said Taylor. "I see."

"He said he might call you."

"That's fine."

"You filed a missing persons report on Ellen, right?"

"That's right."

"Detective Harris asked if I'd done that."

Taylor was silent for several moments. "This is all very frightening. If what you're thinking is correct, Ellen could be in desperate trouble."

"I know. And someone in Dallas is involved."

"Why? What do you mean?"

"Someone breaks into the house and steals nothing but Ellen's computer, and then her car is set on fire. That's no coincidence."

"No, of course not." Taylor sounded a little confused. Pete realized he was dumping a lot on him all at once, and Taylor hadn't looked all that well yesterday at the bank.

"I'll let you go, Taylor," he said.

"Pete," he said. "What are you going to do now?"

"Find Franklin Walker."

CHAPTER 18

Ellen washed her hair in the morning. Carefully, she shampooed the back of her head for a long time, trying to get it as clean as she could. Her head was still very sore, but overall she was beginning to feel much better, remarkably well considering the injuries she'd received. She wasn't sure how many days she'd been in Los Angeles. Whenever she tried to think about time, she got confused. She'd fall asleep, wake up and not be sure if she'd slept one hour or four or eight. She had no sense of day and night.

The murderer was waiting in the hall, she knew. He always kept a close watch on her when she wasn't tied up. Last night they had talked in such a friendly way that she'd thought she might actually convince him to let her go. This morning, however, he wasn't in a good mood. Something was bothering him. Maybe he had a hangover. Ellen had smelled beer on his breath last night. Whatever the cause, his mood worried her. She didn't want him to be angry or upset, even if it didn't have anything to do with her.

Ellen dried off, combed her hair as best she could, and got dressed. At some point the murderer had taken her dirty clothes to a laundromat and washed them. This was a good sign. No reason to wash her clothes if he were planning to kill her. Still, something had to happen eventually. He couldn't keep her tied up in his bedroom forever. And this morning he was sullen and cold. Ellen wondered if she should try to improve his mood or ignore it.

As he had made his habit, the murderer sat with her as she ate a bowl of cereal in the bedroom. He had nothing to eat, only a cup of coffee.

"Something wrong?" she asked him after they had been sitting together silently for several minutes.

"Not really," he said.

She finished her cereal. The murderer asked if she wanted more. Ellen didn't, but she said she'd like a cup of coffee. He left and brought her a cup.

"Thanks," she said.

He sat back down.

"Is it a problem for you to miss so much work?" she asked.

"I've got vacation time coming. Even if they fire me, I don't care. It's not that good a job."

She thought a minute about how to phrase her next question. "Have you thought anymore about how we can turn our situation into a positive one?"

He stared at her, and Ellen thought maybe she had made a mistake. She'd tried to sound sincere, but maybe he'd detected a note of sarcasm in her voice. All she needed was for this guy to think she was making fun of him.

"Yeah, I thought about it."

He was touchy today. Maybe it would be best to just let him alone for now. Ellen drank her coffee.

"I felt sorry for you that day," he said. "You were so scared. It was a horrible thing to happen to a little girl."

"What happened to my father was worse."

"I guess so." He put his hands together. "Tell me about those bad dreams."

"I already did."

"They always the same?"

"Not exactly. There are parts that change a little bit."

"You dream about how you got outta there?"

"No."

He nodded, not saying anything.

"Why?" she asked.

"I wondered."

"One of the policemen got me out."

"That in your dream?"

"No. I always wake up when I'm inside the office. It's full of smoke and I'm choking."

"Why do you think a cop got you out? They tell you that?"

"I think so. They were the only ones there. The building was on fire. I think by the time the firemen got there the place was pretty much gone."

"Yeah."

"Somebody got me out. It must've been a policeman. There's smoke in the office. It's very thick and I can't breathe. Sometimes I dream about someone grabbing my ankle. I wake up then."

He looked at her a long time, so long Ellen became uncomfortable. The murderer's gray, almost colorless eyes seemed void of all emotion to Ellen. She started to worry that he was thinking about killing her.

"It was me," he said.

"What?"

"That got you outta that building."

Her face burned and she looked away. Ellen rejected the idea immediately. He was lying to her. He wanted her to like him, wanted her to think he was a hero instead of a killer. Maybe this was how he thought he could make the situation positive, by telling her a lie. *Asshole*. She wished she'd shot him dead when she had the chance

"We was gettin' out the back," he said. "The cops had come up to the front and we was runnin'. I saw the smoke comin' out the window as we got to the alley. I didn't know he'd started a fire till then. He was runnin' away. But I stopped. I was lookin' up at the window and all that smoke. He screamed for me to come on, but I didn't. I went back inside and up the stairs. It was so black I couldn't see. I bumped along tryin' to find the office where you was. Then I got down on my hands and knees. I could see a little bit then, and I found it. The smoke was getting blacker and the floor underneath my hands was hot. I yelled for you, but I didn't hear nothin'. Then I remembered the desk, so I went around feelin' with my hands till I bumped into the chair. I pushed it outta the way and reached under the desk and felt your leg. I pulled you out and crawled to the stairs, holdin' you under one arm. I couldn't see nothin'. I could barely breathe, I was chokin' so much. I was about to faint by the time I got to the stairs, but I got down 'em. The next thing I knew we was both outside. You were lyin' on the blacktop cryin'. I was still chokin', and I was dizzy but I knew I had to get away. I got to my feet and started down the alley. I didn't get too far."

Ellen was sick to her stomach. She didn't remember. She didn't remember anything. There was no way to know if he was telling the truth, but the story he told seemed too detailed for a lie. Ellen didn't think he was smart enough to make something up that was that convincing. Could it be true? That the man she'd hated her entire life had saved her from the fire?

After a while she said, "Who was with you?"

He looked at her, surprised.

"You said someone screamed at you to come on. Who was it?"

"The one who killed your daddy."

"What was his name?"

"I told you he was dead," he said.

"That's a lie. I can tell when you're lying. The story you just told me is true. You did save my life."

"Yeah."

"Is he alive?"

The colorless eyes stared at her for several moments. "Yeah. He's alive."

"Have you told him about me?"

The murderer nodded. "Yeah."

The bastard. Now she knew why he'd been so moody. The other guy was coming to kill her. He'd saved her life once, but now he was going to help kill her. Shit. She had been so close. The murderer would have given her the other man's name eventually. If only she hadn't been distracted by the knock on the door. But she had been, and she had turned her head and everything changed.

"What's his name?"

"Alan Barton. But I don't even know if that's his real name. I don't think it is. It's what he went by back then."

"Does he still use it?"

"It's what I call him. He lives in New Orleans. I have a number to call. He calls me back after I leave a message."

"What did he say when you told him about me?"

"He said to wait a few days. Keep you tied up."

"Why?"

"He wanted to check things out."

"What things?"

"Things in Dallas. He wanted to see if anyone knew what you were doing."

"No one does."

"That's what he figures."

"How'd he check up on me?"

The murderer shrugged. "He knows a lot of people."

"What kind of people?"

"I guess the kind of people who can find things out."

"What's he want to do now?"

The murderer chewed on his bottom lip for a minute. Ellen knew what he was going to say. "He wants me to kill you. That's what he wants me to do."

"Let me out of here," she said. "I won't tell anybody. Please."

"Thing is, if I don't kill you, Alan's gonna have us both killed. I let you go, first he'll find me, then he'll find you."

"Why? I don't know who he is or what he looks like. I don't know where he lives. I can't hurt him."

"He's not gonna take that chance. You found me. He figures you might be able to find him. You won't be safe in Dallas, you won't be safe anywhere." Walker chewed on his lip again. "You and me is in a fix," he said. "And I don't know exactly what the best thing to do is."

Suddenly Ellen was panicked. *I've got to get out of here. I've got to get out as soon as I can.*

The murderer cuffed her, tied her ankles and taped her mouth closed. He left, closing the door. Ellen listened, hoping to hear him leave the apartment, but she heard nothing. She didn't know if he was there or not, so she couldn't do anything about trying to get away. She wondered if he had been telling the truth. He seemed frightened of this Alan Barton. So frightened he probably would kill her to save himself. Ellen needed more time. She had to convince the murderer not to kill her. Make this Alan Barton come out and do it himself.

She heard a noise and knew he was still in the apartment. Since she couldn't try to free herself now, she decided to lay down and rest. She was tired again and supposed it was because she hadn't fully recovered from her injuries. She lowered herself onto her left side, her right side was very sore, and pulled her legs up. At least he hadn't hogtied her ankles with a rope to the handcuffs. Ellen scooted back away from the edge of the bed. She felt better lying down. Walker had told her it was Wednesday. That meant it had only been six days since she had talked to Pete. Not long at all. It was possible he wasn't even that worried about her yet. After the incredibly awful last two weeks, her anger and disgust with him, it would only be natural for Pete to assume she was staying away out of spite. He might figure she needed a week or so to cool off. But he hadn't wanted her to go, and he had been upset that she wasn't at Susan's as she had said she would be. On Thursday when she talked to him, she'd thought he was merely angry at her. Angry that she did something on her own, without letting him know. But now Ellen thought she'd been wrong. It wasn't just anger in his voice, he was also worried about her. And if he was worried, maybe he'd call the police, though how the police could help, she didn't know. How would they ever figure out that she'd flown to Los Angeles to confront Walker?

Soon, Ellen fell asleep.

CHAPTER 19

Pete drove to the police station on Venice Boulevard about eight miles east of his hotel. He arrived before Marvin and waited outside the main entrance to the large brick building. Marvin pulled into the parking lot a few minutes later, and they went into the station together.

Roy Trenton came out to meet them almost immediately. He was a short, husky man with metal-gray hair. He led them back to a large room with a dozen cubicles in it. Trenton grabbed a couple extra chairs and pulled them over to his cubicle. They all sat.

"I talked to Lamar Harris in Dallas about an hour and a half ago," Trenton said. "They still can't locate Franklin Walker. He wired out a photo they got from the state prison system. It's somewhat out of date." He passed a sheet of paper over to Pete. It showed a thin man of fifty with short gray hair. The man stared blankly at the camera. He had a large chin, and his heavy eyes drooped at the corners.

Marvin leaned toward Pete to look at the photograph. "How long ago was it taken?"

"Eight years ago."

Pete said, "Detective Harris was trying to trace him through employment records."

"Yeah. There hasn't been any income reported under his Social Security number for over two years. California DMV has addresses for three Franklin Walkers. Two are not our guy, and the third has moved."

"Where was the last place he worked?" asked Marvin.

"In Fort Worth for a year while he was on parole. By the way, we dusted the inside of the car Mrs. Donelly rented and got some prints. Most seem to belong to one person, probably Mrs. Donelly. We're getting a set of Walker's prints to use for comparison purposes." Trenton then told them that most of the television news programs would be running a story on Ellen's disappearance that evening. "They'll show her photograph and then a phone number to call if someone has any information on her," he said.

"They going to show a picture of Franklin Walker, too?"

"No," said Trenton. "At this point we don't want him to know we're looking for him."

Trenton made copies of Walker's photograph for Pete and Marvin before they left. Marvin was going to circulate the photo at the shopping center where Ellen's car had been found. Pete was heading back to the area around the post office where Ellen had purchased the money order in August.

Pete started with the post office. The manager remembered Pete from his prior visit. She carefully studied the photograph of Franklin Walker, but he didn't look familiar to her. She took Pete behind the service counter, and he showed the photo to the clerks working there. No one remembered the face. Before Pete left, the manager made a photocopy of Walker's picture for the letter carriers to look at when they returned in the afternoon.

Pete then went up and down both sides of the street, two blocks in each direction. He spoke to many of the same people he'd shown Ellen's photograph to previously. No one recognized

Franklin Walker. Discouraged, Pete went back to his car. It was two in the afternoon, and he was very hungry. He drove west to La Brea and turned north. Stopping at a taco stand, he bought a couple of chicken tacos and a soda. The man who took his order stared at Walker's photograph without recognition.

After he ate, Pete continued up La Brea. Two blocks further north he passed a large supermarket. A block past the store Pete thought he might as well stop. Walker had to buy food somewhere.

He turned right, drove a block and turned right again, circling back to the market's parking lot, which was crowded. Pete found a spot near the rear of the lot and walked across the asphalt to the store. It was Wednesday. A full week had passed since Ellen left. *Please. Please let her be okay.*

The assistant manager of the supermarket, Larry Kellums, came out of his small office near the entrance to the store and looked at the photograph of Walker.

"Yeah," he said after a moment, instantly giving Pete goose bumps. "He shops here. He looks a little older now. But I recognize him. He in trouble?"

"He might be," said Pete. "You're sure you recognize him?"

"Yeah. I've seen him in here a lot of times. He's a regular. Are you a cop?"

"No. But the police are trying to find him. I'll call them in just a minute. They may want to talk to you." Pete was trembling with nerves now.

"No problem. Come over here." Pete followed Larry to a checkout line where a thin Asian woman was scanning items and sliding them down to the bagging area.

The checker glanced back at Larry and Pete.

Larry said, "We just have a quick question, Gloria." He

started bagging the groceries for her until a boxboy stepped up and took over. When the customer had paid for his groceries, the checker came over.

"What's up?" she asked.

Larry took the photo from Pete and held it up to her. "Recognize him?"

"Yeah."

"Do you know his name?"

"No. He always pays in cash, and he's not too talkative."

Larry briefly told her why Pete was looking for him.

"You don't know where he lives, by any chance?" asked Pete.

"No," said Gloria. "No idea."

"You see him in here often?"

"Two or three times a week. He's always coming in to buy cigarettes. Usually I see him in the early evening. I think he stops on his way home from work."

Pete punched Marvin's number into the pay phone outside the market. Louise answered. Marvin wasn't home, but Louise said she'd page him. Pete gave her the number of the pay phone. Next he phoned Trenton at the police department. Trenton promised to be there in fifteen minutes.

Marvin returned his call several minutes later. Pete gave him the location of the supermarket.

Trenton arrived with another detective, a black man named Carpenter. Pete sat in the back seat of the silver Chevrolet they were in, and repeated everything the assistant manager and the checker had told him. Trenton went into the store to talk to them himself while Pete and Carpenter waited in the car. Pete was beside himself with anxiety and excitement. Walker would come to the store within a day or two, surely, and then they would have him. If only there was a way to find him now. Waiting for him to come to the store for cigarettes or food would be unbearable. He must live somewhere nearby. Maybe within a few blocks. There had to be a way to find him.

Trenton returned to the car. He said, "All right. When he shows, the manager and the young woman know not to act any differently toward him. We'll stay here until the store closes at midnight. If he doesn't show, I'll have someone here all day tomorrow."

"What if he does show?" asked Pete.

"We'll follow him. We question him here, and he might not tell us where he lives even if we arrest him. And we definitely need to locate his house or apartment."

"What can I do?"

"Best thing would be for you to leave."

"If I stay, I can help. The store's crowded and big. He could show and you'd miss him."

Trenton smiled. "Don't worry, Mr. Donelly. We won't miss him. I promise you that. If you stay, you'll be a nervous wreck the entire time."

"I'll be a nervous wreck if I leave."

"I know. But unless we're lucky, this could take a few days. It'd be better for you to be a nervous wreck someplace else."

Carpenter left the car and went into the store, where he was going to push a shopping cart around while Trenton remained in the vehicle watching the entrance. Every couple of hours they would switch places.

Marvin arrived, talked with Trenton briefly, and then he and Pete left. Pete followed Marvin to his apartment building. As they rode up in the elevator, Marvin told Pete that he'd had no success showing Walker's photograph around the shopping center where Ellen's rental car had been abandoned.

Inside his apartment Marvin spread out a street map on the table. With an orange marker he drew a dot to mark the location of the post office, another dot where Ellen's car had been found, a third dot on the spot where the supermarket was. They were all within three miles of each other.

"She must be somewhere around there," said Pete.

"It's looking likely."

"I wish I'd stayed at the grocery store."

"It's best you didn't," said Marvin. "Trenton can do a better job if he's not worrying about you going berserk when you see Walker."

"I wouldn't go berserk."

"Trenton doesn't know that."

"True," said Pete.

"Besides, you can't really say how you'd react if you came face to face with Franklin Walker, can you?"

"No," said Pete. "I guess not."

CHAPTER 20

Walker drank a beer at the kitchen table. He couldn't decide what to do. It was an impossible situation. Barton would be calling soon. Either that or he'd be sending Dale by. Walker could lie, tell Barton he'd done it. Say the body was two hundred yards from a dirt road in the Mojave, buried four feet under the hard, cracked dirt. That would buy a little time, and he could take off, get a different car, drive to—where? Idaho or Montana? But Barton would be looking for him soon enough, and Walker didn't think he could hide for very long. And Ellen. What would she do? Go back home, he supposed. But she wouldn't be alive long. Barton would know exactly where to find her.

The previous night Denise had insisted on coming into the apartment, and Walker realized that to keep her out would cause more trouble than to let her in. First thing she asked about was the spot on the carpet, the stain still visible even though Walker had used two different stain removers on it. He told her he had spilled some wine. This seemed to satisfy her, even though she knew damn well he never drank wine. She sat down, lit a cigarette and asked if he might have a drink for her. Walker just wanted to get her out of the apartment, so he said he felt like going out. But Denise didn't want to go out. Walker fixed her a couple of drinks and then she started hinting around that she'd been missing something else for a few days, started rubbing Walker's leg and giving him the look. God, the next thing she'd do would be to stand up and head for the bedroom. What the fuck would he do then? Finally, he told Denise he was out of gin. She was so suspicious that she went into the kitchen to look for herself, which pissed him off. If he said he was out of gin, why'd she have to search the place? Walker had read in one of Eddie's books that two people can't have a successful relationship if they don't trust each other. He'd have liked to read that to Denise and see what she thought. Probably go right over her head. Walker did have a quart of Gilbey's under the sink, but Denise didn't look there, so then she believed him. They went up to her place, and Denise had a couple more drinks before they went to bed. When they finished and she was asleep, Walker left.

Most of the afternoon Walker sat in the living room smoking. The phone rang, but he didn't answer it. It was either Barton or Denise. It rang eleven times and stopped. He heard people coming and going from their apartments. Walker knew that around six Denise would be by. The thought made him shudder. He had to find a way to end things with her. One of Eddie's books talked a lot about screwed-up relationships between men and women and how to improve them. Walker decided he should read that section again, but he really wasn't much interested in improving things with Denise anymore.

It was six-thirty, and Walker was thinking about putting the first dinner in the microwave, when Denise rang his doorbell. She was in a dress, he supposed it was a nice one, and she had done up her hair.

"You aren't ready?" she asked when he opened the door. It took him a moment, then he remembered. Fuck. It was the night he was going out with Denise and her sister. "You didn't forget, did you?" she asked.

"No. I need to grab a shower, that's all."

"You forgot," she said, disgusted. Denise took half a step into the apartment.

"No," he said. "Go upstairs. I'll be there soon as I get a shower."

With a pained expression on her face, she backed out, and Walker closed the door, locking it. He knew he'd have to hurry or she'd be back at his door ringing the fucking bell. He put a dinner in the microwave and then jumped into the shower. He had to go into the bedroom to get some clean clothes. The woman was awake, lying on the bed, bound and gagged.

"Sorry," he said to Ellen. "I got to go out tonight, but I've got your dinner in the microwave." He took his clothes out to the living room and changed. Walker didn't own a sport jacket, but he had a sweater Denise had given him for his birthday. He'd wear that and hopefully it'd put her in a better mood, make her a little less pissed off.

He took dinner in to Ellen, untied her hands, removed the tape from her mouth and told her to eat quickly, since he had to go. Ellen finished in five minutes, went to the bathroom, and then came back into the bedroom, where Walker quickly bound and gagged her again.

"I hope I'm not gone too long," he told her. "We need to talk about things. I got some ideas." He smiled as he turned off the light and closed the door on her.

ELLEN LISTENED for the sound of the front door closing but never heard it. She waited a long time, not moving, thinking about what the murderer had said to her. They needed to talk about things later.

Ellen felt stronger, her mind clearer. Her ribs on her right side were still very sore. The back of her head was tender if she touched it, but otherwise she felt good. She knew she could roll off the bed; whether she'd be able to get out of the bedroom or not, she didn't know, but she was going to try. Then a thought struck Ellen. Maybe the murderer had said he was going out merely to see what she would do. He'd never told her anything like that before, and it might be a test to see if she tried to escape. She hadn't heard the door close. The murderer might be right outside the closed bedroom door, listening. What if he was? If he was going to kill her, he was going to kill her. It really wouldn't matter much if it was now or later tonight or tomorrow morning. The murderer had said that if he didn't get rid of her, the other man would kill them both. It wasn't much of a choice. He was going to have to kill her. Ellen took a breath and rolled off the bed.

She landed on her left side. It jarred her and the back of her head started throbbing, but she was okay. Ellen waited a couple of minutes, listening for any sound in the apartment. There was none. The pain in her head faded. Walker must have left, just as he said. He had been quiet and moody today. Probably feeling guilty about having to kill her, she thought. Well, he should feel guilty. Ellen was consumed with an overwhelming desire to get out of the apartment and live. She wanted to see Susan and Caitlin. She wanted to see Taylor. Pete, too. Pissed off as she had been at him, his affair didn't seem so important now. She was getting over the shock of it, she supposed. Ellen rolled onto her back, which was uncomfortable since her hands were cuffed behind her, her legs drawn up close by the cord that ran from her hands to her ankles. Now what? She tried to sit up and get on her knees, but she couldn't. She started scooting on her butt, sliding her feet an inch or two, then bouncing her body forward. It was painful progress, the handcuffs digging into her wrists and back as she moved along. It took five minutes to get to the end of the bed, but then the closed door was only a few feet away. If only she could get to her knees. She continued moving along until she was completely away from the side of the bed. There was more floor space here. For a few minutes she lay on her back resting, then she moved herself sideways so she was next to the end of the bed. She lifted her back up again as if trying to sit up and twisted toward the bed, hoping to prop herself up. She missed and landed back on the floor, sending a searing pain through the back of her head. The next time she was successful. She easily turned enough so that her back was propped up against the edge of the bed. From here Ellen was able to move herself up a bit, then lean forward and fall over onto her knees. This was better. It was simple to move her knees back and forth slowly, and bit by bit make her way to the door. But there was no way to stand up, no way to use her hands cuffed behind her. Ellen tried to grip the doorknob between her chin and neck. It didn't work. She stared at the doorknob in front of her face, thinking. There had to be a way to get out. She could try her mouth and teeth, but to do that she had to get the tape off. Ellen couldn't afford to waste time. Maybe it wasn't the best thing to try, but she couldn't think of anything else. She fell back onto her side, waited for the pain to ease, and began rubbing the side of her face against the carpet, hoping to get the edge of the tape turned back. Once the tape was off, she felt certain she could get the door open. And once in the other room, she could get to the phone. Ellen remembered the small counter it sat on. She would pull it off the counter and use her tongue to dial 911. She would not die.

As she thought about this, rubbing her face back and forth on the carpet, she heard the front door open and close.

Ellen held her breath and listened. For several long moments there was no other sound. Then she heard the floor creak and knew the murderer was really back. What was he doing? If he came in and saw her, she knew he would hurt her. Ellen's skin went damp and ice cold. Why had she been so stupid? With all her heart, she wished she had stayed on the bed. Ellen was more afraid than she'd ever been in her life. She wished she could scream out, scream so loud the whole neighborhood would hear her. She waited, trembling, feeling sick to her stomach at the thought of what was in store.

Ellen heard the door open and close again. She waited. Her nausea passed, but she couldn't stop the shaking for several minutes. Slowly, she began rubbing her cheek on the carpet again, but her skin was getting sore. Maybe this wouldn't get the tape off. Rolling over, Ellen began trying the other side of her face.

Fifteen minutes later her face was burning with rug irritation, and she had felt nothing to indicate that the tape was pulling away. She had to try something else. Rolling onto her back, she scooted herself around so that her head was toward the door. She pulled her shoulders up off the floor as she inched her butt back and was able to prop herself partway up against the closed door. She did this again, then leaned forward and was back on her knees. Stretching back and up, she tried to get the doorknob under her arm. Several attempts at this failed; she just couldn't get high enough. Exhausted, Ellen rested a moment before stretching up as high as she possibly could. The knob hit her just above her armpit, and there was no way to get higher. The cord between her ankles and wrists had been pulled to its limit; she'd felt the handcuffs digging into her wrists as she tried to lift herself up. Ellen stopped again, her back against the door. She'd have to grab the doorknob between her chin and neck. It hadn't worked the first time, but it was the only way. She'd keep trying until it did work.

Ellen painstakingly inched herself around. The first thing she realized was that she couldn't grab the doorknob straight on, as she'd tried to do before. Her face got in the way. Turning sideways, she tried to get hold of it and succeeded. She had the knob pinned, not tightly, between the left side of her chin and neck. Rolling her head forward, she tried to turn the knob and slipped off. Ellen straightened herself, grasped the knob and tried again. It slipped away again, but Ellen wasn't discouraged. All she needed to do was grip the knob a little tighter and it would turn. If she turned it just a bit, the door would pop open. Once she was out in the other room, Ellen knew she'd be able to get free.

CHAPTER 21

Pete had the television on in his hotel room, but he couldn't sit down and watch it. He paced back and forth across the small room, sat down for a moment, then got up and paced some more. Detective Trenton didn't know exactly when the news broadcasts would do the story on Ellen. Pete had turned on Channel 7 at five o'clock and anxiously walked around his room through the entire hour of news. Ellen had never been mentioned. Now he was ten minutes into the six o'clock news, and still nothing. Pete went to the window. Pico Boulevard was ten stories below him. Across the street was a high school; a few students and faculty were still walking around. If Ellen had come out here to find Franklin Walker, which must be the case, then something had definitely gone wrong. And whatever had gone wrong might have cost her her life. The thought made Pete physically ill. He couldn't let himself think this. It was still possible that she was alive. Pete thought of Trenton waiting in the supermarket parking lot. If only Franklin Walker would show up tonight. If he did, Pete wondered how long it would be before he heard about it.

At six-twenty, after the weather report, they ran the story on Ellen. As the anchor spoke, a photograph of Ellen was superimposed on the screen. A police phone number was shown along the bottom. The whole thing lasted a half-minute or so. When it was over, Pete realized he was crying. *Fuck, fuck, fuck. Why did this have to happen to us?* He turned off the television, blew his nose, went into the bathroom, and washed his face. When Marvin phoned a short while later, Pete had calmed himself. Marvin told him that four of the six stations with evening news broadcasts had run the story. Plenty of people would call the police about Ellen, he said. The problem was that most of these people wouldn't really have seen her, they'd just think they had.

Pete drove to a Yucatán restaurant on Lincoln Boulevard where he was meeting John Ericson, Ellen's friend from Iowa. The restaurant was in an old coffee shop that had been repainted with yellow trim and vibrant murals of tropical jungle scenes. John was waiting inside for him. Pete hadn't seen John for several years, but he hadn't changed much. His hair was thick and full, and there wasn't a hint of any gray. John had made a name for himself as one of the stars of a minor sitcom that had been popular for a couple of years, though it never became a top ten hit. Since the show was canceled, Pete knew John had done several pilots, but so far none had been picked up for a regular series run.

They sat at a small table covered by a paper tablecloth with a small votive candle in the center. There were paintings on the walls done on wood and then intricately carved into designs that gave them an eerie, three-dimensional effect.

The food was very good, but Pete took no pleasure in it. He felt as if his entire life was imploding, racing inward toward the moment that would come tomorrow or maybe the next day or maybe next week when he would finally find out what happened to Ellen.

Pete said, "One thing I wanted to ask you was if Ellen ever mentioned that she was writing a play."

"Yeah, she did. Did she ever finish it?"

Pete nodded. "She tell you what it was about?"

"No. I don't think so. She told me she was doing it for fun. I never really thought about it again."

"It was about her father being killed."

"Seriously?"

"Yeah. She never told me anything about it. But I found a copy on her computer. It's pretty scary."

"I imagine it would be."

"Did Ellen talk about me to you?" Pete asked.

"What do you mean?"

"You know, talk about our relationship. There are so many things in her life she didn't tell me about. I'm starting to wonder if she really loved me."

"She loves you. I think Ellen kept these things about her father's death inside her because she had to. I don't know if she ever talked to anyone about it; she never did with me."

After saying goodbye, Pete drove his car up Olympic Boulevard all the way to La Brea and then cruised past the supermarket. He spotted Trenton's car parked in the same spot it had been earlier in the day. So Walker hadn't shown. Shit. Pete didn't know if he could stand waiting more than one more day.

He drove back to Santa Monica, going all the way to the ocean, turning onto the pier, and parking. Pete walked the length of the pier, past the fun zone, which was closed, and the small gift shops and restaurants. There were quite a few people about. Some young couples, their arms around each other staring down at the waves. Homeless people huddled on the benches under grimy blankets. Pete stopped for a few moments and watched the surf breaking into the shallow water beneath him. Some people walked behind him, talking, and Pete remembered the voices and distant rumble he'd heard when Ellen last called him. That rumble had been surf. He was sure of it. Pete turned around and looked across the pier at the small shops and restaurants. About a hundred feet further along was a public telephone.

Fishermen cast their lines from the end of the pier, though you had to wonder what they could catch this close to the shore. The men were wrapped in jackets with bait buckets and tackle boxes next to them. A few drinking from thermoses, a few sipping quietly from bottles. Maybe it didn't matter if there wasn't anything to catch. Maybe it was just a place to be and something to do. Pete reached the end of the pier and looked out at the dark sea, the dark night. It was cloudy, and there were no stars to be seen, no moon, just black. As far as he could see, it was black. It seemed to go on forever.

CHAPTER 22

The night didn't go well. It started when Walker first stepped into Denise's apartment. The television was on, and Walker looked at it and saw Ellen's picture filling the whole fucking screen. It stopped him dead, and for a few seconds he didn't hear anything, the roaring in his ears was so loud. It meant the cops were looking for her now. If Barton found out Walker hadn't killed her yet, he'd be coming to take care of both of them. Walker felt sweat running down the underside of both his arms. He had to get away.

Denise took him by the elbow, and he pulled his eyes from the television. Someone, it was Denise's sister, said, "The poor thing, she must be dead." Then the TV was turned off. Walker found himself being introduced to Darlene, who was younger than Denise, overweight and had tightly curled hair with blonde streaks running through it. She smiled weakly when introduced to Walker, glancing down at his pants and shoes with a look of mild disgust. *Jesus, what's she got against me?* Maybe Denise had told her that he was an ex-con. Just like Denise to do that. Not thinking it was a big thing herself and assuming her sister'd feel the same way. Of course, Denise didn't know he'd done time for murder. He'd told her it was for armed robbery, which didn't seem to be a problem for her.

Darlene's husband, Randy, wore a suit and tie. He was the service manager at a Pontiac dealership in Missouri. Randy drank vodka martinis and talked football. He discussed quarterback ratings, the relative merits of the run-and-shoot, the intricacies of nickel defenses. The poor guy said the St. Louis Rams were his favorite team. Walker listened to him and tried to show some interest, but he couldn't stop thinking that the cops were searching the city for Ellen and that somehow they'd manage to pick up her trail and follow it to his apartment. He'd be charged with kidnapping and attempted murder. No one would give a fuck that she'd come there to kill him. Walker felt cold. He was practically shivering.

"Walker, you feeling okay, hon?" Denise asked.

He looked at her. "Sure," he said.

"Look a little pale, is all."

"I'm fine."

Glancing at Darlene, he saw a clear look of disapproval in her eyes. Fuck her if she didn't think he was good enough for her alcoholic sister.

They drove to a Mexican restaurant on Western, and Walker had four beers with his dinner, which calmed his nerves some. Ellen had been missing for some time now, he told himself. It wasn't surprising she was on the news. And it didn't really matter. There was no way the police could track her to his apartment. No way in the world.

Walker picked up the check, looked at it, and Randy asked what the damage was. Walker said he'd take care of it, since they were out-of-town guests.

"That's not necessary, partner," Randy said.

"No, it's my treat," said Walker. He had his wallet in his hand and had pulled three twenties out.

"Randy," whined Darlene.

"Honey, if the man insists, what can I do?"

"Please," Walker said, looking right at Darlene. "It's my pleasure." She gave him a sour look but didn't say anything else. She wanted to, though, Walker could see that.

They stopped by the Inkwell for a couple of drinks, and Darlene insisted Randy pay this time when the waitress brought the first round.

"I just don't feel like owing," Darlene said after she was well into her second Mai Tai at the bar.

Denise said, "What're you worried about? Nobody owes anybody anything. Walker only paid because he wanted you to have a good time. Isn't that right, hon?"

"Sure," he said. "That's absolutely right. We're all having a good time, aren't we?"

"I sure the hell am," said Randy. Walker figured Randy must be on his seventh martini of the night.

"It just don't sit right with me," said Darlene. "I know you meant well by it." She glanced in Walker's direction for a moment with a halfway pleasant expression on her face. *A miracle*, thought Walker. *She managed to stop acting like a total pain in the ass for at least five seconds*. Walker figured he'd handled himself pretty well through all this. Darlene obviously hated his guts, but Walker hadn't lost his temper and told her to go fuck herself. Through his effort what could have been a very negative situation had turned out halfway decent.

They said good night in the courtyard. Walker shook hands with Randy, who gazed at him with glassy, half-closed eyes. He grunted at Walker and then leaned onto Darlene for support. She struggled to keep him on his feet.

"God, Randy, you're making a hell of an impression!" she complained.

Randy grunted and tried his best to stand up straight.

Darlene turned him around and they started slowly up the stairs. To Walker's dismay, Denise stayed by his side. He was going to have a scene with her, and there was nothing he could do to avoid it. He hated to waste the time because he wanted to talk to Ellen about his plan. There was no time to drink with Denise and wait for her to pass out.

"Thanks for going tonight," Denise said to him.

"I don't think your sister liked me much."

"She's funny about some things. I thought it was real nice of you to pay for the dinner. Real nice." She slipped her arms behind his waist.

"You probably better get up there and help them get settled down for the night."

"They can take care of themselves. They're sleeping in my bed. I got it all ready for them. I thought I could spend some time with you."

"I'm pretty beat," he said. "Not much in the mood."

"We don't need to do nothing."

"You know how I am," he said lamely. "I have trouble sleepin' 'less I'm alone."

She removed her hands from him and took a half-step back. "Walker, what the hell's the matter with you?"

"Nothin'."

"I don't have a bed to sleep in tonight."

"Seems like you could go up there and change the arrangements. You got that fold-out sofa."

"I don't want to go up there. I want to stay with you."

"I'm not in the mood for that tonight."

"You mean to tell me you won't let me sleep in your bed? You're gonna make me go up and sleep on the sofa?"

Walker was afraid somebody would hear her. He tried to think what he could do. Maybe take her to a motel, screw her and let her sleep it off. Get back to Ellen and explain what they must do.

"I haven't been myself lately," he said to Denise. "Sorry."

She softened, touched him again. "It's okay. I don't mean to snap at you. Come on. Let's go inside."

"We can have another drink," he suggested. He thought if he got a couple more glasses of gin in her, he might get lucky and she'd pass out on his sofa. It'd happened more than once before. If she didn't, he'd offer to take her to the motel, try to make it sound romantic or something. He wondered how much he could get a room for at the Crest on La Brea. Couldn't be much, the place was a dump.

"That sounds good," she said.

Walker slid the key into the lock and opened the door. Denise went in ahead of him. Walker followed and turned on the light as he closed the door. Turning around from the door, he bumped into Denise, who stood frozen, hand clenched near her face. Sounds came from her mouth, high-pitched, like an animal in pain. Walker didn't know what was wrong with her.

Then he saw Ellen on the floor near the counter. The phone was on the floor near her head, the receiver off the hook. Jesus. Her hands and feet were still bound, tape still covered her mouth. How the fuck did she get out of the room? For a second he panicked, thinking someone had been in the apartment and killed her. Then Walker saw that her eyes were open, staring up at him.

Denise backed toward the door, the little animal sounds still coming from her mouth. Walker grabbed one of her arms. It was like a piece of wood.

"Listen to me," he said. "She came here with a gun. She was going to kill me." Denise didn't look at him. Her eyes, fixed on the bound body on the floor, twitched back and forth rapidly. Had she even heard what he said?

Denise started to scream.

Walker clamped his hand over her mouth. "Don't! She came with a gun! I didn't have no choice in this!"

But she was still trying to scream. Denise pushed away from him. Walker grabbed her around the neck and pulled her to the floor. She began screaming again, but he got his hand over mouth quickly. Jesus! If she'd just shut up and fucking listen to him for a minute.

"She was gonna kill me," he told her. "She had a gun. She was gonna shoot me! Understand?"

Denise shook her head back and forth, trying to get free of the hand that smothered her mouth. Her body writhed under him, trying with every ounce of strength to get loose as he pushed down harder on her mouth, the muffled screaming getting more and more frantic. *Fucking alcoholic bitch!* She bounced under him like some pathetic fish. He should never have gotten involved with her. It wasn't worth the trouble she put him through. Always wanting his attention. Wanting him to feel sorry for her because she was getting old and lonely. Screw her. He didn't feel sorry for her. She wouldn't even listen to him when he tried to explain a simple thing.

There was a noise at the door. Walker twisted to look at it. In horror, he watched the doorknob jiggle back and forth. Now she'd done it. One of the neighbors had heard her scream. Walker removed his hand from Denise's mouth, and she gulped in air. He stared down at her.

"One word outta you, and I'll kill you," he whispered. "Swear to God I will." He got to his feet and stepped to the door. The handle jiggled back and forth again.

"Yeah," said Walker. "Who is it?"

"Franklin?" a man said. "It's me, Dale. Remember?"

Mother of God. What the fuck do I do now?

"Let me in, Franklin," Dale said. "We need to talk."

"Listen, man," said Walker. "This ain't a good time. I've got a lady in here. We're tryin', you know, to have a date."

Denise was sitting up now, rubbing her throat where Walker had been holding it. Walker looked at her and put his finger to his lips, shaking his head back and forth.

"Catch the news tonight, Franklin?" asked Dale. "Let me in. It's important."

"I've got my girlfriend in here," said Walker. "Give me a break and come back tomorrow morning."

Denise cleared her throat. "What the fuck is this?" she asked.

Walker turned to look at her just as Dale forced the door. It bashed into Walker, and Dale pushed in. He glanced quickly around the room, then closed the door. Walker saw the small gun in Dale's hand, probably a .22, with a silencer screwed onto the end of the barrel. Dale looked from Walker to Denise, who was staring at him with her mouth open, to Ellen.

"Shit," said Dale. "This is a fucking mess. Looks like you need some help after all."

Walker was silent.

Denise grunted as she got to her feet. "I don't know what the fuck's goin' on here, Walker, but I don't want any part of it. I'm goin' upstairs for a drink."

Dale shot Denise in the throat, the sound barely noticeable, a whisper of a noise. Denise stood for two or three seconds, a look of astonishment on her face, the hole in her neck noisily sucking air in and out. Dale fired a second time and hit her in the forehead. The sucking noise stopped, and Denise dropped to the floor without making a sound.

"Sorry, Franklin," said Dale. "But she seemed like a pretty big cunt." He turned his gaze to Ellen. "So this is the bitch that's causing all the problems, huh? How come she ain't dead?"

"I hadn't . . ." Walker said and hesitated.

"Hadn't what?" asked Dale as he took a step closer to Ellen. "You were supposed to take care of her."

Walker wrapped a hand around the brass pole lamp he'd bought on sale a year ago. Denise had talked him into buying it. Said it would add some class to the place.

"I hadn't had time," said Walker.

"Hadn't had time? What the fuck you talking about? It doesn't take any time at all to kill somebody."

Walker got his second hand on the lamp and swung it like a baseball bat, the cord ripping out of the wall as the base flew toward the ceiling. It came down and hit Dale across the side of the head with a sickening crunch. The man went down as blood spurted from the dent in his head. But he wasn't unconscious. He actually tried to push himself up, and he still had the gun in his hand. Walker stomped on Dale's wrist twice, causing him to let go of the small pistol. Walker grabbed the piece and pointed it at Dale, but he couldn't hold the weapon steady. It bounced all over the place. Dale groaned.

Walker got down on one knee, putting the gun to Dale's head. He glanced at Ellen. She was watching him in wide-eyed horror.

"Turn your head away," he said to her. She didn't move. "Turn away! Don't watch this!"

Ellen turned her head so that it was facing the wall. Walker pushed the gun against the back of Dale's head, closed his eyes and fired. Another little whisper. Walker stood and backed away, tasting bile in his mouth. Fucking hell. There was no doubt he was cursed. He stared at Denise's pathetic, twisted body. God knew he'd never wanted anything like this to happen to her. Now, if Barton didn't kill him, Walker would be spending the rest of his life in the penitentiary. No way they'd ever believe he had killed Dale to save Ellen. He might as well put the gun in his mouth right now and end his misery.

Ellen moaned, and Walker looked at her. She was shaking uncontrollably.

"It's all right," he said, trying as best he could not to sound panicked. "She wouldn't listen to me. I told her to go home, but she never would listen to me." He stepped over to the phone, picked it up and replaced it on the counter. Walker bent down on one knee and looked at Ellen. Her eyes were shut tight, and waves of spastic shaking ran through her body. It reminded him of a newborn puppy. As he slid his arms underneath her, she let out another moan.

"Nothin' to worry about now," he told her. "We have to leave, but we were gonna have to leave anyway." He carried her back into the bedroom and set her on the bed. "I got a few things to take care of," he said. "You wait here. We'll be gettin' out soon enough." He patted her on the head and walked out, closing the door.

IT WAS A LONG TIME before she could stop shaking. Ellen had closed her eyes when she realized the woman had been shot, but she had seen enough and she couldn't stop seeing it again and again in her mind. The woman's neck blossoming with blood, the sound of the air sucking in and out of the ragged hole made by the bullet. God, who was that man? She'd opened her eyes again and seen him lying on the floor, bleeding from the head. Then Walker put the pistol to the back of the man's head and told her to turn away. She'd done as she was told, but she still heard the quiet sound of the gun and felt the floor shake as the man's body jerked. *Oh, please, God, help me to get away from all this.*

She wondered now if she'd ever have had the nerve to shoot either one of her father's murderers. It didn't matter now. Walker said they were leaving. That meant he was taking her with him. Why? What would he possibly want with her now? He was supposed to kill her. She'd heard the man say that. What would Walker do? If he didn't kill her, Alan Barton would surely kill him. What choice did he really have?

Ellen was exhausted. The effort to get the door open, then awkwardly move herself across the living room to get to the phone had drained her. She had spent hours trying unsuccessfully to dial 911 with her nose. Ellen wanted to sleep, but the image of the dying woman continued to flash into her mind. She felt partly to blame. If she hadn't been trying to escape, the woman might still be alive. Why did the murderer bring her into the apartment when he had Ellen in the bedroom?

People in the apartment building would know the woman went out with Walker. When she was missing, he'd be the first one wanted for questioning. When the bodies were discovered in the apartment, the police would be searching for Walker. This could be a hopeful development if Ellen stayed alive. When they caught him, they'd find her. If she could stay alive. But how soon would the murders be discovered? The woman lived alone. It was possible no one would miss her for a couple of days. Tears sprang to Ellen's eyes, and she began to weep. She wouldn't be alive in two days. She might not last the hour. Oh, Lord. She'd never see Pete or Susan again. God, she didn't want to die so soon.

Incredibly, Ellen fell asleep. She dreamed about Pete as a young man, in his mid-twenties, the age when she first met him. Together they were looking for something in an old house that she'd never been in before. They went from room to room opening closets, looking under beds, rummaging through dresser drawers full of clothing she'd never seen. Pete kept telling her, "We'll find it. It has to be here somewhere." But she had no idea at all what they were looking for.

The murderer shook her by the shoulder, startling her.

"We're goin' now," he said.

She sat up. He untied her feet and hands. Ellen thought about Pete in her dream. When they had first met each other they had both been so thoroughly in love. Her chest heaved, nearly causing her to cry out loud. She had loved him so much.

The murderer let her use the bathroom. Sitting on the toilet, Ellen realized she should leave something in the apartment, something that would let the police know she'd been here. She thought of her shoes, but the murderer would notice that immediately.

He knocked on the door. "Hurry it up," he said quietly. She flushed the toilet, stood and pulled up her jeans. At the sink she put one hand up to the mirror, pressing it firmly against the surface. *That should leave some good prints.*

The murderer put the handcuffs back on her, reminded her that he had her gun, and then marched her to the front door. Ellen squeezed her eyes shut as they went through the living room so she wouldn't have to see the bodies lying there. Once they were out the door, she felt better. The cool night air enveloped her, and she opened her eyes and breathed deeply. It felt wonderful to be out of the apartment. She glanced up and was exhilarated by the sight of a few stars in the hazy black sky.

Walker kept one hand clamped on her left arm. At the end of the building he turned her to the left, guiding her through the opening into the carport and then past his car to a blue Taurus. He opened the back door.

"Lie down with your face against the seat."

Ellen climbed in and did as she was told. The murderer crouched behind her, tying her ankles and then running the cord up to her wrists and securing it. He reached a hand around her face, and for a moment Ellen thought he was going to strangle her right there. Her heart smashed like a fist against the inside of her chest, and she thought of Pete dressed in the black suit he had worn the day they married, his hair cut too short, his eyebrows pressed close together in anxiety.

All the murderer did was remove the tape from her mouth.

"We get out from the city, I'll untie your feet and you can sit up," he said. "But you gotta promise to be good." Ellen didn't reply. He climbed out, closed the door, and got in behind the wheel. He started the car and they backed out of the carport and then drove slowly down the alley. Twisting her head, Ellen could look up and see out the back window. She watched streetlights, telephone poles and trees go past her small field of vision. After being trapped in the murderer's apartment for all those days, she found she couldn't close her eyes. She wanted to take in every light and tree limb she could. After about ten minutes they stopped under a concrete bridge. Ellen heard the rumble of freeway traffic. Soon they turned left and she felt the car accelerating up an incline. They were getting on the freeway. She kept her eyes open, watching lights and freeway signs pass by. The murderer turned on the radio, switching stations until he found country music. Ordinarily, Ellen didn't care for country music, but right then it sounded wonderful to her.

They drove for a long time and Ellen saw the sky lighten: fuzzy gray at first, then white and finally a misty blue. Ellen was hungry but didn't dare say anything. About an hour after they started she felt the car slowing. It headed down an off-ramp, stopped momentarily and then started again. The sound of the freeway traffic faded away. Ellen wondered if they had already reached the place where he was taking her. She wondered if it was the place where he planned to kill her.

A few more minutes and the car slowed again. Ellen felt it turn off the road. Through the window she saw they had stopped under a large tree. The murderer turned off the engine.

"I'm going to untie you now," he said. He opened the back door and undid the cords around her ankles and removed the handcuffs. *Please don't kill me now. Please, God, let me live another day. Just one more day.* She sat up and looked around. They were on a rural two-lane road in the middle of a flat expanse of farmland, no buildings anywhere in sight. The nearby fields were full of brown tomato plants. He could kill her here and no one would know. There would be no one to hear her scream or see her fall. He could leave her body under this tree.

"We're out past Riverside," Walker said. "About sixty miles from Los Angeles. Why don't you get out and stretch your legs?"

Ellen shook her head at him. She wasn't getting out of the car. If she got out of the car he was going to shoot her.

The murderer frowned. "You don't want to get out?"

She shook her head again and slid away from him until she was jammed against the opposite door.

Walker looked at her, still puzzled, then his face changed, and he looked down at the ground for a moment. When he looked up again there was sadness in his eyes. "You're scared a me. That's it, isn't it?"

Ellen said nothing.

"I don't blame you for wantin' to get away," he said. "But it wouldn'ta done you no good. Alan Barton would find you. He's not gonna let you get away. And when he finds out about Dale gettin' shot, shit, he's gonna kill us both."

"Please," she said. "Please don't kill me."

"No," he said. "I ain't gonna do that. No way I could ever do that."

It wasn't joy Ellen felt, but relief. It pushed up inside her with such force that for several seconds her ears were ringing and her eyes clouded over. She bent her head to her knees and cried and cried.

"There's no reason for you to be doin' that," said Walker.

Ellen nodded her head, still bent over her jeans, which were getting soaked with her tears.

"Come on now," said the murderer. "Get outta the car and get some air. You'll feel better in a minute." Ellen sat up and slid toward the open door. Taking hold of her arm, Walker helped her out. She stood next to the car, putting her hand against the door to steady herself.

Walker said, "See? That's better, isn't it?"

Ellen nodded. She wiped her eyes on the sleeve of her shirt.

"Here," said the murderer. He moved to the open front door and leaned into the car. A moment later he emerged with a white tissue in his hand and held it out to Ellen.

"Thank you," said Ellen. She took the tissue, wiped her face and then blew her nose. There were birds singing in the tree above her. In the distance Ellen saw a highway overpass. Cars crawled over it silently.

"Okay now?" asked Walker.

"I think so."

"The thing is, we're still in trouble." His face, covered with gray stubble, brightened. His eyes flashed at her. "We need to work together against Alan Barton." He smiled then, showing his crooked, stained teeth.

"Work together," Ellen said.

"To kill Alan Barton. Once he's dead, our chances are a lot better."

"Right." Ellen took a deep breath, calming down now. She had to go along with whatever he said to stay alive. He said he wouldn't kill her, but Ellen didn't think she could trust him. Walker was a psychopath—if he lost his temper he might kill Ellen before he could stop himself. He'd feel bad about it after the fact, but Ellen would still be dead.

"Why'd Barton kill my father?" she asked.

"I don't know. I truly don't. He hired me to help him rob the place. I thought we was there just to take the typewriters and adding machines. That's God's truth."

Ellen looked at the car. "Where'd you get the car?" she asked.

"I had to borrow it. They'd be looking for mine."

"Did you steal it?" she asked.

"Sorta," he said. "It's Denise's car."

"Oh." For a moment the look on the woman's face after she was shot flashed through Ellen's mind. "Won't they be looking for it?"

"I got somebody else's plates and put 'em on. It should be okay for a day. Then we'll get another. If you're feelin' better, we should get goin'."

He walked around to the other side of the car and opened the front door for her. Walker got behind the wheel and they drove off. After half an hour, he left the highway and drove through a McDonald's. Ellen ate two Egg McMuffins and drank a cup of coffee. She felt much better and thought again about what she must do to stay alive. She couldn't make Walker angry or suspicious of her. Maybe they'd actually have a chance to kill this Alan Barton. It was what she'd set out to do, and he deserved to die. It'd be viewed as justifiable homicide now, she reasoned. She'd been held prisoner for almost a week after being savagely beaten. No one would charge her for killing to get free.

"Where are we going?" she asked.

"New Mexico. The mountains."

"Why?"

"There's a place there Barton owns. He knows I'll go there. He'll show up."

"To kill me?"

"To find out if I did it or not. He'd kill you when he saw you was alive. Me, too."

"Because of that man at the apartment?"

"Yeah. And the police are lookin' for me by now. I get caught, Barton will be afraid what I might say about him."

"What does this man do?" Ellen asked. "How does he live?"

"He pulls in a lotta money now. He's the one sent me money when I was in Huntsville. He helped me get the job in L.A. He's got connections with Vincent Davore in New Orleans. You heard a him?"

"No."

"He's the outfit in New Orleans."

"Outfit?"

"You know. Organized crime. Mafia."

They passed the turnoff for Palm Springs and continued east through the desert. A sign said Phoenix was 200 miles away. Walker turned on the radio again, and they listened to a country station out of Needles. Ellen couldn't help but think of her poor mother. What would she say if she knew Ellen was traveling across the country with the hated murderer Franklin Walker? That now, after nearly being killed by him, she was allied with him? *Mama would scream. She'd scream and tear at her hair. Pound her fists.* But her mother didn't know that Walker had saved her life as a girl. If not for him, she would have perished in the fire over thirty years ago.

After a half-hour or so Ellen thought of something she wanted to ask Walker, but when she glanced over at him, he seemed so intense, listening to the music, holding tightly to the steering wheel, that she decided to wait and ask later. It was going to be a long drive. They'd have plenty of time to discuss the plan to kill Alan Barton.

CHAPTER 23

When Pete woke, the message light was flashing on his telephone. He called the desk, and learned that Trenton had left him a message at one in the morning. There had been no sign of Walker. They would be back at the store when it reopened.

Pete left his hotel at nine and drove to Main Street, a trendy shopping area four blocks west of the hotel. Pete spent nearly two hours showing Ellen's photograph to the merchants and restaurant managers in the area. No one recalled seeing Ellen. Back at the hotel Pete checked for messages and then drove east to the grocery store Trenton was staking out. He passed the lot but didn't see Trenton's car. The police must be in a different car today, parked in a different spot.

Pete stopped at a convenience store to get something to drink. After buying a bottle of ice tea, he used a pay phone outside the store to call Marvin.

"It's good you called," said Louise. "Get over to this address right away: Twelve-twenty-four Aviary. It's about eight blocks east of La Brea between Pico and Olympic. Marvin left ten minutes ago."

"Is that where Walker lives?" asked Pete.

"They think so. Trenton called twenty minutes ago, they had

an all points out for a Franklin Walker. The age and description match."

"What's he wanted for?"

"I don't know. Marvin said you should get over there. That's all."

Pete stared at the cold bottle of tea sweating in his right hand. There wasn't a thought in his head. Barely, he was aware of the slow thump of his heart in his ears.

"Pete? Pete?" he heard Louise say. "Pete, are you there?"

"Yeah," he said, suddenly back in reality. "I'm here."

"Are you all right, dear?"

"I think so. What was the address again?"

Louise gave it to him, and Pete hung up.

Pete drove as fast as he could to Olympic, turning east. He changed lanes constantly, racing around the slower-moving traffic. *Please, God. Please don't let her be dead. Please, Jesus and Mary, let her be alive.* By the time he pulled onto Aviary Street, only ten minutes had passed. The street looked familiar. Pete thought he'd driven up it at least once when he was canvassing the neighborhoods around the post office.

The police had the block cordoned off. The mantra still repeating in his head, Pete parked on a side street and walked back. His insides were twisting with tension as he approached the motorcycle cop standing on the corner.

"I'm supposed to see Detective Trenton," he told the officer.

Pete waited while the man talked on his two-way radio.

"Go ahead," the cop said after a minute. Pete moved past him and went toward the building in the middle of the block. There were a half-dozen police cars parked in the street, along with a coroner's van. *Oh, God, no. No. No. No.* He crossed the street, passing the van, looking at it. Everything seemed to be moving in slow motion. Pete's steps were glacial. The man standing next to the van lifted a cigarette to his lips in one-quarter time. Pete deliberately rotated his head back toward the building, continuing as if he weighed a thousand pounds, each deliberate step taking many, many seconds. The people he passed moved their mouths and eyes incredibly slowly. Pete thought he was losing his mind. In the courtyard of the apartment building, police were knotted outside a downstairs apartment on the left.

Pete spotted Marvin standing by himself on the perimeter of the scene, and time crashed back to normal speed. Police radios spat out static and voices. There were hushed conversations all around. Pete reached Marvin and clutched his arm.

"I saw Trenton," he told Pete. "They found two bodies inside, neither one is Ellen."

"You're sure?"

"Yeah. One victim was an upstairs neighbor. Somebody the suspect went out with. The other is a white male. They don't have an ID yet."

"It's not Walker?"

"No. He's too young."

"Okay," said Pete.

"Don't think the worst. Trenton told me there wasn't any sign that Ellen had ever been here, but they're still going over the apartment."

"She was here. It's the reason she was in L.A. It's the only thing that makes sense."

"You might be right."

"I know I'm right, Marvin. Jesus. What else could it be? God knows what our chances of finding her are now."

They stood in silence for a few moments. It was still possible, Pete thought. It was still possible to find her alive. It had to be. *Please,* he prayed, starting his mantra again. *Please let her be alive.* Marvin turned and looked at the apartment's front door. Trenton stepped out of the apartment and walked over to them.

"There's nothing inside that indicates your wife was ever here, Mr. Donelly. They've found a few different sets of prints inside the apartment. We'll see if any match your wife's." He pulled a pack of cigarettes from his shirt pocket, tapped one out, quickly lit it and took a deep drag. "It's a goddamn mess in there," he said.

"The woman who was found was his girlfriend?" Pete asked.

"Yeah. For quite a while, I understand."

"Any idea what happened?"

"No. They went out to dinner last night with the victim's sister and brother-in-law. Maybe they got into a fight and Walker lost his temper. I don't know how the male victim fits in. He's sporting a nice set of prison tattoos, so I don't think we've got a model citizen on our hands."

"You're sure it's the right Franklin Walker who lives here?"

Trenton nodded. "The victim's sister identified him."

Marvin walked Pete out to the street.

"She was here," Pete said.

"Maybe. But we might end up back at square one, Pete. Don't forget that. Anything is possible."

"No. Franklin Walker is the reason she came to Los Angeles. The reason she didn't tell me or her sister what she was doing. He's the reason she had a gun."

"Mr. Donelly?" It was Trenton. Pete and Marvin stopped. Trenton came toward them from the courtyard between the apartment buildings. Something was in his hand.

"Glad I caught you. Do these look familiar?" He held up a

plastic bag that contained a pair of women's underwear, bright green with a white elastic border along the top. They weren't new or clean. Pete felt pinpricks up and down his arms and across his back. It was like an electric current running through his body.

"These were found inside the apartment. In the bathroom trash can," Trenton continued. "The victim was wearing underpants, so I thought there was a possibility . . ."

"Yeah," Pete said. "Ellen had underwear like that."

"You're sure?"

"I'm sure."

All three men stared at the bright green cloth in the plastic bag.

"There's a stain on the carpet," said Trenton. "It's blood, maybe a week old. A lot of it. Looks like the suspect tried to clean it up with something. I thought I should tell you."

Walking down the street, Pete's arms and legs went numb, and he had a sensation of floating, as if his feet were rising right up off the sidewalk. He stopped and took a couple of deep breaths. It was as if all the life had been vacuumed out of him. There was nothing left, and now he was floating away.

"We don't know anything for certain yet," said Marvin.

"I don't think she's dead," said Pete. "If she was, she'd be in there with the other two. She was here, but she left. Either on her own or with Walker."

"You think she really planned to kill him?"

"I don't know. Susan told me that her mother always agonized over the man who got away after Ellen's dad was killed. Maybe Ellen thought she could get his name from Walker. I don't know what the hell she thought she was doing." He stopped as he reached his car. "It's so crazy, and Ellen wasn't crazy. So maybe she didn't want to kill anybody. I guess I don't know what I think anymore. I'm all mixed up. I need to go home."

"That's a good idea," said Marvin. "You need to rest. I'll keep on top of things here."

Pete followed Marvin's car to his apartment. There, Pete called the airline and made a reservation to fly home. Louise made an early dinner for them. Pete wasn't hungry, but he ate anyway.

"I haven't even told my parents about this," said Pete.

"They don't know Mrs. Donelly's missing?" asked Louise.

"I didn't want them to worry. I don't know how I'm going to explain it to them now."

Marvin and Louise went downstairs with Pete and walked him to his car. Pete shook hands with Marvin.

"Maybe I should stay," Pete said. "Walker's probably somewhere in Los Angeles."

"He could be anywhere. Go back to Dallas and get some rest. I'll let you know what's going on here. You can always fly back."

"Okay." He looked down at his feet for a moment. "I keep wondering if things would've been different if we'd had kids."

"Did you think about having children?" Louise asked.

"A few years back we talked about it. But Ellen said she wasn't ready."

"Having children changes the entire world," said Louise. She stepped toward Pete and reached out with her hand, finding his shoulder and squeezing it. "'Bye, Pete. Take good care of yourself. I'll miss you."

"Goodbye, Louise." He leaned forward and hugged her.

At the hotel Pete packed his suitcase and then sat down on a bed and stared at the phone. It was eight o'clock in Texas. Pete knew he couldn't wait until the morning to call Susan. It wouldn't be right for her not to know what had happened.

The phone rang four times before she answered.

"Hello."

Pete paused a second, wishing he wasn't doing this but knowing he had to. His head was bowed. His eyes were shut tight.

"Hi," he said. "It's Pete."

CHAPTER 24

THEY REACHED FLAGSTAFF in midafternoon. The sky was bright, more white than blue, with a few gray clouds bunched around the mountains to the north. Walker was dead tired, so he pulled off the highway and drove through the city until he found a dilapidated motel with an empty parking lot. He rented a room from a shrunken, dark-skinned woman who spoke little English. The room was surprisingly clean and neat; the two beds had fuzzy cotton bedspreads that reminded Walker of the ones his mother had used when he was a boy. The curtains were a cheerful blue-checked pattern.

Ellen showered, then Walker tied her wrists to the bedposts and took a shower himself. Ellen was asleep when he came out of the bathroom. Walker lay down on the other bed and was soon asleep too.

When he woke, the room was dark. He called Ellen's name and there was no answer. For a second he thought she'd managed to run off and he leaped from the bed, but then he saw her, still on the other bed, sound asleep. Walker put on his shoes and left the room. Two other cars were now parked in the motel lot. Walker had planned to get another car but decided all he really needed was to change the plates. He drove several blocks from the motel and turned into a neighborhood of small, tired bungalows crowded so close to one another that there was barely room for a man to walk between them. He cruised through the quiet streets, parked the car and then walked back a block to where a rusted pickup was parked. He unscrewed the plates and was back in his car driving away in less than five minutes.

Pulling into the motel parking lot, Walker got a shock when he saw a light on inside the room. He pulled the key from his pocket and checked the number. Eighteen. The headlights of the car were right on the door—Eighteen. How the hell did she turn on the light when she was tied to the bed? Fuck. She'd gotten away. She might be talking to the cops right now. Walker hit the car lights, killed the engine and hurried to the room.

Ellen was sitting on the edge of the bed when he came in. Walker was so astonished that he stood staring at her in disbelief for several seconds, the door wide open behind him.

"I needed to use the bathroom," she said. "I worked at the ropes and managed to get one hand free."

Walker closed the door and locked it. She could have run away, but she hadn't. Barton was going to try to kill them, and she knew it. Most people would run, call the cops. She was staying with him even though they were in a hell of a spot, and this gave Walker a good feeling inside. He held out the paper bag that was in his hand.

"You hungry?" he asked her. "I stopped at Arby's and got us some sandwiches."

A few hours later they were on the highway driving through the predawn blackness. Walker had stopped a few miles outside Flagstaff and changed the plates on the car. He felt safer with the Arizona plates on. Once they were in New Mexico he'd change them again.

"You coulda run away back there," he said.

"I thought about it."

"How come you didn't?"

He heard her take a breath. She looked out the window to her right. Miles away a few lights blinked in the dark. *Some sort of ranch out there.* Ellen turned her head back so that she was again staring at the road ahead of them.

"I want to find the man who shot my father." She laughed softly to herself. "It's just happening in a different way than I planned."

The sky ahead slowly lightened, then turned orange and pink as the stars overhead faded. There were thin slivers of clouds in the sky, dark against the dawn. When the sun actually appeared over the horizon, it was right in Walker's eyes and he put on sunglasses. Even then he had to squint to see the highway in front of him.

Just over the border of New Mexico there was a truck stop with a Zuckey's store and coffee shop. Walker pulled off the highway and parked near the entrance. He noticed Ellen holding her arms tightly in front of her chest.

"You cold?" he asked.

"A little."

"I got your things in the trunk."

He opened the trunk and lifted out her suitcase, putting it down on the pavement. Ellen took out a sweatshirt and put it on. Then they went into the coffee shop together. There were a dozen other people eating in the restaurant. Walker felt some apprehension taking her into a public place, but she walked quietly to a booth, sat down and picked up a menu as Walker slid into the seat opposite her. He was hungry and ordered a big breakfast. Ellen ordered one egg with biscuits. She ate most of it, then sipped coffee quietly.

"What're you thinking about?" he asked her.

"Nothing, really," she said. "It's nice to be out in the world again. One summer when I was little my mother drove us up to New Hampshire. We stayed there for a month. I think I remember more about driving up and back than I do about the place we stayed. That was the only time we drove across the country when I was a girl. I remember stopping at coffee shops just like this."

She seemed tired. No wonder, after all she'd been through in the last week. Recovering from her injuries and being tied up for days. It had to wear you down. Walker was glad that this trip reminded her of the vacation she had when she was a girl. It was a nice thing to say. He wondered if she missed her husband. She hadn't said much about him. It seemed to Walker that it must not be a very good marriage.

Walker finished his breakfast and they walked back to the car. The morning was cool and breezy, and there was a smell of wood smoke. Walker unlocked the car door for Ellen. She got in. He moved around the car, stopping for a moment to look at the yellow-brown desert stretching out for miles around him. He felt a strange sensation in his chest. A thickening tightness that felt good and somewhat painful all at once. His heart thumped. Walker breathed in and out deeply. He thought he knew what this feeling was, though he'd never felt this way before. Walker believed he was happy.

When he got in the car Walker said to her, "Eddie Rollins would be proud a us. We're turnin' this situation into something more positive every day."

On the highway, however, he began to think about Barton and what they'd have to do once they got to the cabin. It had been a couple of years since Walker had been there, but he remembered the terrain and layout well enough. There was a dirt road that you took off the two-lane highway that ran into the mountains. Walker remembered that the road wound through the thick pine trees for more than three miles, then went up a steep grade to the cabin. A small shed, used for storage, stood behind the cabin. There was no garage, which was too bad because it would have been a good way to hide the car. Walker knew it must be freezing up there now. He wasn't sure of the elevation of the cabin, but it was high.

"We have to talk about how to handle things," he said.

"All right," said Ellen.

"This cabin I'm drivin' to is way off by itself. Barton's had it a long time, ever since I've known him. He goes up there for huntin' and fishin' once or twice a year. He'll figure I'll head there."

"Why?" Ellen asked.

"It's the place where we were supposed to meet if anything went wrong back when we robbed places together. I been there a couple times just for a vacation."

"Oh."

"He might not be positive I'd go there, but he'll check to see. I know that."

"What do we do when he shows up?"

"I got it figured out," he said, turning down the volume on the radio. "You'll have to hide outside the cabin somewhere. When he comes I'll tell him you're already dead. I killed you in L.A. and buried your body out in the desert. Then when he's relaxed, not worried about nothing, I'll shoot him."

"That's it?"

"Yeah."

"All I have to do is stay out of sight?" she asked.

"Since we don't know when he'll show up, you'll have to hide soon as we get there. He'll probably be comin' tonight or tomorrow morning, but it could take a few days. There's a shed out back a the cabin. I thought maybe you could stay there. There used to be some sleeping bags up there."

"What kind of shed is it?"

"I don't know. Just a shed. He keeps tools and stuff in it."

"There are a lot of trees around the cabin?"

"Yeah. Like I said, it's in the mountains."

"I'll go a few hundred yards away from the cabin so that I'm out of sight. I'll sleep outside for a night or two if I have to."

"It'll be awful cold."

"I'm not sitting in some dark shed waiting for this guy to show up. I spent too long tied up in your apartment."

She had a mind of her own, that was for sure. Long as she was a good ways off, it would probably be okay, Walker figured. Barton drove up and saw her, then they'd have a big fucking problem, but she was smart enough to stay out of sight. If she half froze to death the first night, the shed might not seem such a bad place after all. At least for sleeping.

Ellen asked, "It won't be hard to shoot him?"

"If he's just sittin' there, not expectin' it, should be easy."

"I mean, you won't feel bad doing it? He's your friend. He sent you money all those years while you were in prison."

"Only 'cause he didn't want me to talk. I spent fuckin' thirty years inside, and he didn't do no time at all."

"So you'll just do it. You won't hesitate or freak out."

"I have to do it. He'll kill us both if I don't."

She didn't ask any more questions. Walker wondered where Alan Barton was right now. He might not even know what had happened yet. But he'd hear soon enough. If he heard today, Barton could fly to New Mexico and possibly be at the cabin sometime tonight. Walker figured he and Ellen would make it there by the early afternoon. That wouldn't give them a lot of time, but he supposed it was all the time they needed.

CHAPTER 25

IT WAS PAST MIDNIGHT when Pete turned his car into the driveway. After he showered and changed, Pete went into the kitchen to find something to eat. He poured cereal into a bowl, but there was no milk, so he ate it dry. Then he lay down on the bed and slept fitfully for several hours. His mind played through a confusion of images: Ellen when he kissed her for the first time. The picture of Walker he'd gotten from Trenton. Ellen getting into her car the day she left home. Eating dinner with Marvin. Ellen's underwear in the plastic bag.

At nine in the morning he called Detective Harris, who answered on the second ring. Harris had talked to both Marvin and Trenton in Los Angeles, so he knew that Franklin Walker had not yet been apprehended. Harris told Pete that Walker was believed to be driving the dead woman's car, a Ford Taurus.

Pete walked out into the back yard. The grass hadn't been mowed in weeks now and was over four inches high. He unlocked the garage door and got the mower out. There wasn't much gas in it and the can was empty, so he drove to the gas station and filled the can. When he got back Brian's car was parked at the curb in front of the house. Brian stood on the front porch. Pete parked and walked to the porch, carrying the can of gas in one hand.

"I was driving down Central, so I thought I'd swing by and see if you were back," he said.

"I got home in the middle of the night."

"Things bad?" he asked.

Pete nodded. "Things aren't looking good."

"God almighty," Brian said slowly. "I'm sorry. Really sorry."

"Yeah. I know."

Pete set the gasoline can on the front porch and unlocked the door and they went in, sitting in the living room.

"So what's happened?" asked Brian.

"They found two bodies in an apartment, and some of Ellen's clothes were there."

Brian groaned. "I can't believe this, Pete. How could this happen?"

"There's still a chance she's alive. I think she is alive."

"Is there anything—" He stopped in midsentence.

"I don't think so. But thanks."

"Call me if you need anything. I'll be praying that this turns out all right." Brian hugged Pete and started to leave. "I almost forgot. I did a Nexis search on that company, Delta Partners."

Pete nodded. "You find anything?"

"Yeah. The company dissolved about fifteen years ago. They were being sued by a group of people who invested in oil partnerships through them. Delta Partners settled the suit and went out of business."

Brian left and Pete went back outside. He filled the mower with gas, started it and mowed the front lawn. The routine took part of his mind off Ellen for a while, though even when he wasn't consciously thinking of her, he was aware of a dull pain in his midsection that he'd had for days but was now worse than ever. A pain he'd carried around without giving it much thought. It was part of him, it felt like something that would never go away, though as time passed maybe he'd notice it less.

The back yard was covered by a carpet of orange-brown leaves. Pete raked these up, filling two trash cans. When the back yard was mowed, Pete carried the cans out to the curb and a neighbor drove past, beeping his horn and waving. Pete waved back. *They don't know. They might not have even noticed that she's been gone.*

Harris drove up before Pete went back into the house. Pete waited for him at the front door.

"How you doing?" Harris asked as he walked up.

"The best I can, I guess."

"I'm truly sorry things don't look better at this point, Mr. Donelly."

"Thanks."

Pete invited Harris in, and they sat, as they had before, in the living room.

"I wanted to fill you in on a couple of things," Harris said. "First off, there's no progress to speak of in the arson investigation. No one saw anything, and there's not much physical evidence to go on. The device placed under your wife's car was a glass bottle filled with gasoline, they know that much. I talked to the officer who located the car, and he says he didn't tell anyone but Taylor Reed about it, so that's kind of at a dead end at the moment."

"Did you get a copy of the file on Victor Samuels's murder?" Pete asked.

"I did, and I've read through it and spoken to the detective who was in charge of that case. Truth is, the best piece of evidence they had was the murder weapon. There were prints on it, but they never did match them. They tried to get Franklin

Walker to talk about who was there, but he never would."

"What about trying to match the prints from the gun now?"

"I thought about that myself," said Harris. "But I can't locate the evidence box at the moment."

"What?"

"Well, it's in storage. I called the warehouse to have it sent up to the station, and they couldn't locate it."

"Shit," said Pete.

"I'm sure they'll find it," said Harris. "It probably got stuck in the wrong place somehow. That happens."

Pete walked Harris out to his car. The detective shook Pete's hand warmly.

"I'm really very sorry, Mr. Donelly," he said. "Call me if there's anything I can do for you."

Harris drove off, and Pete went to the back yard to put away the lawn mower. Inside the garage he looked at the cardboard boxes lined against the back wall. There were a dozen of them, all plainly labeled by Pete on the side. All except one box. It was on the floor to the left of the others. Pete let go of the mower and walked over to it. Usually, Ellen's car was parked on the left side of the garage, and if her car had been there now he wouldn't have noticed it.

Pete pulled the box away from the wall. It was heavy. *Probably more old college stuff or a bunch of Ellen's sketch pads.* He used a screwdriver to cut through the tape that sealed the top, but as soon as he opened it, Pete saw that it wasn't old papers or sketches. It was what he'd been looking for since he discovered Ellen hadn't gone to Susan's. He was so fucking stupid. He'd turned the house upside-down, but he hadn't thought to look in the garage. It never occurred to him that she would put anything important in the garage, which was exactly why she'd done it.

The first thing he pulled out was a typed report dated over five years ago from an investigator who had researched the background of Franklin Walker. A more recent report from a different investigator gave an address for Walker in Los Angeles. Pete noticed that the address was different from the apartment where Walker had murdered his girlfriend and the man. In another folder he found some pictures of an apartment building with the address written on the edge in black ink. He pulled out a folder dated August of this year. Inside were notes in Ellen's handwriting. She had the make and license number of Walker's car. What time he left for work. The address where he worked and the type of street parking nearby. Ellen had noted a place he went for lunch one day. There was a description of Walker's girlfriend, which Pete read with a growing sense of vertigo. Ellen had followed them into a bar where they went to have drinks. She described the now dead woman like this: "Her hair is bleached of all color and her skin is a pale yellow. Can't tell if she's stained from the cigarettes she constantly smokes or if she's suffering from the first stages of cirrhosis. Certainly drinks enough to have liver damage. Walker doesn't seem to treat her well. Acts like she annoys him."

Pete couldn't look at it any more. He picked up the box and carried it into the house, leaving it in the kitchen and going to the living room. He sat and stared out the window. Ellen had stalked Walker, trying to figure out the best way to kill him, he supposed. It was so cold and calculated. She must have hated him very much. Pete thought of her waking up in the night screaming at the top of her lungs. If she had killed him, would the nightmares have stopped?

Pete went back to the kitchen and lifted the box onto the table. As he started to take everything out the phone rang. It was

Susan. She started crying, and Pete said what he could to comfort her and found himself starting to cry too. They talked for almost an hour, Susan telling him that she had called Taylor and told him the news from Los Angeles. Taylor had taken it badly, she said. Pete had been planning to see Taylor later in the day. He was relieved that Susan had spoken to him first.

Pete finished removing the contents from the box. There were some old, yellowed newspaper clippings about Ellen's father's murder and the arrest of Walker. Walker's photograph was in a couple of the stories—a hollow-eyed young man with that severe chin and greasy hair. Pete looked again through the reports on Walker's background. He was born and raised in Midland and still had a sister there who was married to a man named Watkins. She was three years younger than Walker. While he was in prison she wrote to him with some regularity and visited him several times. Walker received a money order once a month from someone. It was enough for him to have all the spending money allowed in prison. Two guards said the envelopes were postmarked from various places: Fort Worth, Austin, Amarillo, Santa Fe. Never Midland. Therefore the money was assumed to come from someone other than his sister.

On another piece of paper was a handwritten note that said Walker took a vacation after his first year of work for Margold Video. He went out of town, but the investigator didn't know where. The note was not in Ellen's writing. Pete thought it was her mother's, but he wasn't certain.

Pete went to the phone and called information in Midland, asking for the number of Walker's brother-in-law. He wrote it down in the margin of the investigator's report. Pete waited a minute, thinking about what he should say to Walker's sister if he got her on the phone, finally deciding to tell her the truth.

But it was her husband who answered. "Hello," he said.

It stopped Pete for a second. He hadn't thought about what he would say to her husband.

"Hello?" the man said again.

"May I speak with Christine Watkins, please?" asked Pete.

"Who's calling?"

"Pete Donelly."

"Are you somebody else calling from California?"

"No," Pete answered. "I'm calling from Dallas. But it has to do with her brother out in California."

"She's been talking to you people for half the day. Can't you let her have a minute's peace? It's all been very upsetting to her."

"I'm sure it has, and I'm sorry to have to bother her again."

"Lord knows she's had enough heartache from that brother of hers. She sure didn't need any more."

"I understand, Mr. Watkins. I'm sorry. I only wanted to ask her one thing. You might be able to help me, actually."

"How's that?"

"You could go in and ask your wife the question for me. That way she wouldn't have to get up and come to the phone. I assume that after a day like this one she's probably lying down."

"You're right about that. I feel like it myself. Last time I was in there, she was still crying."

"It must be terrible for her."

"You don't know."

"But if you could ask her just one question for me?"

"Well, all right. What is it?"

"Ask her if she recalls anywhere her brother might have gone for a vacation since he's been out of prison."

"Why in the world do you care about that?"

Pete told the man about Ellen, how she was missing and that

it looked like she had been with Walker during the last week.

"Lord," he said when Pete finished. "I thought you were another policeman. Hold on. Let me see what she says."

Pete heard the man put the phone down. He waited for several minutes and then Mr. Watkins came back on the line.

"You still there?" he asked.

"Yes," said Pete.

"She said she don't remember her brother ever taking a vacation. Maybe he did, but he didn't tell her about it. They weren't all that close, really. She felt an obligation to him since he was her brother, but he was never nothing but trouble."

"Okay," said Pete. "Thanks for your time."

Pete didn't phone Taylor Reed before driving over to his house, which was on Armstrong in Highland Park. It was an enormous brick structure, set far back from the street. Parking at the curb, Pete hiked up the long walk to the massive oak door. It was cool and breezy. Pete looked to the west and saw the sky erupting into bright crimson as the sun fell below the horizon.

Pete raised the large brass knocker and let it fall.

Taylor's housekeeper, Anna, let Pete in and escorted him through the living room to the study. Pete sat in the leather armchair. Taylor entered a few minutes later, dressed casually in a cashmere sweater and cotton slacks. Taylor was extremely pale. If anything, he looked worse then when Pete had seen him a few days before at the bank. Pete stood and put out his hand. Taylor took it in both of his.

"Oh, Pete," he said weakly.

"It's horrible, Taylor."

Taylor let go of Pete's hand, and Pete sat down. Taylor slowly settled onto the sofa.

"I know you spoke with Susan," Pete said.

"Yes. I still can't quite believe this nightmare returned after all these years."

Pete asked, "Did you know?"

"Know what?" he asked, surprised.

"That Ellen and Lois were planning something so insane? Did you ever have the slightest inkling that something like this could happen?"

"No. Never."

"You were close to Lois. I thought maybe she might have said something once. Maybe something you didn't even take seriously."

"No. I never had any idea. If I had . . ." His voice faded away.

"Did you love her, Taylor?"

Taylor looked at Pete. "Lois?"

Pete nodded.

"Yes, I did. For some time I even hoped we might marry. But Lois didn't want to marry again."

"That must've been hard for you."

"For a time it was. But after a while I accepted her decision. We remained very close, as you know. I enjoyed her friendship for many years." Taylor put a hand to his face and wiped his eyes. "Now poor Ellen is with her mother. They both suffered so much from the tragedy of Victor's murder."

"Maybe she's not dead. I keep thinking she's not."

"You think that's possible?"

"Maybe."

"God, if that were only true."

PETE SAT in a lawn chair on his back porch that evening. It was cold. He'd pulled on a jacket before going outside. Next door he could hear his neighbors through an open window. The television was tuned to the evening news, and he heard the sounds of dinner being prepared: a pot being put on the stove, water running, the clink of plates and glasses being removed from a cupboard. Pete tried to think about what his life would be like without Ellen, but he couldn't really grasp it. Living without her just didn't seem possible. He couldn't imagine dinner alone every night, sleeping by himself in their bed, waking up and not having her to talk to. It sickened him to think that just two months ago his life with Ellen and their love for each other had meant so little to him that he was seeing Tracy every chance he could.

"I'm sorry," he whispered quietly, hoping somehow Ellen could hear him. "I'm sorry."

He stayed outside for a long time. The stars glittered in the black sky, and a quarter moon worked its way up over his neighbor's roof to the east. He didn't go inside until the phone rang. It was half past eight.

Pete picked up the phone. "Hello," he said.

"Hello," said a man. The voice was familiar to Pete, but he couldn't place it. "Is this Pete Donelly?"

"Yes."

The man said, "This is Arnie Watkins. My wife is Chrissie Watkins. You called her earlier in the day about that brother of hers, Franklin Walker?"

"Yes. That's right."

"I told my wife all about why you called. You have to understand that this is her brother. And with all that he's done, he's still family. You can understand that, can't you?"

"Yes."

"She was thinking about you and how you must feel, your wife missing and all, and she said she wanted to tell you about a postcard she got from him one time. He sent it from a place in New Mexico. Chrissie believes he was there for a vacation of some sort."

"Where was the postcard from?"

"I've got it right here. Chrissie saved it. It's from Lantrow, New Mexico. Picture on it is of the mountains, so I guess it's up there somewhere."

"Thank you, Mr. Watkins. And thank your wife for me, too."

"I'll do that. Good luck to you."

Pete hung up and went to the living room, where they had an atlas. Lantrow was about seventy miles north of Santa Fe, east of Taos. Probably a ski area. He'd never been to northern New Mexico. Why had Walker gone there? he wondered. He wished he'd asked Mr. Watkins what Walker had written to his sister. It might have said something about what he was doing, where he was staying. He thought about calling him back but decided against it. If he found it necessary, he could call Chrissie Watkins again. The important thing was that he had a lead on where Walker might go. He wondered if he should call the police in Los Angeles and tell them. It didn't seem necessary. After all, there was no real reason to suspect that Walker was headed to New Mexico now. It was just a hunch. The police wouldn't be impressed with this information.

Pete left the atlas, went back into the kitchen and got the phone book. He opened the Yellow Pages to the airlines and picked up the phone. He would catch a flight to Albuquerque that night.

CHAPTER 26

When Ellen awoke they were in the mountains. She pushed herself up in the seat and saw a grove of aspens shimmering yellow-gold in the sunlight. The grass on the hills was brown. A small creek ran through the grove of trees, a cold, frothy blue. Warm air blew on her from the car heater. Ellen put her fingers to the window next to her; the glass was cold.

"Have we passed Santa Fe?" she asked.

"About forty minutes ago," Walker said.

That meant they were almost to their destination. To her right, Ellen could see the mountains rising thousands of feet to a rocky peak. A line of flat clouds surrounded it. Pete loved the mountains. Ellen wondered what he was doing right at this moment. Was he looking for her? Were the police? *He must be mad with worry by now.*

Pete had seemed truly anguished about things the day she had left. At that point Ellen hadn't felt she could ever forgive him. Now, though, his infidelity seemed much less important. He said he still loved her. She still loved him. That was what was important.

They reached a small town and Walker pulled into a gas station. While he filled up the tank, Ellen got out of the car and headed for the restroom.

She splashed water on her face, then looked at herself in the mirror. Though the swelling had gone down, the bruises on the right side of her face were turning a deeper shade of purple—the color of a ripe eggplant, fading into green along the edges. The white of her right eye was still blood red. She looked like she'd been in a car wreck.

Ellen sat inside the car, waiting for Walker. He came out of the men's room and sat behind the wheel, then said he wanted to stop at the deli across the street to get something to eat.

It was a small store with a wooden porch in front of it. A red neon sign in one of the windows said "COORS." Next to the front door a chalkboard had the prices of eggs, Delicious apples and roast beef sandwiches. The prices, Ellen noted, were high compared to Dallas.

Walker emerged with a paper bag in his arms and returned to the car. He pulled a large bag of tortilla chips from the sack and tore it open, setting it in the space between them.

"I got a few apples and some cookies. You want any, help yourself," he said.

"Thanks."

He pulled out of the parking space in front of the store and headed back onto the road. Walker ate the chips as he drove. The radio station they were listening to slowly faded into static. Walker punched the tuning button, trying to find a strong signal. A couple were faintly audible behind the static. Walker gave up and turned the radio off.

"How much longer until we get there?" Ellen asked.

"Two and a half, maybe three hours. I'm not really sure. It's been a while since I been up here."

"How long?"

"I came up right after I got outta Huntsville and then a year ago last summer."

"What for?"

"See Barton."

"What about?"

"First time he wanted to talk about what I was gonna do since I was outside again. He helped me get that job in L.A."

Ellen stared out the window for a few minutes. It was beautiful country. The mountains were stark and muscular, with deep shadows and spectacular angles of jutting rocks. She'd never been in this part of New Mexico before. It was no wonder people flocked here.

"Why didn't you kill me that first night?" she asked.

"I didn't want to do that."

"It would've been easier if you had. You probably could've gotten away with it."

Walker thought about this for a short while. "I kept thinkin' about you as a little girl," he said. "I felt like I knew you."

"I was threatening to kill you."

"I hit you when I got the chance, didn't I? But I felt bad after I saw how you was hurt."

"I guess I should thank you for saving my life back then. In the fire, I mean."

"You don't need to."

"I've lived thirty-four years thanks to you."

She saw him clench his jaw as he stared straight ahead. He said, "It didn't seem right to leave a little girl in that building."

He and Barton had ruined the lives of her mother, Susan and herself. Yet he had risked his life to get her out of the building and spent thirty years in jail because of it.

The car began to shudder. The engine nearly died, then lurched forward as Walker stepped on the gas.

"Fuckin-A," he said.

The car stalled and Walker pulled to the side of the road, stopping with the right wheels on the narrow gravel shoulder. He tried to restart it. The engine cranked but didn't come close to starting. After several tries Walker stopped. He put both hands on the steering wheel.

"What do you think's wrong?" she asked.

"Fuck if I know," he said. He reached under the dash and popped the front hood before getting out of the car. Ellen climbed out, too. She watched him prop open the hood and look at the engine.

"Get in and try to start it," Walker said.

Ellen got behind the wheel and turned the key. The starter whined, but the car wouldn't start.

"That's enough," he said.

Walker put the hood down and came around to the window next to Ellen.

"We'll have to walk back to town," he said. "Fuckin' sonofabitch!" He kicked the front bumper of the car.

Ellen grabbed the keys and slipped out of the car. "How far back do you think it is?"

"Five or six miles. Fuckin' cop runs these plates and we'll be in for it."

It was cool and they were walking downhill, so they made good progress. Occasionally a car or truck would pass going in their direction and Walker would stick out his thumb, but no one stopped. After forty minutes they started going uphill and their pace slowed. Ellen found herself getting out of breath rather quickly, the ribs on her right side aching. Walker was even more winded than she was.

"Let's rest for a few," he said. They sat on a couple of large rocks in the shade. Walker took out his cigarettes and lit one.

"How far do you think we've walked?" Ellen asked.

"Maybe a couple a miles."

They sat there for five minutes and then they heard a car in the distance coming up the road in their direction. They both stood and waited for it to come around the curve.

"Maybe this one'll stop," said Walker. He put his thumb out.

The car came into sight. It was a green sedan with a light bar across the roof—a Forest Service car.

"Shit," said Walker. The car slowed as it approached them. "You won't try nothing?" he asked Ellen.

"No."

The car pulled off onto the shoulder and rolled to a stop. A man in an olive green uniform got out. He was tall and thin, around thirty years old, with long brown hair that was tied back in a ponytail.

"Hi," he said. "You people leave that car up the road?"

"Yeah," said Walker. "We was headin' back to town to see about a tow truck."

"I'll give you a lift. Bob at the gas station oughta be able to give you a tow."

Ellen rode in the back seat of the car. Walker sat in front next to the ranger, who was named Scott Burrows. He'd been working for the Forest Service for seven years now, he told them. This was his third assignment. He'd been in New Mexico for the last year and a half.

"What's wrong with the car?" he asked.

"Don't know. It just died," said Walker. "We hadn't been having any trouble with it before now."

"It's probably nothing too serious," he said. "Bob, back in town, will get you on the road okay. You folks from Arizona?"

"Yeah," said Walker. "Phoenix."

"Where you headed?"

"A friend's cabin up near Lantrow. Just trying to have a few days' vacation."

Scott took them to the gas station where they had filled up the car an hour earlier. Bob was a heavy man in his fifties working under a car in the garage bay. He said he would be with them in a minute. Walker, Ellen and Scott went outside the garage to wait. Walker thanked Scott for the ride, and the ranger drove off.

"I hope to hell he don't run the plates on the car," Walker said.

"Why would he?" Ellen asked. "He didn't seem suspicious."

"Sometimes they do it for no reason at all."

Five minutes later Bob emerged from the garage. "Just let me get the keys to the truck," he said, heading into the station office. Walker followed him. The two men spoke for a few moments. Walker then came out.

"You mind waitin' here?" he asked. "I'll ride with him to the car."

"No. It's fine."

Ellen watched the truck disappear up the road and then walked across the street to the store. She figured she had at least twenty minutes before they got back. There was a pay phone outside the store entrance, but Ellen didn't have any change. She opened the screen door and went inside. At the counter a woman gave her three dollars' worth of quarters. Ellen went back out and inserted one of the coins into the pay phone.

For a few seconds she froze, not able to remember her own phone number. She concentrated. The area code was no problem. *214. 214. 214 what?* When she remembered it, she wasn't positive it was right. She thought she might be remembering the number of the bookstore or Taylor's house. No, it was her house.

It had to be. She quickly dialed it and was told to insert $2.25 for the first three minutes. She listened as the call went through. It rang twice. Her heart leapt as it was answered, but fell when she heard her own recorded voice speaking back to her from the answering machine. If only he'd been home. She waited and left a message, telling Pete she was fine and would be home in two or three days. She was sorry she'd missed him, she knew he was worried, but she hoped he wouldn't worry so much now. Ellen hung up. She didn't have enough money left to call Susan. Pete would get the message at some point today. He'd call Susan and let her know.

Ellen turned and saw the Forest Service car pulling into a parking spot just a dozen feet away. Scott Burrows got out of the car.

"Hi," he said. "Bob go to get your car?"

"He just left," she said. "Walker went with him."

Scott stepped up to her and stopped. "He a relative of yours?"

"No. Just an old friend."

"At first I thought he might be your husband."

God, what a thought. She almost laughed out loud. "No."

"I know he's a lot older than you, but sometimes you see that."

"Yeah."

"He's a family friend, I guess?"

Ellen nodded her head in agreement.

"Looks like you were in some kind of accident."

The comment surprised Ellen. He was the first person to say anything about her appearance, though she had noticed people looking at her when they stopped at gas stations and restaurants. "Yeah," she answered. "A car accident."

"You okay now?"

"Yeah. I had a concussion, but I'm fine now."

"That's good. Well, I'm going to go in here and say hi to Doris and then I'll be on my way. Good luck with your car."

"Thanks. Thanks again for giving us a lift."

"Happy to help."

Ellen went back across the street and waited at the service station. There were two molded plastic chairs along one wall of the office. Ellen sat in one. She realized it would be hard to convince anyone she was being held hostage by Walker now. The ranger was bound to remember her and this conversation. Walker was far away. If she wanted to escape, what better time than now? Well, there was nothing to be done about it. Maybe the police would believe she had been brainwashed. Hell, it might even be the truth.

It was twelve-thirty. More than an hour since the car had broken down. If it took long to fix they wouldn't get to the cabin until after dark.

The tow truck returned, pulling the Taurus behind it. After Bob had it unhitched, Ellen and Walker went to the coffee shop down the block and sat at a table. They ordered lunch.

"There may be a problem paying for the car if it's expensive," Walker said. "I only got about a hundred-sixty dollars left."

"I have credit cards," Ellen said.

"I thought about trying to get another car, but in a place like this they'd figure it was us that took it and then they'd run the license on the other car. Pretty quick they'd know who we was. Better to wait for this one to get fixed."

"What if Barton gets to the cabin before us?" she asked.

"I don't know. Let's just hope he can get the car fixed quick."

They finished the coffee and walked back to the gas station. Bob was on his phone in the office when they arrived. He put his caller on hold when they stepped in. "It's your fuel injector," he said. "I'm seeing when I can get the part up here."

"You don't have one?" Walker asked.

"No. We get our parts from Santa Fe. I'm probably not gonna be able to get one here until tomorrow."

"There's nothing closer than Santa Fe?"

"Nope. That's it. Usually they send the parts up on the Greyhound bus."

"What time does it arrive?" asked Ellen.

"Ten-thirty in the a.m.," Bob said.

Walker and Ellen slowly made their way to the Pueblo Motel two blocks away on the edge of town. They stepped into the tiny office, where a three-foot counter ran along one wall. There was a sliding window above it. A thin man, all nose and cheekbones, wearing plastic-framed glasses held together with black tape above the nose, rented Walker a room for the night.

The room was small—the two beds squeezed into it with only a foot between them. In the narrow bathroom was a rust-stained shower with an endlessly dripping shower head. Walker and Ellen walked to the gas station, retrieved their luggage from the trunk of the car and carried it back to the motel.

"I'm not sure how we'll work things now," Walker said sitting on the edge of one of the beds.

"He'll get there before us, won't he?"

"Good chance he will. I figured he'd be up here tonight or tomorrow morning. But, shit, he could be drivin' by us right now." Walker stopped for a second. "If we're lucky he won't make it here that fast. I don't know. Eddie Rollins says people make their own luck. Guess we better try to make some."

"We'll have to be careful when we drive up tomorrow," said Ellen.

"That's for damn sure."

"I'll get out of the car before we get there. That way you'll be alone if he's already there."

Walker nodded in agreement. "If he's there, I'll take care of him soon as I can. If he's not, then we'll wait for him same as we planned."

Later, as they walked to the restaurant for dinner, Ellen carefully watched the lone car that passed on the road going north. A middle-aged woman was driving. Ellen and Walker ate quietly, hardly saying a word to one another. There were only two other customers in the restaurant.

After they finished Ellen went into the store and bought a paperback novel. She needed something to do until it was late enough to sleep. In front of the store Ellen looked at the pay phone and wondered if Pete had heard her message yet. He must have. He was probably waiting by the phone now, hoping she would call again. Should she try calling later? She could tell Walker she was going for a walk and come back here. Ellen crossed the street, heading back toward the motel. Walker had gone to the gas station to check with Bob about the car again, still worried that Bob or someone was going to get suspicious and call the police. Walker might believe Eddie Rollins when he said that people create their own luck, but it seemed he had little faith that he could accomplish this himself.

Inside the motel room Ellen sat on one of the beds and began reading. She could escape now, leave the motel, call the police and then hide somewhere in the dark. Unlike the other night in Flagstaff, it wasn't fear that stopped her. Now she realized she wanted to go to the cabin, wait for Alan Barton and finish what she had started.

A half-hour later Walker returned and sat down, a worried expression on his face.

"I don't know," he said. "I'm thinkin' maybe we oughta just get the hell outta here tomorrow. Drive a long ways away."

"You said that wouldn't do any good. He'd find us."

"Maybe I was wrong."

"No, you were right. We won't be safe until he's dead."

"Yeah," he said, rubbing his jawline with his hand. "Thing that worries me is that Barton's smart. Smarter than me. Maybe smarter than you."

"He won't expect that you're going to shoot him. Why would he? You do it soon as you can and it'll be over."

Ellen went back to reading the paperback she'd bought. Walker went outside the room to smoke. He came in once and said he was walking to the store. He returned with a six-pack of beer. Ellen had one of the beers, sipping it while she read. Later she left and walked to the phone booth. She stood next to it for a few minutes trying to decide if she should call Pete again. She put a quarter in the phone, started to dial the number, then hung up. She was afraid to talk to him. Afraid of the questions he'd ask, afraid he might talk her into getting away now while she could.

When she returned to the motel Walker was on the edge of his bed, writing on a pad of paper.

"What're you writing?" she asked.

"Letter to my sister," he said. "Remind me to mail it tomorrow."

They took turns using the shower. Ellen lay on her bed in a clean T-shirt and sweatpants.

"You awake still?" Walker whispered after some time had passed.

"Yeah."

"What you thinkin' about?"

"My sister. My husband."

"You don't talk about your husband much."

"I guess not."

"Things not so good?"

"They've been better. It's been hard the last couple of years. I guess we've both been to blame."

"I never was married."

It was quiet for a while. Ellen heard a car go by on the road. *That could be him. That could be Alan Barton driving by right now.*

"I didn't want anything to happen to Denise," Walker said after several minutes. "She bugged the crap outta me, but she was still good in some ways. I just can't stop thinkin' about it."

Ellen remembered the woman dying and shuddered.

"It wasn't your fault," she said.

"I shouldn't a let her come inside."

They didn't speak again. Soon Ellen was asleep. She slept soundly for several hours. Then she had the dream.

CHAPTER 27

"THIS SOUNDS LIKE an extreme long shot," Marvin said after listening to Pete explain what he was doing.

"I know. But it's worth looking into, and I'm going to do it. If I call the cops and tell them about this, all they'll do is send out a bulletin to the New Mexican authorities."

"I can fly out there and meet you in Albuquerque," suggested Marvin.

"No," said Pete. "Like you said, it's a real long shot."

"Well, you get lucky and find something, don't do anything stupid."

"I won't."

After landing in Albuquerque early Saturday morning, Pete reached Santa Fe in just under two hours. He pulled off the highway there and drove through a Burger King, getting coffee and a hamburger. Back on the road, he continued north. The mountains were stunning. He wouldn't mind coming back here sometime for a vacation. A vacation. The idea seemed ridiculous. How could he have a vacation without Ellen? But he would. Even if the worst had happened, his life would continue. He'd have Christmas and New Year's. His birthday in March. Winter, spring, summer, fall. Eventually he'd feel like a normal person again. Do normal things. Take a vacation. It seemed wrong for things to ever get back to normal. But he supposed they would. He'd have to go back to work soon. He'd already missed more than a week. The thought of seeing Tracy again made Pete feel ill.

It was only 10:30 and he was halfway there; he'd be in Lantrow by 2:30. He had the photograph of Walker. He'd ask around, see if anyone recognized him or had noticed a Taurus with California plates. He assumed it would be a small town. If there was a real estate office that did vacation rentals, he could start there.

He listened to the radio as he drove. He thought about a lot of things, but he kept coming back to Ellen and her plans to find the man or men who killed her father. He remembered the first time he'd been with Ellen when she had a nightmare. It'd scared the shit out of him, and then when it was over and she was sobbing and embarrassed because she'd wet the bed, he tried to comfort her. They were in his apartment, and he didn't have any other sheets, so they put down towels over the bed, unzipped his down sleeping bag and huddled under it.

"I'm sorry," she said.

"There's nothing to be sorry about," he told her. "I'm sorry you had such a horrible dream. You want to tell me about it?"

"Not now." She turned her head and kissed him on the side of his neck. "Thanks."

It was the first time he'd seen her vulnerable. Up until then Ellen had always been so confident and capable, always in control of every situation. It was wonderful to feel like she needed him. It was the first time he'd felt that way since they met.

The next morning as they sat in his small kitchen eating waffles, he asked her again what the dream had been about. She hesitated for a few moments, tears welling in her eyes, and he was instantly sorry he'd asked.

"Never mind," he said.

"No. I'll tell you. But later," she said. "It's too hard to talk about. And it's embarrassing too because I wet the bed. I wish I would stop doing that. You'd think I could just scream and wake up."

A week passed before she told him, in a low voice, about her father being killed. Pete clearly remembered the shock he felt. It was a horrifying story, and he was overwhelmed with a deep longing to protect Ellen and keep her safe from the evil that slithered into her dreams once or twice a month. But he didn't learn the entire story until their wedding reception more than a year later. Taylor took him aside and handed him an envelope with a check in it, saying it was a little something to help them get their feet on the ground. Pete thanked him, and Taylor went on to say how pleased he was for Ellen and Pete.

"I've worried a lot about Ellen over the years," he said. "I'm so glad she's found happiness."

"I hope she'll be happy," said Pete. "I think she will be."

"I think so, too. She had a tough time there for a while after she lost her father."

"I know. That was a tragedy for everyone."

"I think about Victor a lot," said Taylor. "And poor Ellen. To have been there when such an awful thing occurred. Horrible thing to happen to anyone, let alone a child."

Pete was paralyzed, head to toe, and was unable to say anything coherent to Taylor. A week later Pete asked Ellen about it. Reluctantly she told him it was true, but that she remembered nothing about that day.

She said, "I wouldn't even know I was there except people told me I was."

"You never mentioned this before."

"I don't like talking about it. Not to anyone."

Pete asked, "In your nightmares, are you there?"

Ellen's face drained of color and she hung her head, which was enough of an answer.

"I'm sorry," he said. "Forget I asked."

Pete rarely brought the subject up again. When Ellen had a nightmare, he'd wake her up, calm her, help change the sheets and try to go back to sleep.

Once he suggested she might consider hypnotism as a way to stop the nightmares.

"You think a hypnotist will make me forget my father was shot in the head?" she asked.

"Of course not," he answered. "But maybe it would stop you from dreaming about it."

"It's been thirty years. I'm never going to stop dreaming about it."

Now Pete wished he had been more understanding and had tried to talk with Ellen about the nightmares even though she insisted she didn't want to. If he had, perhaps she would have told him of her desire to find Franklin Walker and the other man. *If she'd only done that; talked to me or someone other than her mother about it, then it wouldn't have happened. She would have realized the insanity of it, and none of this would have happened.*

Pete drove north through Pojoaque, Espanol, Albiquiu and Cebolla. It got cool as the road moved higher into the mountains. He was glad he had thought to bring a heavy jacket. It was past three when he drove into Lantrow, which was set in a narrow valley surrounded by tall rocky peaks on three sides. Pete drove the length of the town, then turned around and came back. It consisted of the highway and two streets that intersected it. There were several restaurants, a real estate office, two motels, a couple of gift stores, a bar or two, a grocery store, a modest church, a hardware store and a Texaco station at the south end of town on the highway. Pete stopped to get gas, putting on his jacket as he got out. The man working there recommended one of the restaurants, Cathy's, which Pete found a half-block up on the right.

The restaurant was empty when he entered. Pete took a small table next to a window where he could keep an eye on the highway. He wanted to make sure he noticed if a Taurus happened to drive by.

Pete ordered a sandwich and coffee. When he finished, the waitress brought him the bill, and Pete told her he was looking for a man who might be in the area. He showed her the photograph of Walker.

"Are you a policeman?" she asked.

"No. I'm trying to find my wife. This man might know what happened to her."

She took the photograph from him and looked at it closely. She didn't recognize Walker, but promised to keep an eye out for him. As he left, Pete asked her which motel in town was the best. She told him to go to the Aspen Pines.

It was a white U-shaped building with forest-green trim. The office was at the front on the left side. There were newspaper racks next to the glass door that led inside. Pete rented a room for the night and pulled the car in front of his door. There were two beds in the room and charcoal-colored carpet that still smelled new. The TV was mounted on the wall. Pete picked up the remote and clicked on the TV, running through a few channels before turning it off.

He went on foot to the real estate office and spoke with the woman working there. Walker's name wasn't familiar to her, and she didn't recognize his photograph. She looked in her files for his name, but didn't find it, which meant he hadn't rented anything through her office for the last four years. Pete thanked the woman and left.

He then went from building to building, asking people if they remembered seeing Walker or a Ford Taurus with California plates. Only one man, a bald man in his sixties who owned the grocery store in town, thought the photo of Walker looked familiar. He couldn't say when, but he thought he'd seen the man before.

"Could it have been a year ago in the summer?" Pete asked.

"Might've been. He looks familiar. I haven't seen him recently. I know that."

Pete said, "There's a chance he might be showing up in this area again. If you see him, give me a call. I'm staying at the Aspen Pines down the street." Pete wrote down his name and room number on a small piece of paper and left it with the man.

From his motel room, Pete tried phoning Marvin. The grocer's ID gave Pete some hope that Walker might show up here again. Marvin didn't answer. Pete left a brief message with the number of the motel.

Then Pete called home to check his machine for messages. When he heard Ellen's voice it was as if a hand had gripped his heart and tried to yank it, still beating, from his chest. He was so shocked he didn't understand a word she said. The message was over before he could even begin to think.

A mistake. It was a mistake. An old message that somehow hadn't been erased. Pete was shaking violently. He dropped the phone in the cradle.

He waited half a minute before calling back. It couldn't be an old message, he realized. It had been a week since he'd heard from Ellen. The tape had been erased and recorded over several times. Was his mind playing tricks on him? Pete redialed his number. Even though he was prepared the second time he listened to it, it still shook him deeply. But he was able to understand what she said this time, and he knew that this was a new message, a message Ellen had left today.

Pete dialed Susan's number, silently praying she would be home. She was.

"She's alive," he said. "Ellen's alive."

PETE COULDN'T IMAGINE where she'd been or what the hell she was doing now, but she was alive and it made him positively joyous. He tried phoning Marvin again to tell him the news, but he still wasn't home. Pete felt like celebrating, but that wasn't appropriate. Ellen might not be out of danger. She had been in L.A. to find Walker, and she had been in his apartment. Now Ellen and Walker were missing, and Walker's girlfriend and the other man were dead. And Ellen had called to say she'd be home soon. If she was still with Walker, she was in extreme danger. Maybe she wasn't with him. She sounded calm in her message, not frightened or anxious, not like a kidnap victim or a person in danger. She said she'd be home soon. Walker could've forced her to say that, he supposed. But why would he?

Pete thought about driving back to Albuquerque immediately and flying home. But he was tired and still felt shaky inside, and there was something else. He thought Ellen might be near. He felt he was right about Walker fleeing to New Mexico and that Ellen, despite the calmness of the message she had left, could be with him.

He put on his jacket and went outside. The sun was behind the mountains now and it was chilly. The sky was lavender blue, cloudless. It looked like it would crack if you tapped it with a spoon. Pete wandered up and down the length of the town, stopping in a couple of places. He looked through the postcard rack at one store, wondering if any of the cards were the same as the one Walker had sent to his sister in Midland.

It was seven when he went back into Cathy's to have dinner. Many tables were occupied now. Pete requested the same table he'd been at earlier, still interested in the occasional car driving by on the road. Pete ordered and waited, thinking about Ellen and how wonderful it would be to see her again. Things would be better between them now. He'd make damn sure of that.

Pete ate quickly, anxious to get back to his room and try Marvin again. He'd call Taylor, too. Taylor would be overjoyed to learn Ellen was alive.

A man stepped up to the table. He looked about sixty, with graying hair and dark eyes. His face was remarkably unlined for a man his age. He was thin and wore a brown leather jacket over a plaid flannel shirt.

"I heard you were asking about someone who might have been around here looking to rent a cabin?"

"That's right," Pete answered. "I was."

"Mind if I sit down?" he asked. "I might know something that could help you."

"Please."

The man pulled out the chair opposite Pete and sat. "I know Angela, who works in the real estate office here. I own a couple of cabins and she rents them out for me. She told me about you. You're looking for someone from California?"

"That's right," said Pete. "He might've arrived yesterday or today. He's in his sixties, about five-nine. His name is Franklin Walker."

"Angela said he's wanted for a crime?"

"He's wanted for a murder in California."

"Jesus," said the man, shaking his head. "After Angela told me about you, I thought I better try to track you down. Last night I was having a couple of beers at The Divide, right across the street here, and this man was there asking about renting a place. I told him that I had a couple of empty cabins. He paid for a week in cash, so I gave him directions and a key I had with me. He told me his name was Art something or other. What was it?" The man paused, thinking. "I can't remember it now. I asked where he was from and he told me Colorado. I suppose I shouldn't have rented to him without a little more checking, but he had the money right then, and he wanted a place. The cabins are empty so much of the time, I hate to lose an opportunity to rent one."

"Did you see what kind of car he had?" Pete asked.

"No, I didn't. Sorry."

Pete picked the napkin off his lap, folded it and set it on the table. "Did the man have a prominent jaw?" Pete asked.

"I guess you could say that," he said. "Now that you mention it."

"How old was he?"

"Looked like he was in his sixties to me."

"I've got a photograph of Walker back at my motel room. I'll go get it."

"All right. Why don't you meet me down at the bar? You know where it is?"

"Yeah. I saw it," Pete said. "There wasn't anyone with him, was there?"

The man knit his brows, trying to recall.

"A woman in her mid-thirties. Light brown hair?" asked Pete.

The man stared at Pete for several moments.

"There was a woman there," he said slowly. "Quite a bit

younger than he was. I didn't think she was with him at first because he was alone at the bar when I was talking to him. But when he left, this woman stood up at a table and followed him out the door."

Pete's stomach knotted and for a second he feared he was going to lose his dinner right on the table. He stared at the man sitting across from him for several moments. He must have looked stricken, for the man asked if he was all right.

"I'll be okay," Pete said quietly. "Did you see what she looked like?"

"Not too well, but she was a lot younger than the man. And she did have light hair, light brown or blonde."

Pete tried to think. Ellen had sounded okay when she left the message. Not frightened. Not under duress.

"You're sure they were together?" Pete asked.

"Not a hundred percent. I noticed she followed him out last night, and I wondered if she was with him or not, but it was hard to tell."

Pete pulled out his wallet and flipped it open. He tried to steady his hands as he removed the small photograph from the plastic holder in his wallet. He got it out and passed it across the table to the man.

"Is this the woman who was with him?"

The man held the picture of Ellen to the light and looked at it for several seconds. "Her hair's longer here, but it looks a lot like the woman I saw. Who is she?"

"My wife," said Pete.

The man frowned and looked from the photo to Pete. "What the hell's she doing with him?" he asked.

"She's being held against her will," said Pete. "He's kidnapped her. Until this afternoon I'd thought he might have killed her."

"What happened this afternoon?"

"She called our house and left a message on the phone machine. I hadn't heard from her in a week, and there was evidence that she'd been in Walker's apartment, but I was still hoping—then today I called my house to check messages on my phone machine and there was her voice." Pete hesitated. "It shocked the hell out of me."

"I guess so. So she called your house today?"

"Yeah."

"She didn't say where she was?"

Pete shook his head. "No. I—God, I don't know what to do now. How far away is that cabin?"

"About fifteen miles from here. But the road off the highway is bad. It takes at least an hour to get there. We should probably give the sheriff a call."

"How far away is the sheriff?"

"The station is a good eighty miles from here."

"Can you give me directions to the cabin?"

"I can, but I have to tell you it'd be almost impossible for you to find it in the dark. You go up this dirt road several miles and there are a couple of turns. You make the wrong one and you end up on a fire road that goes forever. You should wait until the morning."

"She's my wife. Every hour she's with that man she's in danger. I've got to find her. I can't wait until tomorrow."

The man stared at him, then slowly nodded his head. "All right. But I better take you up there. You'd never find it yourself."

Pete said, "I can't ask you to do that."

"You won't find it in the dark. Wait until tomorrow and you could see where the turns are."

Pete knew that made sense, but it was out of the question. "I can't wait until tomorrow," he said.

"Then I'll have to give you a ride."

"It might be dangerous," said Pete. "He's probably got a gun."

The man set his jaw, thinking. "Do you have a gun?"

"No."

"I could borrow a rifle from a friend," the man said. "I'll call the sheriff, too. A deputy might not get up here until the morning, but I think we better let them know this character is around."

"Good idea," said Pete. "You sure you want to do this?"

"Well," he said, "you couldn't find it in the dark, and it seems to me you might need a little help."

"I probably will," Pete admitted.

"Maybe he'll listen to reason. He didn't seem totally off his rocker or anything. If he had, I wouldn't have rented the place to him. Still, if he's wanted for murder . . ."

Pete stood up. "We better go. By the way, my name's Pete Donelly." He put out his hand.

The man took his hand with a firm grip and stared directly into Pete's eyes. "Nice to meet you, Pete," he said. "I'm Alan Barton."

CHAPTER 28

ELLEN STOOD next to the hole in the wall. Her daddy was on his knees next to her. There had been a metal screen on the hole, but her daddy had taken it off with a small screwdriver.

"I'm scared," she said.

"I know, darlin'. But go ahead. It'll be all right." He spoke softly, almost in a whisper. Ellen knew he didn't want the bad men to hear him. "Go right through to the next office. There's no cover on the vent there. Look through and you can see. It's only a couple of feet. Go to the phone on the desk there and dial 0. The operator will answer. Tell her you're in trouble and to send the police to Nine-thirty-five Hamilton Street. Tell her there are men with guns. Then go out to the hall and walk to the front and leave if you can. Run down the street and wait at the corner. When you see a police car, you wave at it. The policemen will stop for you."

"Daddy, I'm scared."

"You don't need to be scared. Do like I told you. Go on now."

Ellen stared at him for several moments, not wanting to move but knowing she would have to, knowing she would obey him. Finally, she turned and got down on her hands and knees. She put her head into the small opening. Daddy was right. She could see the opening into the next office. Ellen crawled in and wiggled along the cold metal duct. It was barely big enough. She felt the smooth sides rubbing against her as she moved. It only took a few seconds to get to the other opening. She pushed her arms through and pulled herself out. Ellen stood up. The room was a lot like her daddy's office. She stepped to the desk and picked up the phone. There was no dial tone. Ellen went to the door, opened it and made sure no one was in the hall. She didn't know where the bad men were. To her left was the front part of the office, where she had seen another phone. The hall was carpeted. Ellen walked slowly, not making a sound. No one was in sight. She wanted to go back to her daddy, but she didn't want him to be mad. Her heart beat in her ears as she continued on toward the front office and the phone.

Ellen picked up the telephone and heard a dial tone. She dialed 0.

"Operator," a woman said. Ellen opened her mouth but said nothing.

"Hello, operator," the woman said again.

Ellen put the phone back down. She was too scared to talk to a strange person on the telephone.

She looked at the door that went to the stairs. Her daddy had said to go outside and run down the street. But Ellen was afraid to leave. She turned back to the hallway. Ellen wanted to be with her daddy. She walked quickly down the first section, turned the corner and heard the voices. There was a doorway open now that had been closed before. The voices came from there. Ellen didn't want to walk past the door, but it was the only way to get back to her daddy.

"I need to know what to do with them," said a man. Then there was quiet. "No. She hasn't seen me." More quiet. Ellen realized the bad man was talking on the phone. She was just about to try hurrying past when the bad man with the silver tooth looked out the doorway and saw her. His eyes popped and he yelled, "Sonofabitch!"

He grabbed Ellen by the arm and pulled her down the hall toward the office where her father was.

"What the hell you doin'?" the bad man asked her. "Huh!?"

Ellen wanted to cry, but she didn't want to cry in front of him.

"Listenin' to us talk? That what you doin'?" He stopped moving but kept his grip on her arm. "What'd you hear, anyway? Tell me now!" Ellen didn't answer him. "Goddamnit!" he said.

He marched her back to her father's office and unlocked the door. Ellen ran to her daddy, burying her face against his shoulder.

"Keep her in here or you'll both be sorry," the man shouted. Then he slammed the door shut. Ellen started to cry.

"It's okay, darlin'," her daddy said. "Don't cry."

But Ellen couldn't stop. She wanted to leave. She wanted her daddy to get up and take her away. Go home. To Mama and Susie.

"Hush, now," he said. "That's enough. Did you phone the operator?" Ellen shook her head against his shoulder.

"It didn't work," she lied.

"Okay," he said. "Okay, then."

Then she was standing up next to her father. He was looking out the window. She could hear sirens.

The bad man stood in the open doorway. His gun pointed at Daddy. "Fuckin' sonofabitch!" he screamed. He put the gun right in her daddy's face. Ellen squeezed her eyes shut. Her fists were so tight her hands hurt. Something touched her face and she opened her eyes.

Daddy's face was close. His hand was on her cheek. His

mouth opened and closed. He was telling her something, but Ellen couldn't understand what it was. The bad man yanked her daddy's arm and took him out the door.

Ellen waited. She wanted to get away, but she was scared. She went to the window, stood on a chair and looked out. There were four police cars. Some policemen were walking toward the building. There was a pop and the police fell to the ground. Three more pops, then the police got up and ran back behind their cars.

Smoke. She smelled smoke, but she didn't open her eyes. If she waited quietly, was a good girl, everything would be fine. Daddy would come and get her. They would drive home in his car, stopping for ice cream cones on the way. Ellen started to choke and opened her eyes. The room was black with smoke. It was curling under the edge of the desk, filling the space where she hid.

"Daddy!" she screamed. "Daddy!"

She opened her eyes again and saw nothing. The smoke scratched at them. There was no air left to breathe. Only smoke. She put her face down on the carpet, hoping to find some air left there. Something grabbed her leg and pulled her from under the desk. Daddy! She was under his arm and he dragged her across the floor. She heard cracking and hissing. Far away there were sirens. Ellen was lifted up in his arms and she felt him going down steps. Then he fell and Ellen landed on her side, her face hitting the edge of one step. Ow! Her face hurt. Her side hurt. It was too black to see. Too black to breathe. There were red and white spots in front of her eyes. She thought she saw Mama wearing her pretty white dress standing in front of the dining room table. Her makeup was beautiful. She looked like a princess.

Ellen was bumping along now. She couldn't see anything. Then she saw Mama again, smiling at her. Her head bumped again and again. *It should hurt. My head should hurt.* But it didn't. Mama in her white princess dress was dancing with Daddy all around a beautiful ballroom. Daddy wore a gold crown on his head and a white suit.

Bright light, and the sirens were louder. Ellen was choking. She heard Daddy choking nearby. She could see something now through the red and white spots. They were outside. She could see the tire of a car. Ellen tried to sit up but couldn't. Her body wouldn't work. She tried to move her arm. She couldn't feel her arm.

A hand took her chin and moved her head. She looked into the soot-stained face of the bad man. Blood dripped down the side of his head. A face appeared next to the bad man. It was Pete.

ELLEN SHRIEKED and woke up. Her stomach heaved and she swallowed back the vomit in her mouth. She clenched her teeth, trying to keep her food down. She had soaked the bed. Walker stood over her, worried.

"Christ's sake," he said. "You all right?"

Ellen tried to tell him she was okay, but she couldn't. She shook her head at him.

"You have a bad dream?" he asked.

She shook her head yes, keeping her hand over her mouth, tears still streaming down her face. The murdering bastard had saved her life. He really had.

He sat back down on his bed and waited. She supposed he was ready to help if there was anything he could do. *I'm thirty-eight years old, and I still wet the bed when I have nightmares about my father's murder. Help me if you can.*

Ellen sat up and walked into the bathroom, stripped off her

wet clothes and showered. She changed, went back into the room, took the wet sheets off the bed and tossed them in a corner.

Sleep was out of the question. She stepped outside and stood in front of their room for a while. It was four in the morning and very quiet. No sounds at all except for some crickets still around this late in the fall. Ellen had put on a jacket, but she was damp from her shower and it was cold. She was shivering but didn't care. She needed to get out of that room, away from Walker. The cold air smelled good. The quiet felt good.

The dream had unnerved her. She had never dreamt about being rescued before. Well. It didn't change what they were going to do today. The car would be fixed. They would drive to the cabin. If they were lucky, Alan Barton wouldn't be there yet. They would wait and Walker would kill him. Then she would go home, and Walker would try to evade the law. She doubted he'd be free for long.

Back in the motel room, she put a towel on the bed, lay down and closed her eyes. Soon Ellen fell into a mercifully dreamless sleep.

CHAPTER 29

In the pitch black, bouncing along the winding dirt road, Alan Barton never drove more than five miles per hour. All they could see was a hundred feet of the uneven track ahead of them and the dark, indistinct shapes of trees and boulders lurking along the perimeter. They were in Barton's Jeep Cherokee, which was a good thing since the road was so bad Pete wondered if the car he'd rented would have been able to make it to the cabin. Barton drove methodically, keeping his eyes riveted on the road. He knew the way well enough. They'd passed two places where the dirt road forked. Barton had known which way to go without hesitation.

"I hope we're doing the right thing," Pete said.

"You and me both," answered Barton.

Before leaving the restaurant, Pete watched Barton call the sheriff from a pay phone across the parking lot. When he returned he reported that, as he'd suspected, the sheriff's station wouldn't be able to send a deputy over until tomorrow morning.

An hour later Barton had picked Pete up at his motel. When he got in the vehicle, Pete saw a rifle on the back seat of the Cherokee. He showed Barton the photo of Walker, and Barton confirmed that Walker was the man who had rented the cabin the previous night.

"You never told me how your wife got kidnapped by this man," Barton said.

"I don't know exactly how it happened. I know Ellen went looking for him because he was involved in the murder of her father about thirty years ago."

"He killed her father? She knows that?"

"Yeah. He spent a long time in prison for it. He was only released three years ago."

"Good God."

"Ellen didn't tell me what she was doing. She left and lied about where she was going. At first she called, but then she stopped. It was lucky that I found out she'd gone to Los Angeles."

"You think she planned to kill this man? She wanted revenge?"

"I don't know. Maybe. It's hard to believe she could actually do it. I think she wanted to find out who had been with Walker the day her father was killed. She and her mother had always anguished over the fact that this other man was never arrested."

"You mean two people murdered her father?"

"Two people were there. Franklin Walker was arrested, but he'd never say who the other man was. That's why I think she tracked Walker down. She wanted to force him to tell who his partner was."

"What about your wife's mother? Did she know what your wife was doing?"

"She's dead. She died eight months ago."

"So you wife did this all on her own?"

"Yeah."

"Never told anyone?"

"Not so far as I know."

"If this man kidnapped her, I wonder why he'd let her call you?"

"I don't know. That doesn't really make sense."

"No."

"When you saw her, did she seem scared or nervous?" Pete asked.

"I didn't notice that. Like I said before, I didn't really get a good look at her."

Pete asked, "Was Walker planning to drive up here last night?"

"I told him he should wait until daylight."

They drove along an extremely bad stretch of road. Barton slowed the Jeep to a crawl.

"Is there any way this Walker would think you could trace him up here?" Barton asked.

"No." He explained about calling Walker's sister in Midland and how that led to his flying to New Mexico this morning.

"How far do we have to go?" Pete asked.

"Five point two miles from the highway. We have to make a turn in a little while. You can't really see that there's a road there in the dark."

"How far have we come so far?"

"Over a mile and a quarter now."

Pete looked at his watch. They'd been driving on the dirt road for almost fifteen minutes. At this rate that meant nearly an hour to go.

"He'll hear us coming, won't he?"

"Yeah. I was thinking we should stop about a half-mile away and walk in. If he's awake and hears the car, he might think it stopped at another cabin."

"There are other places nearby?"

"Closest is about a mile away. But you can hear cars from a long ways off."

"So we walk up to the house," said Pete. "What do you think we should do then?"

"Don't ask me," said Barton. "This was your idea."

"Yeah." Pete knew he couldn't knock on the door and politely ask Franklin Walker to let his wife go. But he didn't know how to shoot a rifle. He didn't know how to sneak up to a cabin in the middle of the night and rescue someone.

"If we're quiet, maybe we can look around without waking him up," Pete said. "We locate Ellen, maybe we can get her out without him knowing."

"It's not a very big cabin," Barton said. "And the sound of the car will probably wake him if he's asleep. Doesn't seem like he's going to let your wife go voluntarily."

"We have the gun."

"You'd shoot him?"

"She's my wife, Mr. Barton. I'm getting her away from that man."

The thing to do was surprise Walker. If Pete kept the rifle on him, Barton could tie him up. They'd leave with Ellen, and the sheriff's department could go back and arrest Walker tomorrow.

"We'll have to try to surprise him," said Pete.

"There's an idea," said Barton. His tone was sarcastic, and Pete looked at him. Maybe it was a stupid thing to say, but it was strange for Barton to make light of it. Shit, Ellen's life was in danger. Their own lives could be in danger.

Barton said, "Hey. That sounded wrong. I didn't mean anything."

Pete was silent.

"I just thought it went without saying that we'd be trying to surprise him," he continued. "That's why we're walking the last part."

"Don't worry about it," Pete said. But there was something about Barton that was starting to bother him. Something he didn't like. Pete hadn't noticed it initially, but now he felt Barton had an attitude. It wasn't snobbishness. More like he felt he had something on you. Or that he was smarter than everybody else.

They drove for a long time. It seemed endless. Pete couldn't stop agonizing about Ellen. Was she all right? What was she doing with Walker, and why had she called today to tell him she'd be home in a few days? All he wanted was to get to the cabin and get Ellen away from that man. He didn't care what Walker did or said; Pete would get her away.

Another half-hour went by. Barton stopped the car and put it in park. "We're less than half a mile from the cabin," he said. He killed the engine and flipped off the headlights.

Pete got out of the car. A cold, dry breeze stung his face and skipped through the branches of nearby trees. There was no moon out. It was as black as a grave.

Opening the back door of the Jeep, Barton reached inside and bent down. Illuminated by the Jeep's dome light, Pete saw him pick up the rifle. He closed the door and they were in blackness again.

"Ready?" Barton asked.

"Yeah."

He turned on a flashlight and pointed it on the road in front of them, and they started walking. Pete moved carefully over the uneven ground. There were loose rocks and holes in the hard dirt. They hadn't gone fifty yards when Pete caught a toe on something and stumbled before catching his balance.

"Careful," said Barton quietly.

They trudged along. After a few minutes the road took a sharp turn to the right and rose steeply for a hundred feet. Pete was quickly winded.

Barton said, "When we get to the top of this rise, we can see the cabin."

They reached a flat part of the road and Alan pointed up through the trees. "It's right up there. If there was a light on, we'd be able to see it."

They continued. The road was level for a couple hundred yards before turning steep again. They scaled the hill and Barton clicked off the flashlight.

"Just to the right up here," he said quietly. They moved slowly around a bend and Pete saw the cabin less than fifty yards away. His eyes had adjusted to the dark now, and he could see quite well. The cabin was in a clearing, and the sky, marbled with stars, provided some light.

It was a single-story structure, larger than Pete had expected. It looked like it had a couple of bedrooms. Pete could see a porch along the front. The tin roof above the cabin was steeply peaked.

"No car," Pete whispered.

"No."

"Think they didn't get here?"

"I don't know. I thought he'd be here by this morning. He paid for it. You want the rifle?"

Pete reached out his hand and took it.

"I don't think anyone's here," said Pete.

"Better take a look. Don't step on the porch. It creaks."

Pete started slowly toward the cabin. He tried to move silently. He stopped once, thinking he'd heard something, then realized it was only Barton moving behind him.

Pete halted near a side window. He knew Walker could be watching from inside. If Pete went up to the window, he could get shot point-blank in the face. Pete took a step, stopped and looked back.

"I think you better try to see inside before we go in the front door," Barton whispered.

Gripping the rifle tightly, Pete took the last two steps to the window and put his face to the glass. He saw a room with two beds in it, both unoccupied. There was no sign that anyone had been there. Pete turned to Barton and shook his head. He crept along the side of the house. Curtains were pulled across the next window, and he couldn't see in. Continuing around the back of the cabin, Pete saw a shed fifty or sixty feet away. Too small to put a car in. Pete tripped over a tree branch and stumbled, going down on one knee with a gasp. He held up the gun so it wouldn't hit the ground. He and Barton both waited, watching the windows of the cabin, but there was no sound or movement inside. Pete got to his feet and went to the first window at the back of the house. Curtains were drawn here also, but there was a two-inch gap between them. Pete tried to see through the gap, but it was impossible.

Barton said, "Check out the kitchen. Down at the end."

They continued the length of the cabin and stopped. Pete put his face against the window and looked in. There was no food out. No plates or glasses.

"Doesn't look like anyone's been in there," said Pete.

They circled back to the front porch, and Pete rapped on the door. There was no answer. Barton took out a key and unlocked it, and they went inside.

Barton turned on the flashlight again and they walked through the place. It was clear that no one had been there. The men stopped in the living room, where there was a sofa, a couple of chairs and a coffee table.

"I wonder what happened to them?" Pete said.

"Maybe they got lost. I wrote out directions for him, so he should've been able to find it in the daylight no problem. What do you want to do?"

"I don't know." Pete was exhausted. He'd been wound up tight thinking they were going to find Ellen; now all that energy had evaporated. "If you don't mind, I'd like to wait for them. They might show up in the morning."

"Okay." Barton sat in a chair. "I'd rather not drive back down the road in the dark anyway." He put the flashlight on the coffee table pointing straight up, making an oval of milky light on the ceiling.

Pete said, "We'll wait until midday. If they don't show up by then, something must have happened and they're not coming."

"That's fine."

"You sure? I've got you involved in this, and if you want to take off . . ."

"We can wait," Barton said. "It's kind of exciting in a way. I guess I should move my car. If he drives up the road tomorrow morning we wouldn't want him to see it sitting there."

Barton left, and Pete went through the cabin again. He opened the closets and found them all empty. In the kitchen cupboard he saw a set of cooking pans and some old plates and glasses. There was a refrigerator, but it wasn't working. Pete went to a light switch and flipped it. Nothing happened. There must be a generator somewhere, but there was no point in turning it on now.

Ten minutes after Barton left, Pete heard the car start. It was faint: You wouldn't notice it except that there was no other sound. He listened to the Jeep's engine for several minutes, then it stopped. More time passed and Pete heard footsteps outside. From the window he saw the flashlight approaching. Pete went to the door and opened it as Barton stepped onto the porch.

"I put the car off the road. He won't see it now."

"I could hear it pretty clearly," said Pete.

"Good. We don't want Franklin sneaking up on us, do we? I'm going outside to turn on the water." He went into the kitchen, and Pete heard a drawer open. Barton returned with a wrench in his hand and headed outside. A minute later Pete listened to the squeak as the valve on the water main opened.

When he returned, Barton said, "I'm going to go lie down and get some sleep. You should probably do the same."

"I'll sit up for a while," Pete said. "I'm still too wound up to sleep."

"Okay." Barton went into the hall that led to the bedrooms. Pete heard his shoes drop to the floor as he took them off.

Pete sat on the sofa, the rifle next to him. It was cold in the cabin, but he had his jacket on and was reasonably comfortable. Even though he was grateful to Barton for driving him up here, the crack he had made in the Jeep still troubled Pete. It was a strange thing to say, especially for a guy who seemed to be such a Good Samaritan.

Why hadn't Walker and Ellen come to the cabin today after renting it last night? Ellen's call had been made during the day, and she said she was fine. But Walker might have been arrested since then. For a moment the thought thrilled Pete, then he realized it wouldn't mean Ellen was all right. There was no telling what Walker would do if he was facing imminent arrest.

• • •

Pete woke up, still sitting on the sofa, cold and stiff. A misty gray light seeped in through the windows. For several moments Pete didn't move, carefully listening for the noise of a car coming up the road. He heard nothing. He stood, stretched and walked over to the front window. Outside everything was wet with dew. It was very still. There wasn't even the sound of a bird singing. Pete put the back of his hand against the glass and was surprised at how cold it was. He looked at his watch. It was past 7:30.

As quietly as he could, Pete opened the front door and went out. The cold air nipped at his face as he went around the place and covered the sixty feet to the shed. He guessed the temperature to be in the low thirties. Pete urinated behind the shed, steam rising from his water where it hit the ground. He was scared. Walker was a murderer. If he showed up, how the hell was Pete going to free Ellen without getting them both killed? He hoped a sheriff's deputy would arrive soon. He hoped there would be two of them.

Pete hiked into the woods, climbing the hill that rose behind the shed. There was a thick layer of pine needles on the ground and the air was full of scent from the trees. At the top of the hill he sat on a rock and looked back down at the cabin and the shed. He could see part of the road they'd driven up last night. To his right the mountain was obscured by a gray-white cloud. Barton had called Walker "Franklin," Pete remembered. He said, "We don't want Franklin sneaking up on us." Pete hadn't thought anything of it then, but now it struck him. Barton knew the man's name, of course, Pete had told it to him. But Barton said the first name in such an offhand, familiar way. As though he knew the man personally. Pete shivered at the thought.

He stood and made his way down the hill, stopping to look at the shed. It was an old structure, weathered gray, though still sturdy. It had once been painted white, but there were few traces of the paint left. The door was secured with a heavy padlock. Pete went around to the side where there was a window. He tried to look in, but the glass was dirty, the interior dark. All he could see were a few cardboard boxes stacked under the window.

He continued around the cabin and out to the road. Pete tramped down it, looking for the spot where Barton had driven the Jeep into the woods. He went at least a half-mile without seeing any place that looked wide enough for a car to drive through. Pete found tire tracks, but the road was so rocky they were impossible for him to follow more than a few feet. And he couldn't find where the tracks headed off. It didn't matter. Pete wasn't really sure why he wanted to see the Jeep anyway.

He turned back. The morning was brighter now. The top of the mountain that vaulted up behind the cabin was illuminated by direct sunlight. The trees there shimmered with dew. Above the mountain a few fingers of clouds floated by. Pete heard a woodpecker somewhere in the distance.

Approaching the porch, Pete saw Barton watching him from the front window. Pete raised his hand, and Barton returned the gesture. Pete climbed the steps and opened the door.

"Good morning," he said as he walked inside.

"Did you get any sleep?"

"Yeah. A little bit. I woke up about an hour ago and decided to take a look outside. It's beautiful up here."

"Thanks. I like to come up whenever I can. Usually manage it a few times a year. Sometimes I do some hunting in the fall."

Pete sat down. "I guess now we just wait and see if they show up."

"Not much else we can do." Barton walked over to the doorway that led to the kitchen. He leaned against it, staring at Pete with a strange expression on his face. "I could use some coffee."

"Me too. Think we should wait till noon?"

"I don't know. Maybe into the early afternoon. We'll be starving by then."

"I'm already starving," Pete said.

"Guess we'll just have to put up with that. I could drive out and get some food, but by the time I got back it would be afternoon anyway, and he might show up while I'm gone."

Pete watched Barton step over to the front door. "I think I'll go stretch my legs a bit, too."

"All right," said Pete. "See you later."

He left, and Pete was glad he was gone. Something wasn't right with Barton. He was probably being paranoid, but he couldn't help it. The guy was weird. That was all there was to it. He had said something else that bothered Pete. He'd said he came up here for hunting. If that was the case, why did he have to borrow the rifle last night?

Pete looked to his left and noticed that the rifle was no longer standing in the corner. He remembered clearly that Barton did not have the gun in his hand when he left. Getting up, he looked around the room. He went into the kitchen, then into the bedrooms. He looked under the beds and in all the closets. He checked in the bathroom. Finally, he went back into the living room, looking behind the sofa and under it.

"It's got to be here somewhere," he said out loud to himself. Then he went through the entire cabin again.

But the rifle was gone.

CHAPTER 30

COUNTING DALE, Walker had killed four people in his life. All occurred more or less accidentally. At least, this was what he told himself, and there was some truth to it. Something had gone wrong or events had gotten out of hand, and there was no way to avoid it. Like with Dale. He didn't really want to kill him, but things had definitely gotten out of hand, and there was nothing to do but make sure the prick was good and dead.

Planning to murder anyone would unnerve him, but planning to murder Alan Barton was much worse. Walker had decided to ambush Barton before he even entered the cabin. Walker would hide in the trees across from the front door. When Barton arrived and stepped up onto the porch, Walker would shoot him in the back. The trouble with the plan was that it depended on them getting there before Barton did. Because of the car breaking down, that might not be possible. Walker didn't know the best way to work it if Barton got there first.

Once Barton was dead, though, there'd be nothing to stop him and Ellen from doing okay for the rest of their lives. Ellen hadn't told him what she wanted to do, but Walker figured she'd head back to Dallas, maybe go back to her husband. Walker wanted her to be happy, that was all. He thought he could find a place in Dallas too, use a different name and visit her once in a while. They would tell their story to Eddie Rollins, cutting out some of the more gruesome aspects, of course, and Eddie would undoubtedly want to use them in one of his late-night television specials. That meant that he and Ellen would be on TV. Walker didn't know how much Eddie paid the people he had on TV talking about their amazing successes, but he knew it had to be a lot. Everyone on TV got paid a fucking fortune. Whatever it was, it'd be enough. He didn't need a lot of money.

They went to breakfast at eight. Ellen was quiet. She looked at her menu for a minute, then set it down. When the waitress came she ordered, then folded her hands tightly on the table in front of her. She was frowning.

"You okay?" he asked.

"Just thinking."

"About what?"

"The dream I had."

Walker nodded. That had scared the bejesus out of him. She'd been screaming like a knife was being twisted in her. Woke Walker up from a dead sleep, and he didn't know what the fuck was going on.

Ellen said, "I dreamed about things that I never had before. I dreamed about you taking me down the stairs."

Walker was silent.

"Do you remember much about carrying me out of the building?" she asked.

Did he remember it? Walker sometimes thought he remembered more about that day than he did about whole years of his life. He wasn't comfortable talking about this, but he wasn't going to lie to her. He nodded his head.

"Did you fall on the stairs? I dreamed that we were going

down the stairs and you fell. I landed on my side. My head hit one of the steps."

"Yeah. I fell."

"In my dream my father told me something."

"What?"

"I don't know. I can't understand him. He's talking, but I don't understand the words. I thought you might have heard what he said. It was right before you took him away."

Walker squirmed in his seat. "I don't know," he said. "The cops was outside. I wasn't payin' attention to what he said to you."

"Oh."

The waitress brought their orders. Walker had a Denver omelet with toast, but he only ate half of it. Thinking about facing Barton later in the day took away his appetite. He had to regain his confidence. People who believe they will succeed, do succeed. That was what Eddie wrote. Trouble was, Walker had fucked up most of the important things in his life, and he had good reason to worry that he'd manage to do it again.

Heading back to the motel, he said to Ellen, "You sure you want to do this?"

"You said we didn't have a choice. That he'd come after us."

"Yeah. He would."

"Then we don't have a choice, do we?"

Walker didn't answer right away. He knew his weaknesses, but he hated to admit them. "Thing is, I'm scared a him."

They had reached a corner, and Ellen stopped, facing Walker. She put a hand on his shoulder.

"I'm scared, too. That's why we have to do it. Not wait around for him to find us in two weeks or whenever. If we believe we can do it, we can."

It was just what Eddie Rollins would say, and it made Walker smile. If Ellen believed they could do it, then so did Walker. Together, they would do it.

The fuel injector arrived forty minutes late, but the car was soon ready. They put their bags in the trunk and were on their way. The road wound through thick pine forests that seemed to have no end. The air was crisp and smelled wonderful. Small ground squirrels and chipmunks darted around the rocks at the edge of the road as they passed. Walker looked into the forest a few times hoping to catch sight of a deer but saw nothing but more trees, large boulders and a few birds flitting in and out of the shadows.

"So this is it, isn't it?" said Ellen.

"We're gettin' there."

"I want to talk to him first," she said.

"What?" Jesus, she had some crazy fucking ideas.

"I want to find out why he was in my dad's office that day. Why he shot him."

"I told you, we was just robbin' the place. And you don't wanna talk to Alan Barton about nothin'. He walks up to the door, I'm shootin' him in the back and he's dead. That's it. You don't know this guy."

"If you have a gun pointed at him, he can't go anywhere. He can't do anything. All I want is to ask him some questions."

"You had a gun pointed at me," Walker said. "You was askin' me some questions. Look what happened."

"I was trying to tie you up. I got close to you. We're not going to tie him up."

"He's not gonna tell you nothin'. Not even if you torture him."

"I want to ask," Ellen said.

"I thought you wanted revenge. You said that's what you were after. Now you wanna talk to him? Forget it. It's not safe to talk to him. I'll kill him. That's gonna have to be enough for you."

"He shot my father. There was a reason. I want him to tell me what it was."

"He won't tell you shit."

"We'll see."

Walker wasn't going to fight with her. He was the one who'd have the gun. He'd shoot Barton and that'd be that. Ask him all the questions she wanted then.

She didn't say anything else about it, which was good. Walker didn't like arguing with her. Worrying about Barton got Walker to wondering if he might bring someone with him to the cabin. That'd screw up everything good.

"Barton might show up with someone," he said.

"Who?"

"Someone like that asshole back in L.A."

"Why would he do that?"

"He don't know what he's gettin' into exactly, you know? He knows Dale is dead, but he don't know how it happened. He don't know if you're alive or dead. And if you're alive, he don't know why I haven't killed you. He might decide to be careful and bring some help."

"What'll we do?"

"I don't know. They'll both have guns."

They were driving through a narrow valley. The trees were so tall and thick you couldn't see the sky at all except for the narrow line of blue straight overhead.

"We should both have guns," she said.

"There's only the one."

"What about that man's gun?"

"What man?"

"At your apartment."

"I got rid a that back in L.A."

"We'll need to get another."

"In town, there should be a gun shop."

Lantrow didn't look much different from the last time he was there. They stopped at a restaurant to pick up some sandwiches. Walker noticed a waitress giving him a funny look. It scared him for a second, but then he figured it was because of Ellen being so banged up. She must've thought he'd beat her. Probably what the forest ranger had thought, too. Well, let 'em think that. It was the truth, wasn't it? Didn't matter what the fuck they thought.

Next they stopped at the hardware store. There was a counter at the back of the place where guns were sold. Walker purchased a Remington .30-06 hunting rifle and two boxes of cartridges. Ellen used the Visa with the phony name to pay for it. In the parking lot Walker sat in the back seat of the car and slid twelve rounds into the rifle. Walker gave Ellen her revolver, and she slid out the drum, making certain it was fully loaded. She sat in the car holding the gun in her lap. They got back on the highway and drove out of Lantrow.

"How much farther?" Ellen asked after they'd gone a few miles.

"Not far, but you get off the highway and the road's a bitch. Slow going."

"You came here when you took your vacation a year and a half ago?"

He turned his head to look at her. Was there anything she didn't know about him?

"What were you doing?" Ellen asked.

"Like you said. I was on vacation."

"That was it?"

"Why else would I be here?"

“Was Alan Barton here?”

“It’s his place.”

“So he was here?”

“Yeah.”

She could sure ask a lot of questions. Walker wondered if she was always like this or if it was her nerves getting to her. Walker was just the opposite. The sharp, tight feeling he had in his gut right now made him not want to say a thing.

“So you just sat around up here in the mountains?” she asked.

“We was up here huntin’,” he said. If he didn’t tell her something, he knew she’d keep pestering him about it, which meant he’d end up telling her anyway.

“Hunting what?” she asked.

Christ! “Deer,” he said. “We was huntin’ deer. Relaxin’. You know? Catchin’ up on old times. I spent thirty years away. I need all the vacations I can get.”

“You were here in June. That’s not deer season.”

“We was huntin’ out of season. Nobody up here cares. We didn’t get nothin’ anyway.”

Walker glanced in the mirror and saw a green and white Forest Service car behind them. The car was about a hundred yards back, going the same speed as they were.

Ellen said, “What is it?” and turned to look behind them. “Is he following us?”

“Don’t know.”

Ellen watched for a few moments. “He’s probably just driving somewhere,” she said. “That’s their job. To patrol the area.”

“Is it the guy who gave us the ride?”

“I can’t tell.”

“Shit.”

“I don’t think we have anything to worry about.”

"I hope not." Walker looked in the mirror again and saw the car begin accelerating. They had reached a stretch of road where there was room to pass. The Forest Service car moved into the left lane. As the car passed, Walker and Ellen looked over. The ranger was someone they'd never seen before. He glanced at them and raised his hand. Ellen waved back. The car sped past and pulled in front of them. Walker slowed slightly so that the car soon outdistanced them. The road began winding back and forth again, and they lost sight of it. They passed a sign that said "ELEVATION 7,000 FEET."

"The turnoff is a mile up on our left," Walker said.

The road continued switching back and forth as it climbed steeply. Ellen rolled down her window. Cool air washed through the car and blew against the back of Walker's neck. They reached the turnoff in five minutes. It was a narrow unmarked dirt road. Walker slowed and pulled into the opening between the trees.

CHAPTER 31

When he couldn't find the rifle in the cabin, Pete sat down and waited. He'd known something wasn't right with Barton, and this only reinforced it. He thought again of the familiar way Barton had used Franklin Walker's name.

Pete went outside and scanned the area. He stepped off the porch and circled around to the back of the cabin. He looked up the hill where he had hiked earlier. There was no sign of Barton anywhere.

Pete went the sixty feet to the shed and put his hand around the padlock on the door. It was big and heavy, as was the hasp it fit through. Whatever Barton had in there, he didn't want anyone getting at it. Pete stepped around to the side of the shed and stared through the window again. He still couldn't see anything but a few boxes. Maybe it was nothing but junk.

He returned to the cabin, got a glass of water and sat down to figure a plan. He could hike down the dirt road and try to hitch a ride back to town, contact the sheriff's department. But what if Ellen showed up in the meantime? No, he couldn't risk going back to town.

He heard a noise outside, then steps on the porch. The front door opened and Barton came in, holding the rifle in one hand.

Pete was certain he hadn't walked out of the cabin with the gun.

"See anything interesting?" Pete asked.

"Some guy poking around my shed." Barton sat, putting the rifle on the floor next to him. A shadow of a smile crossed his face.

There was ten seconds of silence while Pete tried to think of something to say. His stomach rumbled with hunger. "I was just curious," said Pete.

"There's nothing in there of interest to you."

"All right. How long do you think we should wait?" asked Pete.

"I don't know. It's up to you. I guess I can stand not eating until tonight if I have to."

"You don't have to be back in town for anything?"

"No."

"You were eating dinner in town last night," said Pete. "That must be a long drive from your cabin."

"I have a place that's not so remote," he said. "Just outside of town. I usually stay there. It's more convenient."

"And you're up here to do some hunting, I guess?"

"Yeah. And relax. Get away from it all."

Pete looked at the rifle and said, "Strange you had to borrow a gun if you were up here to hunt."

Barton looked at Pete. "Something bothering you?"

"No. It just seems odd that you didn't have your own gun."

"Why are you worried about this?" Barton asked. "You should be worried about your wife."

"I'm worried about my wife. You know that."

Barton picked up the rifle and looked at it. "I do have my own guns. I didn't bring any this trip. Okay?"

"Okay."

Barton put the gun against his shoulder and aimed it at Pete.

"Even though this isn't my gun, I like the feel of it."

"What the hell are you doing?" asked Pete.

"Nothing. Just testing the feel of this rifle. Am I making you nervous?"

"Why would having a loaded gun pointed at me make me nervous?"

Barton lowered the gun and laid it across his lap. "Sorry," he said.

"Yeah. Right." Pete's mouth had gone as dry as paper. "If they're not here by this afternoon, I doubt they're coming. We should head back."

"What will you do if they don't show up?"

"Talk to the sheriff's office, I guess. Walker and Ellen were in the area."

"Wonder where your wife was when she called?"

"I wish I knew."

"She didn't tell anyone in Dallas what she was doing, huh?"

Barton had asked the same question last night. He was too interested in who might know what Ellen was doing. "You ask a lot of questions," Pete said.

"Guess I do. Just trying to understand this mess."

A little too interested. And acting way too weird while waiting in the middle of nowhere for a murderer to show up. Barton didn't appear at all anxious at the prospect.

"Something wrong?" Barton asked him.

"No. Have you ever been to Dallas, Alan?" Pete asked.

"A couple of times. Why?"

"Just wondered."

Pete finished the glass of water he'd been drinking. He stood, went into the kitchen and refilled the glass. He looked out the window above the sink and drank it down. Pete knew he had to get away, but he couldn't make Barton suspicious. The last thing he needed was this guy following him.

He stepped back into the living room. Barton hadn't moved. Pete sat down. Neither man said a word. Pete stared out the window. After a few minutes he stood and went out to the porch. If he walked off into the woods, would Barton's suspicions be aroused? Pete looked at his watch. It was after eleven. His stomach was growling ceaselessly. He went back inside.

"I wonder where the sheriff is?" he asked Barton.

"I don't know."

"They said they'd send someone this morning, right?"

"That's what they said."

"Taking their time."

"They seem to be."

If Barton had told him the truth last night, if he had really called the sheriff, then someone would be here by now.

"I'm going outside again," Pete said. "I don't feel so hungry when I'm moving around. I won't be far."

"All right."

He went out the door. Stepping off the porch, he turned to his right. Pete planned to walk a hundred yards into the woods and then wait. Find a spot where he could observe the cabin clearly but be far enough away that Barton wouldn't be able to spot him.

Well into the forest Pete halted and looked back. He could see a glint of sunlight reflecting off the tin roof of the cabin. He was too far away. Pete had been walking quickly and was a slightly winded. Waiting, he listened for any sound of Barton coming after him. All he heard was the screech of a jay and the sound of the wind as it swept through the trees. Pete turned up the mountain, angling back toward the cabin. Pete kept his eye on the structure, stopping after ten minutes in an area where several felled trees created a good view. If Barton left, Pete would see him.

He sat on one of the tree trunks that lay across the damp ground and waited. A half-hour had passed when he noticed a faint sound. At first he thought it might be a distant airplane; it seemed to fade in and out. But then it got more distinct, as if it had suddenly jumped a quarter-mile closer. It was a car, moving very slowly. Pete stood up and cocked his head to one side, trying to hear more clearly.

CHAPTER 32

THE CAR LURCHED up and down as they drove up the road. Walker had slowed to a crawl.

"Is it like this the whole way?" Ellen asked.

"Pretty much."

"I hope the car makes it."

"Told you it was a bad road."

A wheel dropped into a hole and the bottom scraped along a rock. They inched along for another hundred feet, then hit a stretch of relatively smooth road. Walker increased their speed a bit.

They heard the clap of a rifle shot in the distance.

"Was that what I think it was?" asked Ellen.

"Yeah. It's deer season now, which I guess you know. That coulda been a long ways off."

"How far?"

"I don't know. Far."

Sheets of dust rose from the sides of the car. The bottom scraped against a rock.

"Will we make it?" Ellen asked.

"I hope so." The left front wheel dropped into a deep hole. "Fuck," said Walker. Maybe he'd spoken too soon.

Ellen said, “If Barton’s already there, he’s going to hear us coming, isn’t he?”

“Probably.”

And if Barton had somebody with him, they were fucked. That was all there was to it. Walker didn’t care that they had the second gun. He and Ellen were no match for Barton and the type of guy he’d have with him.

After another five minutes Walker stopped the car and turned off the engine.

“We’re close enough,” he said. “I’ll walk up first. Then you follow me.”

“How long should I wait?”

“Ten minutes or so. Once you see the cabin, just stop there until I give you a signal to come on.”

She opened her door and slid out, gun in hand. Walker got the rifle from the back of the car. He stared up the road. They were close now. Around the bend the road began rising sharply. It would only take fifteen minutes to walk the rest of the way.

“Walker,” Ellen said from behind, startling him. He turned and looked at her. She was at the edge of the road, facing the trees. Her head was turned toward Walker. “He’s here,” she said.

“Why you think that?”

She raised her left arm and pointed into the trees. “There’s a car hidden back there.”

CHAPTER 33

Pete ran, a slow jog really, moving down the mountain as quickly as he dared. He wanted to intercept the car before it got too close to the cabin. There were rocks, fallen tree limbs, low-hanging branches to negotiate. The ground was soft, carpeted with pine needles, twigs, pieces of bark. At one point Pete got going too fast, tripped and fell, but he broke the fall with his hands and wasn't hurt. He stood and listened again for the car, but didn't hear it now. Pete waited for half a minute, catching his breath, letting his pounding heart quiet. Still no sound of the car. There was no way it had reached the cabin. It hadn't been nearly close enough for that.

Pete turned to his left and headed for the road. He would stop Ellen and Walker whether they were in the car or on foot.

He hiked five more minutes and stopped again to catch his breath. Where was the damn road? He checked his watch. It had been fifteen minutes since he had heard the car.

Pete came to a clearing and scrambled up a fallen tree trunk onto a large jutting piece of rock that angled out of the ground. He looked around. There was nothing to indicate where the road was, but it couldn't be far. He climbed down and rushed ahead, stopping one more time to listen.

Completely out of breath, he reached the road in another five minutes. Pete couldn't believe he had been so far away from it. Looking up the dirt track as he sat to rest, he could see now that it angled up the mountain in a perpendicular direction. As Pete had gone down the mountain, he'd gotten father away from the road. He checked his watch. It had been almost thirty minutes since he had heard the car. Walker and Ellen must have stopped the car to walk the rest of the way. Which meant that Walker thought someone might be up here.

Pete had little doubt now about who the second man had been the day Ellen's father was shot. It had to be Alan Barton. And he was here in Lantrow to meet his partner, Franklin Walker.

CHAPTER 34

It was a dark green Jeep Grand Cherokee. Brand new. Ellen stood next to Walker.

Walker moved directly behind the Cherokee and looked up the narrow clearing it had driven through. He turned back to the Jeep.

"Rental car," he said, poking his toe at a sticker on the bumper. Walker went to the driver's window and looked inside. He moved, staring in the back window.

"Damn," he muttered.

Ellen checked her gun again, making sure it was fully loaded, then stuck it in her jacket pocket. She followed Walker back to the car. He took an extra box of cartridges for the rifle from the back seat.

"Better stay off the road," Walker said. "He'll be watchin' that."

"You know the way?"

"Yeah. The road goes that way, turns and goes up a steep hill. We can cut right through there." He pointed. "It ain't far."

The trees got thicker, and the light faded. The forest was full of the sounds of birds and the wind high in the trees. After a couple of minutes they lost sight of the road on their left. Alan Barton was at the cabin waiting, and he had undoubtedly heard the car if they were as close as Walker thought.

They climbed a steep grade. Walker was breathing heavily. The trees were thinner here, the ground powdery and full of small pieces of black rock. Ellen stopped, picked up one of the rocks. It was flat and thin. She slipped the rock in the pocket of her jeans and kept walking.

There was a crack of a branch breaking to her left. Ellen dropped to a knee and yanked the gun from her jacket. She saw nothing.

"Walker," she said quietly. He turned toward her.

She pointed. They both looked. There was nothing but trees and rocks. Ellen, hands trembling, held the gun in front of her. What had happened to the cool killer she'd been the night she confronted Walker? That was a lifetime ago.

Walker shrugged. "A deer or somethin'."

She nodded and got to her feet. They were nearing the top. Ellen sensed Walker wanted to say something else, but he didn't. He turned and they resumed the climb. Ellen hiked with the gun in her hand. Walker stopped again, out of breath already. Ellen waited next to him.

"We'll be able to see the cabin from up there," he said, nodding his head toward the top of the hill. It was another hundred yards, maybe less. "We get to the top of the rise, then it goes down and the cabin's right there."

She started to move.

"Wait," he said. Ellen stopped. "If things don't work out," he began, then stopped, lowering his eyes.

"If they don't, they don't," Ellen said.

"Yeah, but if they don't, I'm sorry. That's all."

"Let's go," she said.

He turned and started back up, moving slowly. At the top of the ridge they stopped. The cabin was a couple hundred yards directly below them. It had a steep metal roof, redwood siding. No sign of anyone about.

"Think he's in there?" Ellen asked.

"Yeah. He's waitin' for me."

They watched the cabin for several minutes.

"What do you want to do?" she asked.

"Give me your gun," he said. "I'll go around and come up the road. You cover the front from here, in case somethin' happens."

"He'll wonder why you're not in the car."

"I'll tell him it fuckin' broke an axle. Won't be hard to believe."

They swapped weapons. "I've never shot a rifle," Ellen said.

"You're not gonna need it," he said. "I'll get him."

She looked into his anxious gray eyes. They had always appeared nearly colorless to her, but now she noticed flecks of black and gold in them. "Okay," she said.

He said, "Whatever happens, you just wait till I come out and you see me. Otherwise, stay out of sight."

"Right."

"I'll go on, then," Walker said.

"I'll wait right here."

"A man believes in himself and the battle is mostly over."

"I'm sure that's true."

"That always stuck in my mind." He smiled at her, then started angling back down the hill behind them. In a moment he disappeared in the trees. Ellen turned back to face the cabin. She sat on a rock, elbows on knees, and lifted the rifle to her shoulder. She sighted down the barrel at the front porch of the cabin. Ellen thought it very unlikely she could hit anything from this distance.

She heard something behind her and spun her head around, tightening the grip on the rifle. It was a deer, about forty feet away, head bent down to the ground. The animal didn't seem to be aware of Ellen. He moved methodically for a couple of minutes, Ellen watching him. When she turned back, Walker was below her on the road, striding toward the cabin. His anxiety was obvious to her. His shoulders were twisted forward and he moved stiffly. He didn't have her gun in his hand. He glanced up once in her direction. It was brief, but she wished he hadn't done it. If Barton was watching, and most likely he was, he'd know someone was up here.

CHAPTER 35

When he reached the road, Walker stuffed the pistol in the waistband at the small of his back, pulling his shirt over it. He hiked toward the cabin at a good speed, knowing that Barton would be observing him once he was in sight. Walker didn't want to look scared or unsure of himself. That would be a tipoff.

Once he could see the place, Walker studied the windows, looking for some movement. There was none. He glanced quickly up the hill where Ellen was hiding, but didn't catch sight of her.

Walker stepped up to the porch and took three steps to the door. He raised his fist and knocked twice.

"Yeah?" Barton said from inside.

"Barton? It's me. Walker."

"The door's open."

Walker reached behind his back, got his hand around the grip of the gun and pulled it out. He cocked the gun with his thumb and opened the door with his left hand.

It took his eyes a couple of moments to adjust to the dimness inside. When they did, he saw Barton at the far side of the room with a rifle aimed at him.

"Put the gun down, Franklin."

Walker raised both his hands to shoulder level, keeping the gun in his right. "What the fuck?" he asked, trying to sound surprised.

"Put the gun down right now."

"Sure, no problem." Walker lowered the gun and moved over to the coffee table, where he put it down. He was in deep shit now.

"Where is she?" asked Barton.

"I killed her back in L.A. Don't need to worry about it no more. Can you put that rifle down now? It's makin' me nervous."

"Don't lie to me, you stupid fuck."

"What lie? I got rid of her just like you wanted. Dumped the body out in the desert. And I drove a long fuckin' ways to get here. I need help."

"Turn around."

"Come on, man. What's wrong with you?"

"Do what I say."

Walker turned around and heard Barton take a step closer. Heard him pick up Ellen's gun from the table. "There's nothin' to worry about," Walker tried explaining. "I just need a new place to live is all."

"Nothing to worry about?"

"That's right."

Barton pushed the handgun hard against Walker's head. "What about Dale? I guess he's got a little something to worry about, doesn't he?"

"That was a mess. I know it. But it wasn't my fault. That Dale, he just busted in my place with his piece out and I—"

Barton brought the gun down hard on the back of Walker's head, and he went down on his hands and knees, the pain flooding out every other thought from his mind.

"Listen, dumbshit," Barton said, bending over Walker. "Tell me where she is or I'm killing you in one minute. I don't have time to fuck around with you."

"I buried the body out in the desert. I left the freeway and drove about ten miles . . ."

Barton hit him again, and Walker went down flat on his stomach, nearly blacking out. He felt the gun digging into the back of his head.

"You've got thirty seconds," Barton said.

Walker knew all he could do at this point was buy time and hope he'd get a chance to try something. "She's waiting outside," he said.

"For what?"

"For me to let her know everything's okay."

"How'd you know I was here?"

"Saw your car down in the trees."

"Fuck. Get up. You just bought yourself fifteen minutes of life. Do what I say and maybe I'll increase it to thirty."

Walker pushed himself up to his feet.

"Go outside. Signal to her. Get her down here."

He went to the door, opened it and stepped unsteadily out to the porch. The back of his head was bleeding. Walker could feel it running down his neck. At the edge of the porch he looked up at where Ellen was hiding, raised his arm above his head and signaled to her. He saw Ellen stand and return his wave. He watched as she began making her way down the hill.

Nausea swelled inside him, and Walker bent over at the waist until it passed. When he stood up straight, he'd lost sight of Ellen. He'd have to try to work something when Ellen got up on the porch. Barton couldn't watch both of them at once. All he needed was a few seconds. Hit Barton in the back of the head. Get him down. Something. It wouldn't be easy, but fuck, what the hell was?

He saw Ellen near the bottom of the hill coming through the trees toward him. The nausea hit him again and Walker panicked. She was walking to certain death, and he was letting it happen. Walker's arm shot out in front of him, his hand out flat. Ellen stopped less than twenty yards away.

"Run," he cried. Ellen hesitated for a split second, then pivoted and took off for the trees. Walker heard the door jerk open behind him, then something crushed the side of his face.

CHAPTER 36

Ellen was ten yards from the trees when she turned and started running. She was nearly to the first tree when she heard Walker scream. Footsteps banged across the porch. She heard the steps leave the porch and hit the dirt. Ellen held the rifle vertically in front of her as she zigzagged through the trees. After ten more yards the forest thickened considerably. Behind her she heard pounding feet, the tearing of branches, the gasp of the man trying to keep up with her. Ellen thought about stopping, turning and trying to shoot, but she didn't think there would be time. He'd be on her before she could fire a shot.

She headed up the incline toward the spot where she'd been hiding, sprinting as fast as she could, but her legs began to slow in spite of her efforts. Her thighs screamed with fatigue; her lungs were scorched. She prayed the man chasing her was tiring, too. Ellen realized she couldn't hear him any longer, but that might be because her heart was exploding in her ears and she was desperately gasping for air.

Ellen couldn't continue. She stopped suddenly and turned, putting the gun to her shoulder and sighting back down the hill.

There was no one there.

Ellen tried to hold the rifle steady as she scanned the area, knowing he couldn't be far away. Slowly she backed up to the trunk of a large pine, leaning against it, then kneeling. Where the hell had he gone? Ellen tried to remember when she'd stopped hearing the footsteps, but she didn't know. He must be below her, concealing himself behind a tree or perhaps the large rocks that emerged from the ground forty yards back. Ellen crept slowly around the tree so that she was shielded from the area below. Since he'd stopped running, Alan Barton must have been just as exhausted as she was. That meant he was trying to catch his breath too, waiting a couple of minutes before he started after her again. He must have been watching, though. That meant he had seen her stop, kneel down and move behind this tree for cover. Ellen didn't know if she should stay put and wait for him to come after her or keep moving, hoping that he wouldn't be able to keep track as she darted from tree to tree.

She decided to move. Getting to her feet, she stayed low and looked carefully down the hill for any movement. Turning to her left, she took several quick steps to the next large pine and stopped. She looked back toward the cabin and saw no sign of anyone.

For several minutes Ellen continued this pattern, dashing from one tree to another, stopping briefly to look back, then sprinting on. Chest heaving, she stopped again. She'd come a hundred yards from the point where she'd first stopped. She waited a few minutes, watching for Barton and seeing nothing but black-and-white birds darting among the trees. She could circle around now and get a better angle on the front of the cabin, then move closer and wait. Barton would go back to the cabin eventually. When he did, she would get a clear shot at him. Ellen rose to her feet. She heard a sound behind her and spun to look.

He was a good-looking man, trim, with neatly cut gray hair.

Put him in a suit and he'd look like a successful lawyer. His face and hair were damp with perspiration. He held Ellen's gun in his hand. It was pointed at the middle of her chest.

"Put it down," Barton said.

He looked familiar to her. Ellen wondered if she'd seen him the day he'd killed her father. She knew she'd never seen this face in her dreams.

"Put the rifle down. This is the last time I'll ask."

Ellen leaned over and put the gun on the ground.

"Now back away from it," he said.

She took several steps back. Ellen knew she was going to die soon, but she was less frightened now than she had been in Walker's apartment three days ago. She'd found the man who murdered her father. That was something.

Barton came forward, calmly keeping the gun pointed at her as he reached over and picked up the rifle. She couldn't get over how familiar he looked.

"You're a persistent woman," he said. "Normally, I admire that in a person. Start back down now. You try to run, I'll shoot you."

You're going to shoot me anyway. But she did as she was told.

CHAPTER 37

WALKER OPENED his eyes and for a long time the world was spinning and tilting madly around him, and he was sick to his stomach. As the spinning slowed, his eyes focused on the porch roof above him. He remembered where he was.

Walker gently touched the side of his face where Barton had hit him. Fucking thing was all knocked in. Moaning, he managed to slowly get into a sitting position and look around the porch. Barton was gone. Walker crawled to the doorway, used the frame for support and got to his feet. He remembered yelling at Ellen, trying to warn her. Barton must've gone after her. Walker hoped she'd gotten away. Turning slowly, Walker looked out at the trees. He saw no one.

As he stumbled inside, Walker remembered the rifle Barton had pointed at him when he first entered the cabin. His eyes searched the living room, but he didn't see it. Keeping one hand on the wall, Walker moved around the perimeter of the room to the kitchen doorway.

Walker's eyes went over the kitchen as he held onto the doorframe. There was nothing there. Turning, he crossed the living room and went into one of the bedrooms. He checked the closet, then went to the second bedroom and searched there. Barton must have taken the rifle with him, he concluded. Walker returned to the living room window, squinting for focus. It occurred to him to try to make it back to the car, but he knew he wasn't capable of walking that far.

Then, after he lowered himself to the sofa, Walker saw it. The rifle was propped against the chair, right by the coffee table. He stared at it for a long time, not quite able to believe he hadn't spotted it before. Too messed up to see what was right in front of his face, he guessed.

Walker heard a noise outside, then a step on the porch. He sprang to his feet, which sent his head reeling, and he nearly fell as he started toward the gun. He heard more steps, and Walker got to the chair and grabbed the rifle. He turned as the door opened.

Ellen came in first. Her eyes widened in surprise as she saw him. Barton was behind her, and Walker raised the rifle to his shoulder to shoot, his left hand under the barrel, his right hand sliding to find the trigger guard. Ellen was jumping to the side as Barton raised his right arm, Ellen's gun in his hand. Walker's finger found the trigger as he sighted down the barrel of the gun. He squeezed the trigger. And just as he felt the gun kick against his shoulder, there was also something tearing at his chest. The next thing Walker knew he was staring up at the ceiling of the cabin. Barton appeared, looking down at him. His mouth moved, but Walker couldn't hear what he said. Barton went away. Then Walker saw Ellen lean over him, her face much closer than Barton's had been. He saw the fear in her face, the tears in her eyes. Ellen said something to him, but Walker could not hear her voice. There was music coming from somewhere. A piano playing a simple melody that he thought he recognized. A song he had heard as a child, maybe. Walker could hear the music but not what Ellen was saying to him. He tried to tell Ellen it was all right, that he was all right, but he wasn't sure if the words came out. All he heard was that music playing in his ears, slowing, getting louder. Then right in front of him Ellen became the small girl he had seen more than thirty years before. Walker stared into her kind blue eyes, no longer seeing fear and sadness there, but kindness and understanding. And Walker realized that this girl was the only person he had ever loved, and he was so glad she had come to be with him now, staring down at him with those blue eyes. They were the blue of the ocean, the limitless sky, a deep blue that seemed to go on forever.

CHAPTER 38

IT WAS WARM NOW. The afternoon sun was shining directly into his face, and Pete was sweating as he hurried up the rutted road. It took a hairpin bend to the right. Four steps and Pete froze. A hundred feet in front of him a car was stopped. Pete stared at it. It was a blue Taurus with an Arizona license plate. Walker was still driving the car of the woman he'd killed. All he'd done was change the plates.

Pete retreated into the trees. He stopped in a spot where he could clearly see the car and leaned a shoulder against a tree. He was in the shadows. No one going to the car would notice him here.

After several minutes Pete moved out of the shadows and went to the car. Cupping a hand over his eyes, he looked in the side window. There was a paper bag from Burger King on the floor, some sunglasses on the dashboard. On the back seat was a nylon jacket. Below it on the floor was a small box. He moved to get a better look at it but couldn't tell what it was. Pete lifted the handle on the door. Surprisingly, it opened, releasing hot, stale air that smelled of cigarettes. Pete picked up the box from the floor of the car. Something rattled in it. Jesus. It was a box of bullets. Pete opened the box. Four rounds inside. Pete put the box in his jacket pocket and searched the car, hoping he'd find a gun, but all he found was a cigarette lighter. There was no way to tell whether Ellen had been in the car or not. Stepping back, Pete pushed the door closed until it clicked.

He was startled by gunshots, two of them, very close together. The sound echoed for several seconds, then slowly faded away. He had no sense of how far away they were. Pete started running up the road. He ran out of gas quickly but kept going as long as he could, carefully listening for any noise. When he slowed to a walk, he checked his watch. It would start getting dark in a couple of hours. Maybe he'd be able to see in through a window of the cabin. If Ellen was inside, he didn't know how the hell he'd get her out.

It took him more than half an hour to get near the cabin. Pete moved off the road then, stopping at a point where he could sit and have a clear view. There was no sign of anyone there, no face at any window. Pete waited. Soon the light began to fade. Pete checked his watch: past 4:00. He would wait until it was completely dark. Then he would approach the cabin and try to see inside.

Forty minutes later, the front door of the cabin opened and a very thin woman with short blonde hair stepped out. Several seconds passed before Pete recognized Ellen, and then he sat bolt upright, his stomach in a free fall. Alan Barton was behind her. He held a gun right at Ellen's back.

Even from this distance Pete could see that her face was horribly bruised, especially on one side. God. What had they done to her? It looked like she'd nearly been beaten to death. Pete had to fight the urge to jump to his feet and run to her. Exactly what Barton hoped he would do. Well, he wasn't jumping and he wasn't running. That bastard Barton must be worried about him. Good. For all he knew, Pete could be phoning the sheriff right now. Barton said something to Ellen and she stepped off the porch. He followed her as she slowly walked around the perimeter of the cabin. Pete saw no sign of Franklin Walker but knew he must be covering Barton from inside. Coming around to the front again, Ellen and Barton stopped. Barton looked all around, eyes surveying the surrounding hillside for some sign of Pete. He waited a full minute before speaking to Ellen again. She climbed back up on the porch then, and Barton followed her inside the cabin.

Pete had to get her out. But how? Alan Barton and Franklin Walker had guns. He had nothing.

CHAPTER 39

"ALL RIGHT," BARTON said. "Franklin's not here to distract us anymore. Now tell me, who knew you were going to Los Angeles to find him?" He kept the gun pointed in her direction.

"No one."

"Your husband?"

"No."

"Your sister?"

"No." Ellen's eyes went down to Walker's feet, and the pain in her chest increased. She looked away.

"It's hard to imagine you doing something like this without anyone knowing."

"My mother knew. She helped plan it, but she died. I didn't tell anyone else. I intended to murder two people."

"Your husband was looking for you in Los Angeles," Barton said.

Ellen was shocked. "That's impossible," she said.

"The L.A. newspapers say the police know you were in Walker's apartment. They found fingerprints. It says your husband was instrumental in tracking you to that spot."

"I don't believe you," she said.

Barton shrugged. "It's true."

"If it is, I don't know how he did it. I never told him I wanted to find Walker or you." She laughed. "Not that I knew it was you I was looking for."

"Glad you found me?"

"Yes."

He fixed his eyes on her. Ellen didn't look away.

"You killed my father," she said. "I've been waiting for this day my whole life."

Barton moved his mouth slightly. Ellen wondered if that was how he smiled. He said, "Walker told you all about it, did he?"

"I want to hear your version."

"Maybe we'll have time to get to that." Barton cocked his head as if he had heard something. Standing, he went to the window and looked out, then moved to another window and looked. *Who in the hell could be out there?* Ellen wondered.

He turned from the window and came back to the chair.

"Expecting someone?" she asked.

"Not really," he said. "Tell me how you found Walker."

"My mother hired a private detective a few years ago."

"What was his name?"

"Maybe we'll have time to get to that," she said.

It made him move the corners of his mouth again. "We'll get to it," he said. "No doubt about that."

"I'll trade you the name of that private detective for the reason my father was killed."

He looked down at the gun in his hand. Her gun. She wished she was holding it now. The familiar weight and balance of it in her hand. Barton looked like a normal man, respectable even. Ellen wondered if he had a wife and children.

"I dream about that day," she said. "I've dreamed about it once or twice a month my whole life. Walker's in my dream. You never were."

"So?"

"But you look familiar to me. When I saw you in the forest, I knew I'd seen you somewhere."

"You saw me that day in Dallas."

"I don't think so. I wonder if my mother would have recognized you. Did you check up on us or something? Follow us? Watch us?"

"Tell me who you hired to find Walker," he said.

"You haven't told me why you shot my father."

"It was a business decision. I brought along that idiot." He nodded toward Walker's body. "To help make it look like a robbery. I knew your father would stop by the office that day. I never thought he'd bring you along."

"Who wanted him killed?" she asked.

"I didn't say I'd tell you that," he said, sighing. "Who did you hire to find Walker?"

"Tyrus Gallagher. He's in the Dallas phone book." It was a lie, but she didn't see how he could check from here. Even if he could, what could he do to her that he wasn't already planning to do?

"That better be the truth," he said.

"It is. Why did someone want my father killed? It won't matter if I know. I'm not going anywhere."

"No. You're not." He sighed. "Your dad had partners. Let's just say one of them wasn't happy."

"You don't know who?"

"I'm not going to tell you that."

Ellen had to look away from him to keep from losing control of herself. She didn't want that to happen. Not now.

"It doesn't bother you to kill people?" she asked, still not looking at him.

"Most of the people I've killed aren't exactly law-abiding citizens, believe me."

"My father was."

"Maybe."

"Fucker," she spit out. "You fucking murdering bastard."

Barton stood and went to the window again, looking out.

Ellen watched him. "Who do you think's out there?" Ellen asked.

"Your husband," he said.

Ellen went numb. *No. It's not true. He's lying to me.*

"He's quite a detective, that Pete." Barton turned from the window and went to the cabinet next to the wall. He opened a drawer. "He called Franklin's sister in Texas, and she told him that he'd come to Lantrow for a vacation once. Pete was on a plane immediately. Right now he's either hopelessly lost in the forest or he's out there watching the cabin, trying to figure out how to rescue you."

Ellen bent her head and closed her eyes.

"I think he's waiting for it to get dark," continued Barton. "Then he's going to try something. I just hope he doesn't wait too long. I want to get this over."

Ellen heard Barton sit in the chair across from her

"That's why I took you outside. I wanted Pete to get a good look at you." Barton tossed a roll of nylon cord in her lap. "Time to tie you up," he said.

CHAPTER 40

Pete needed a weapon. He thought of the shed behind the cabin and the heavy lock on its door. Getting to his feet, he crept back into the forest and circled around. Pete approached the shed, shielded from the view of the cabin, stopping when he reached the back of it. The only way to get in was through the window on its side. When Pete went to it, he'd be clearly visible from the cabin. He could wait for darkness, but if he did it would be black inside the shed, and he doubted he'd be able to see a thing. Pete would have to hope that neither Barton nor Walker was looking out the back. He picked up a large rock and went around the corner to the window. He broke out a pane of glass, reached inside, undid the latch and pushed up the window. He did all this without even glancing at the cabin. Pete dove through headfirst, not thinking about the broken glass, and sliced open the palm of his left hand. He held the hand against his jeans and sat completely still, listening to his own breathing. There was no sound from the house, no indication that he'd been seen or heard. There were dozens of cardboard boxes in the shed, some tools in a corner: a pitchfork, rake and shovel. Pete opened one of the cardboard boxes and found it stuffed full of files. He pulled a file and opened it. It contained bank statements for a company called Gulf Capital. He picked up the box, moved it and opened the box underneath. Files marked as tax returns and financial statements for several companies. He flipped through the files, reading the names on the tabs. He stopped at one, pulling it half out of the box. At first he thought he was misreading it. But he wasn't. The name on the file was Delta Partners. It was the name of the company that had purchased Ellen's father's business after he died. Pete opened the file carefully, glancing through several pages in disbelief. He looked at the next file in the box, pulled it out and opened it. There was no time to digest what he was seeing, so he just ripped a half-dozen pages out, folded them up and slid them into the back pocket of his jeans. None of this shit was going to matter a bit if he didn't get Ellen out of that cabin soon.

Pete looked again at the arsenal he had available. A pitchfork, a shovel, a rake. None would be much use against a gun.

His only hope was to get Barton out of the cabin and hit him from behind. With the shovel, maybe. But how would he get him outside? And what about Walker? Even if he knocked Barton out, there would still be Franklin Walker to deal with. Then Pete saw a can of gasoline in the corner behind the rake. He grabbed the shovel and the can. Pete lifted both through the window and set them on the ground.

From one of the open cardboard boxes Pete grabbed another handful of papers and stuffed them into his jacket. Then he crawled out the window. A few drops of rain landed on his head. It was getting dark now, and he noticed a faint glow at one of the back windows of the cabin. There was some sort of light on inside. Maybe just a single candle.

Pete picked up the can and the shovel, trudged into the trees and circled back around. When he was in front of the cabin again he saw that the light inside was visible around the curtains, which had been drawn across the front window. Steady rain was falling now, the heavy drops pelting the tin roof of the cabin. Must be loud inside. Pete remembered earlier in the day when he reached under the driver's seat of the Taurus and felt the slender outline of the cigarette lighter. He'd picked it up not knowing he'd ever need it. Pete pulled it from his pocket and flicked it twice, and it lit. He laughed out loud at his good fortune, then jammed it back into his pocket. He moved to the edge of the trees, where he could see the cabin's front porch clearly. He wanted Barton and Walker to be in a panic when they came out. It had to be close enough so they'd see nothing else for a few seconds. If they came out one at a time, Pete could hit the first immediately. Then there might be enough time to hit the second one before getting shot.

Pete considered gathering an armful of small sticks, but the gas would do the job. It only needed to burn long enough to get Barton and Walker outside. The rain suddenly ceased. Pete looked up and saw patches of hard black sky peeking through the low clouds. He was shivering uncontrollably.

It's a weird way to end your life. He hauled the shovel and gas can to the porch. He splashed the gas along the edge of the porch, dousing the steps particularly well. He reached down for the shovel and stepped up on the porch. A few silent steps toward the door and he stopped. His legs felt weak. Pete put the gas can down and moved right up to the cabin, just to the side of the door. He took a piece of crumpled paper from his jacket, his hand shaking wildly as he took out the lighter, flicked it and held the flame under the damp paper. It curled and smoked, but wouldn't light. Pete dropped it and pulled out another piece of paper. He held the lighter beneath it, and the paper lit. *Please, God. Help me. Help Ellen. Help us get away.* He tossed the paper at the gas-soaked porch several feet away.

The gas ignited with a *whoosh* and a blast of heat. The flames soared to the porch roof, curling out over the top, running along the underside toward the cabin. It was so hot that Pete's face was burning. He raised the shovel over his head.

The front door burst open. Barton stepped onto the porch.

"Fuck!" he screamed.

Pete swung the shovel; Barton sensed the movement and leaned to the side. The shovel struck him hard on the shoulder and he bellowed in pain, dropping the gun. Barton's eyes flashed at Pete for a split second, then he turned for the gun as Pete brought down another crushing blow, hitting him between his shoulder blades. Barton collapsed, and Pete dove for the gun. He got his hand around it just as Barton landed on his back, wrapping an arm around Pete's neck and squeezing, cutting off his air and blood. Pete hit back with his arms and legs, trying to get free. Barton leaned his weight against Pete, increasing the pressure on his throat. Pete felt the heat of the fire burning his left side. Out of the corner of his eye he saw that the flames were very close. Using all his strength, Pete rolled toward the flames, Barton on his back. Barton screamed and released Pete.

Pete rolled the opposite way and scrambled to his feet. He still had the gun. Barton was also on his feet. He stared at the gun in Pete's hand, not moving.

"Where's Ellen?" Pete shouted.

Before Barton could answer, Pete noticed that the flames were rushing across the porch now. He saw them reach the gasoline can. Pete turned and jumped off the side of the porch and ran two strides before the gas exploded, knocking him to the ground. He stood and looked back. The front of the cabin was engulfed in flames.

Pete raced around the side of the structure. He smashed

open the first window he came to with the gun. He was met with a wave of black smoke. He broke open the next window. Hardly any smoke at all. Pete knocked away the shards of glass and went in. He stuffed the gun in his jacket, crouched down and moved to the doorway. The smoke coming out of the living room was low and thick, roiling like some living thing. Pete crawled into the burning room.

"Ellen!" he yelled. The fire was roaring, the smoke so thick he could only see a foot in front of him. Burning embers fell from the ceiling. He couldn't see the flames, only an orange glow through the smoke. Pete saw a leg and turned. He touched it with his hand and crawled to his right. It was an old man. Dried blood all over his face and chest. Walker. Dead. Pete moved past, calling for Ellen again.

He was choking. Something fell on his shoulder; Pete brushed it away. The ceiling was going to cave in soon. He bumped into another set of legs. Pete grabbed one and it flinched. He moved to his right and leaned over. Ellen was on her side, tied to a chair, her eyes tightly closed, coughing violently.

"Ellen!"

She turned her head and looked at him, terrified. He leaned over close to her ear.

"Hang on," he shouted.

Pete grabbed the chair and started pulling. Something fell on his head. He swatted at it and felt his hair burning. It curled beneath his fingers as he brushed the embers away. The room was blistering hot. Burning wood fell like flares from the ceiling. He passed Walker's feet and was suddenly at the doorway. The smoke was blanket-thick in the bedroom now. Pete stood, pulled Ellen into a sitting position and tried to lift the chair up and out the window. Smoke roared past him. There was no point in trying to breathe. Something crashed onto his head and he fell. Pete found himself on his stomach, his face against the wood floor. They were so close. Choking, Pete got to his knees. Ellen had fallen over in the chair. He yanked the chair up to the window again, trying to tilt the back of the chair over the window ledge. The chair stuck. Pete pushed harder, but it wouldn't budge. Then, miraculously, it sailed up over the windowsill and out. It happened so fast, Pete couldn't believe it. She had flown away.

Pete put his head and shoulders through the window and let himself fall out on top of Ellen. He rolled off her and dragged her away from the blaze. When he was able to take a shallow breath, it seared his lungs. The fire was incredibly loud. Something crashed inside the cabin, and the wall next to them groaned ominously. He kept moving until they were to the edge of the trees. Pete collapsed next to her and looked down at her smoke-stained face. He was so thankful she was alive.

"You all right?" he asked.

She nodded. "I think so," she said, coughing. "You?"

"Yeah."

A wall of the cabin collapsed into the inferno, sending a fountain of sparks high into the night.

Pete started fumbling with the cords that bound Ellen's ankles to the chair. He got one leg free and started working on the other.

"Pete!" she shouted.

He looked toward the cabin and saw Barton approaching, a heavy branch of wood in one of his hands. Pete stood, reaching into his jacket pocket. Barton kept coming.

Pete pulled out the revolver. Using both hands, he aimed the gun at Barton, doing his best to hold it steady. Pete waited. Barton didn't stop. When he was just fifteen feet away, Pete shot him twice in the chest. Barton fell to the dirt, motionless.

"Oh, Christ," said Pete. "Oh, Christ." He kept the gun on Barton for a full minute, making sure he was really dead. Then he finished untying Ellen and helped her to her feet. Pete put his arms around her, holding her trembling body close to him.

"Thank you," she said. "Thank you for finding me."

"We'll be all right now."

"I know."

"I love you," he said as he started to cry.

"I love you, too."

CHAPTER 41

At the hospital in Santa Fe Pete and Ellen were both treated for burns and smoke inhalation. What was left of Pete's hair was shaved off and his left hand was bandaged. The burns Ellen suffered were relatively minor. They slept that night with oxygen masks over their faces.

It was an experience to walk through the airport the next day. People turned to stare, some with open mouths, others whispering not too discreetly to their companions.

The stewardess couldn't hide her shock when she first saw them. "It looks like you two have been through the wringer. You doing all right?"

"Thanks," said Pete. "We're both doing a lot better."

"I'm glad of that. Let me know if you need anything."

Flying home, Ellen held Pete's good hand. "You know," she said, "he wasn't a bad person."

"Who?"

"Walker."

Pete looked at her.

"He was trying to help me. And he saved my life the day my father was killed. He went back into the building after the fire had started. He carried me out."

"He told you that?"

"Yes."

"You think it's true?"

"I know it is."

Pete nodded his head.

"It's not the only good thing about him." She hesitated. "I know it's hard to believe."

"I believe you."

Ellen gently squeezed his hand.

BACK AT HOME, after Ellen went to their room for a nap, Pete went out to the car and retrieved his suitcase from the trunk. He opened it in the laundry room and removed the plastic bag that contained the burned and smoke-stained clothes he'd been wearing at the cabin. He fished his jeans out of the bag and reached into the back pocket, pulling out the sheets of paper he'd found when he was inside Barton's shed. He took the papers to the kitchen. He hadn't said anything to Ellen about what he'd found there. Pete had hoped there might be some mistake, that he had been confused or misinterpreted what he had read. There was no reason to upset Ellen needlessly. But Pete saw now that there was no mistake. The papers he'd pulled from the Delta Partners file were letters on Arroyo Capital Management stationary. They were addressed to Alan Barton and signed by Taylor Reed.

Pete made one phone call before he opened a kitchen drawer and removed a house key that Ellen kept there. He gathered the letters from Taylor to Barton and left.

It took ten minutes to drive to Taylor's house. He parked in the driveway and walked across the lawn to the front door. Pete rang the bell twice, waited a half-minute, then used the key he'd taken from the kitchen drawer to unlock the door.

The antique clock in the entry hall said 3:35. The clock was over two hundred years old, worth a fortune and kept terrible time. Pete knew it was close to four o'clock. He walked to his left through the living room, which was filled with the fine antiques Taylor had been collecting for decades.

In the den he went around the large rosewood desk and stared at it. Sunlight poured through the leaded glass windows behind Pete, making it unnecessary to turn on a light. There was a neat stack of file folders on top of the desk. Pete glanced at the edges of the files, reading the names of companies that meant nothing to him. He pulled out the chair from the desk and sat, the leather upholstery squeaking as he settled onto it. Drawers lined both sides of the desk. Pete tried the top drawer on the right. It slid soundlessly open. Inside were pens and pencils, a ruler, other supplies. The next drawer contained blank sheets of letterhead that matched the stationery of the correspondence he'd brought back from Barton's shed. The bottom drawer was deep and contained a group of files. Pete flipped through them, but they appeared to contain personal records. Pete opened the top drawer on the left side and found a dozen computer disks. Pete took two out and saw that the labels were in Ellen's handwriting. They had been stolen from her studio during the burglary.

"Hello, Pete." He looked up with a start and saw Taylor standing in the doorway. He was dressed in a gray V-necked sweater and cotton pants. His face was colorless and drawn, his eyes looked terribly weary.

"Hi, Taylor. I rang the bell."

"Yes. I heard it." As Taylor came slowly into the room, Pete saw that he held a small gun in his hand. The old man sat in a chair across the desk from Pete. "Did you find what you were looking for?" he asked.

"I didn't really know what I was looking for. I didn't expect to find these." Pete tapped the disks with a finger.

Taylor sighed. "Barton did that. Broke into the house and took the computer. He had her car destroyed. I told him it wasn't necessary, but I couldn't control him."

Pete said, "There was a shed behind Barton's cabin in New Mexico with lots of boxes of documents stored in it. I found these there." Pete held up a page.

The old man nodded. "It was over thirty years ago, Pete. Why did she have to do this? Why couldn't she just let it be?"

"She never got over it, Taylor. Neither did her mother."

Taylor's elbows were on the arms of the chair. He held the gun loosely in his right hand, pointed toward the floor.

"After I heard what Ellen had done, I told Barton to have Walker let her go," said Taylor. "I hope you believe that. I love Ellen. I never wanted anything to happen to her. Franklin Walker could go to another city, change his name. I would have paid for that. But Barton wouldn't agree. He was convinced that if Ellen could find Walker, she might somehow know about him. He had made up his mind. He wanted Ellen dead. There was nothing I could do to stop him."

"You could have called the police," said Pete. "You knew where Ellen was."

"Yes. I could have. But I was afraid Barton would have me killed and still murder Ellen. However, you're right. That's what I should have done. I've always loved Ellen and Susan. I couldn't have loved them any more if they were my own."

"Why was their father murdered?"

"I was in love with Ellen and Susan's mother. You realized

that. I thought that if Victor was gone, Lois would eventually come to love me." Taylor glanced at Pete, shaking his head. "It was a horrible thing, I know. The irony was that Lois had absolutely no interest in me after Victor died. We were friends, nothing more." He stopped, pushing himself upright in the chair. The gun remained pointed at the floor.

"I can't believe you were involved in such a thing, Taylor."

Taylor ran his hand through his gray hair. "Love is a wonderful thing," he said. "The most wonderful thing in the world."

Pete heard a sound and looked up. Ellen stood in the doorway, her face so devoid of color that she appeared to be a specter, and for a moment Pete wasn't sure if she was really there. She took a step into the room, and as she came into the light, the deep purple bruises on her face were starkly highlighted against her bloodless skin. She stared at the back of Taylor, her hands knotted at her side.

"You bastard," she said.

Taylor jumped as if hit by a lash. He turned and looked at her. "Hello, Ellen," he muttered. "I wondered if you'd come with Pete."

"I didn't," she said. "I heard Pete leave the house and when I got up I found the drawer where I keep your house key open. The key was gone. That's when it hit me."

"What?" asked Pete.

"Where I'd seen Alan Barton. I knew I'd seen him somewhere. It was here. A very long time ago. I came by for some reason and there were several men here. One of them was Alan Barton. That's right, isn't it, Taylor?"

Taylor nodded. "Your memory is very good."

"What made you think Mama would ever love you?"

"Ellen, dear . . ."

"Don't call me that! You killed my father. Tell me why you thought Mama would ever love you."

"All right. All right. How can I . . ." Taylor put a fist to his forehead and held it there. "Your mother and I dated for several months before I had to go into the service. I thought we might marry after I returned, but the war went on for so long, and then I was stationed overseas after it ended. When I got back to Dallas Lois was dating your father. I tried to rekindle our relationship, but she said she loved him."

"That's it?" asked Ellen. "He was murdered, our lives were ruined, just because you wanted to marry her?"

"No. That was only part of it. I had arranged for Alan Barton and his associates to invest a lot of money with your father. Barton and I came up with a plan to pool some of the oil leases that had done poorly into a partnership and sell off shares to individuals. We had some fraudulent geology reports written up to make the leases appear much more promising than they were. It was a brilliant plan, but your father refused to go along. I had already sold hundreds of thousands of dollars' worth of shares, and Victor was threatening to expose the scheme. I did my best to talk some sense into him. I told him that the people who lost money would get big tax write-offs. I told him that he would be rich. He didn't care. He said it was wrong and he'd have no part of it. Alan Barton decided Victor had to go. I told Barton to give me one more chance to talk to him. But then I thought about your mother, and I—I didn't go see your father again. I told Barton I had and that it was no use. That's when Barton decided to kill him."

"I hate you," said Ellen.

"I don't blame you. I can only say that when I saw the devastation Victor's death caused your family, I regretted that I had been part of it. I've never stopped regretting it, Ellen. I swear I haven't."

Ellen stared at him for several moments, then put her face in her hands. "God!" she screamed.

Pete stood, going around the desk. He said, "Taylor, put the gun down now."

"No," he said. "I can't do that." Taylor rose to his feet and aimed the gun at Pete. "Stand over there by that bookcase, Pete. You too, Ellen."

Pete took a few steps back.

"Taylor, please," Ellen said.

"I just need a couple of hours," he said. "I'd let you both go, but I couldn't trust you to let me have enough time to get a flight out of the city."

"Listen," Pete began.

The sound of the pistol firing in the small room was so loud it hurt Pete's ears and left them ringing. Terrified, he looked at Ellen, but she was unhurt. Taylor had shot into the books several feet to Pete's right.

"No. You listen," said Taylor. "I'm going to lock you in that closet right there. In a few hours I'll call someone to come let you out. You'll be all right until then."

Without a word Ellen turned from Taylor and began moving toward the doorway.

"Ellen," Taylor said. "Stop right there."

She didn't stop.

"Ellen!"

She halted and looked back. "I'm not staying here, Taylor. You want to shoot me in the back, go ahead." She continued, reaching the doorway.

Taylor raised the gun, aiming at her back, but then Ellen was gone.

"It wouldn't do you any good to try to get away," Pete said.

Taylor turned to face Pete.

Pete continued, "I called the police before I drove over. They're getting a search warrant. You wouldn't have time to get away."

Taylor eyed Pete. "You're lying," he said.

"No."

Taylor slowly dropped his head to his chest, closing his eyes. The hand holding the gun dangled uselessly at his side.

The front door was standing open when Pete reached it. He went out and saw that Ellen was already in the car. As he started after her, a police car screeched to a stop at the curb in front of the house. A second car was right behind it. Harris got out of the first car. He rushed up the walk toward the open front door.

"You okay?" he asked Pete.

"Yeah."

Two men jumped out of the second car. They followed Harris.

Pete watched the men enter the house. Moments later a black-and-white patrol car arrived on the scene, lightbar flashing.

Pete continued around to the driver's side of the car and got in. Ellen was weeping silently, one hand covering her eyes. Pete started the car, put it in reverse and backed slowly out of Taylor Reed's driveway.

CHAPTER 42

Two nights later Ellen lay awake for more than an hour, her arm wrapped around Pete's chest. It felt good to hold on to him again. *He's a good person.* She remembered when they were in graduate school, and Pete had spent all that time going to art shows, determined to see her again. Ellen had been amazed at his perseverance when he told her about it. And now, when she had needed him most, he had found her again. Found her when Ellen had thought it virtually impossible, and then risked his life to save her.

Ellen carefully removed her arm from around Pete. He sighed but did not wake. Ellen rolled away from him and got out of bed. She checked the clock on the dresser to make sure it was past midnight. Ellen pulled on her robe and stepped quietly out of the room, closing the door behind her.

In the living room Ellen turned on a light and picked up the remote control. She switched on the TV and flipped through a dozen channels before finding the program she wanted.

Ellen sat and watched for fifteen minutes, then the phone number she was waiting for flashed on the screen. Ellen jotted the number down. She picked up the telephone.

"Eddie Rollins Success Line," the woman answering the call

said. "Do you have a personal success story you'd like to share with Eddie?"

"Yes," said Ellen. "I do."

"Well, that's wonderful. Eddie appreciates your call. What's your name, dear?"

"My name's Ellen Donelly. But I'm not calling about myself. I'm calling about a friend. A man. His life was changed by Eddie Rollins, and I'm going to tell you about him."